*A Brockmore house party can be the making of a man... For where the Duke and Duchess of Brockmore lead, all of society follow.*

**SCANDAL AT THE CHRISTMAS BALL,**

a sizzling duet from

Marguerite Kaye and Bronwyn Scott

The Duke and Duchess of Brockmore
are hosting *the* festive event of the year, a whirlwind
of luxury and fun with the possibility of second
chances in the air. But what happens when two
unexpected and decidedly unsuitable couples
find themselves struck with Cupid's arrow?

Read Drummond and Joanna's story in

*A Governess for Christmas*

by Marguerite Kaye

and

Vale and Viola's story in

*Dancing with the Duke's Heir*

by Bronwyn Scott

**Marguerite Kaye** writes hot historical romances from her home in cold and usually rainy Scotland, featuring Regency rakes, Highlanders and sheikhs. She has published almost thirty books and novellas. When she's not writing she enjoys walking, cycling (but only on the level), gardening (but only what she can eat) and cooking. She also likes to knit and occasionally drink martinis (though not at the same time). Find out more on her website, margueritekaye.com.

**Bronwyn Scott** is a communications instructor at Pierce College in the United States, and is the proud mother of three wonderful children—one boy and two girls. When she's not teaching or writing she enjoys playing the piano, traveling—especially to Florence, Italy—and studying history and foreign languages. Readers can stay in touch on Bronwyn's website, bronwynnscott.com, or at her blog, bronwynswriting.blogspot.com. She loves to hear from readers.

# Scandal at the Christmas Ball

## MARGUERITE KAYE
## BRONWYN SCOTT

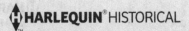

**HARLEQUIN** HISTORICAL

ISBN-13: 978-0-373-29957-7

Scandal at the Christmas Ball

Copyright © 2017 by Harlequin Books S.A.

The publisher acknowledges the copyright holders of the individual works as follows:

A Governess for Christmas
Copyright © 2017 by Marguerite Kaye

Dancing with the Duke's Heir
Copyright © 2017 by Nikki Poppen

Recycling programs for this product may not exist in your area.

www.Harlequin.com

Printed in U.S.A.

# CONTENTS

# A Governess
# for Christmas

## Marguerite Kaye

For all my friends on Facebook who made naming my Brockmore cast such fun. I hope the characters I've written live up to the fabulous names you gave them.

# Chapter One

*Thursday, 24th December 1818, Christmas Eve*

The first flurry of snow had begun to land on his carriage roof as it swept up the long drive in mid-afternoon, as if announcing his arrival, though he'd thought at the time that sunrise might have been more apt. This invitation was, after all, intended to herald a new dawn for him. Now, gazing distractedly out of the tall drawing-room windows in the shadow of the long blue curtains, Drummond MacIntosh saw that the Duke and Duchess of Brockmore's extensive grounds were covered in a glittering and, for the moment at least, pristine seasonal white blanket. This particular window faced due west, but he could see no sign of the sun through the thick, leaden sky. Behind him, the other guests took tea and made polite conversation. He ought to be doing both of those things himself, but now he was here, Drummond was more ambivalent than ever about the reasons for his presence at this party.

It ought to be clear cut. This was the opportunity he had been seeking to forge a new life for himself, to finally escape the purposeless existence he had been forced to endure. Three and a half years since that fateful day which had brought his life crashing down about his ears, it was time to accept that he needed help.

Drummond sighed, reminding himself that he was damned lucky to be here. The unexpected summons and subsequent discussion which had precipitated his invitation to Brockmore was a most surprising Christmas gift, and yet, now he was here at this most prestigious house party, instead of embracing the event, he was prevaricating. Why couldn't he just do as he was told? Of course, if he always had done so, he wouldn't need to be here in the first place.

They would be greening the house later, though seaweed rather than holly would be more appropriate decoration for this particular room. The painted silk wall hangings of the drawing room were cobalt blue. Grotesque sea creatures were carved into the gilded arms and legs of the blue-damask sofas which lined the walls, and the art which adorned the walls also had a maritime theme, the overall impression intended to be, he supposed, that of an underwater cavern. Which by rights should be inhabited by mermaids and denizens of the deep, instead of this collection of well-heeled, well-dressed members of the haute-ton.

It was three years past June since he had attended his last great social occasion, before the tragic events which had precipitated his catastrophic fall from grace. The Duchess of Richmond's now famous, indeed infamous, ball had been held on the eve of the battle of Waterloo. The crime Drummond had subsequently committed had been heinous, and though he still firmly believed that the crime he had refused to commit was even more so, his mutiny had been ultimately pointless. One life had been destroyed, his own changed for ever by the summary justice meted out. It had been justified, there was no arguing that fact. Just as there was no doubt, as far as Drummond was concerned, that he had been right to act as he did, even though his superiors deemed it utterly wrong.

Right or wrong, it was done now, and ancient history, according to the Duke of Wellington, his ex-Commander-in-Chief. It was apparently time for Drummond to re-join society. Drummond himself believed it long past time. After a year moping in the country trying to come to terms with events, he'd taken a deep breath, cast aside his deep regret along with his lingering resentment and his shame, and forced himself back out into the world. But the people who inhabited his milieu had summarily rejected him. Never mind that his military record until that fateful date had been impeccable. Never mind his commendations, his years of dedicated service to his men and to his superiors and his country. Only that last treasonous act mattered. Doors had been slammed. Familiar faces had been averted. He could not deny that he deserved this treatment, for ultimately, he *was* guilty. Yet he could not quell a lingering sense of injustice.

Clearly, none of the guests politely sipping from the dainty Royal Doulton teacups emblazoned with the Brockmore coat of arms either knew or cared about his ignominious past, for all had greeted him politely, not one had snubbed him. Actually, it struck him for the first time as odd that despite his own many connections, he wasn't acquainted with a single person here. Not even his hosts, who had been cajoled by Wellington to extend this most exclusive invitation.

'A Brockmore house party,' Wellington had informed Drummond, 'can be the making of a man. Everyone knows that Marcus and Alicia invite only those and such as those. Men of influence, women of breeding. They can smooth your path to rehabilitation, for where the Duke and Duchess of Brockmore lead, all of society follow. Even myself,' he'd added with one of his ironic smiles. 'You would be a fool to refuse this opportunity, and despite evidence to the contrary, I know that you are not a fool. I have plans for you, MacIntosh, and I am a man who gets what he wants,' the Duke of Wellington had informed him, in that magnanimous tone he had, of conferring great favour which would be accepted unquestioningly with great gratitude. 'You've a practical mind, a cool head, if we are to discount that one aberration, and you've a natural authority that make men inclined to follow you. Between ourselves, though it will not be announced for another two days yet, I am very soon to be in a position where I need a man like you, for Lord Liverpool has appointed me Master-General of the Ordnance. With the Brockmore name firmly behind you, doors will open again, allowing you to make a success of the posting.'

Wellington had proceeded to outline the terms of his rehabilitation, much in the manner he used when issuing his battle plans. 'You have paid the price for your rash actions, MacIntosh. I m willing to make an exception and give you a second chance, but you do not need me to tell you it will be your last?'

Drummond did not need telling and so here he was, with twelve days to impress his hosts sufficiently to earn their patronage and repair the major wound he had inflicted on his reputation. In one sense, he was fortunate indeed, for the other tragic victim of that day's events could have no such second chance. Thinking about that even after all this time made him feel sick to his stomach. So he'd better stop thinking about it and get on with the job in hand.

A guest list had most helpfully been left on the dressing table in his bedchamber along with the agenda for the festivities. The Duke of Brockmore, known as the Silver Fox, had proved to be a handsome man, with a broad intelligent brow under a thick coiffure of white-grey hair that was more leonine than fox-like. Alicia, his wife, her gown of dark blue watered silk the exact same shade as both her husband's waistcoat and the curtains, was the kind of elegant, classically beautiful woman whose looks were timeless.

'They make a striking couple, do they not?' Drummond's solitude was interrupted by a slim, ungainly-looking young man with rather thin brown hair which curled lankly over the high starched collar of his shirt. 'Allow me to introduce myself,' he continued, extending his hand, 'I am Edward Throckton. You, I think, must be Captain Milborne.'

In contrast to the gentleman's rather limp appearance, his handshake was surprisingly firm. 'Drummond MacIntosh, actually. Plain mister.'

Edward Throckton's eyebrows rose. 'How odd, I was sure you must be our military guest. There is something—I think it is the way you survey the room, as if you are expecting us all to fall in to serried ranks. Forgive me, that is a deuced personal remark to have made.'

A vibrant flush of colour stained his cheeks. He was young, perhaps only twenty-two or -three, and judging by the way he was tugging at his cravat, rather bashful.

'I'm glad to make your acquaintance,' Drummond said, 'I don't know a single soul here.'

'Really? I thought I was the only one—that is, I assumed—but I must say, Mr MacIntosh, I'm relieved to hear you say so. There is nothing worse than being—well, not so much an outsider as a—' Edward Throckton broke off, tugging once more at his cravat. 'Not that I can imagine for a moment that you would experience...'

'I assure you, Mr Throckton, I'm feeling every bit the outsider,' Drummond said. 'I've noticed you circulating amongst our fellow guests while I've been lurking here. I'd be very grateful if you'd share what you have gleaned.'

'Are you really interested in my modest intelligence-gathering?'

How many similar eager-to-please lads had he taken under his wing over the years? Drummond wondered. And a good few, once they'd gained a bit of confidence, had been moulded into excellent officers. 'I am very interested,' he said, smiling encouragingly. 'Please, fire away.'

'Well then, let us start with the group at the fireplace. The good-looking young man with the golden hair who is admiring himself in the mirror is Aubrey Kenelm, heir to the Marquess of Durham, and the flame-haired woman beside him is Miss Philippa Canningvale. Miss Canningvale's charms, in that emerald-green gown, are indisputable, but one can't help but feeling there is a touch of bravado in that display—though that is, of course, merely speculation on my part.'

Drummond, who had been expecting nothing more than a bland recitation of names and titles, gave a snort of surprised laughter.

'Beg pardon,' his surprising acquaintance said, blushing predictably, 'I have been presumptuous. I did not mean...'

'Oh, but you *did* mean, Mr Throckton,' Drummond said, grinning. 'You have a very sharp eye. It's a gift that could get you into a lot of hot water, but not with me. Please, pray continue.'

'It is true, I do rather pride myself on being an excellent judge of character, which is why I was so certain you were a military man. It seems I am not infallible,' Edward Throckton said, with a rueful smile. 'Where was I? Oh, yes, the woman in cherry-red is Lady Beatrice Landry. A true beauty, if you are inclined towards marble statues, which I confess I am, rather. Not that Lady Beatrice would deign to notice someone as lowly and as wet behind the ears as I am.'

'A widow, do you think?' Drummond enquired, both amused and slightly bemused.

'I don't know. I do know there is no Lord Landry on the guest list.'

'Which signifies precisely nothing. Who is the equally intimidating young woman by her side?'

'Lady Anne Lowell, daughter of the Earl of Blackton, and one of the most eligible debutantes of last Season. Her name featured daily in the society columns. I am surprised she has not gone off yet.'

'You read the society pages, Mr Throckton?'

'One must keep up with the great and the good, if one has ambitions to enter politics, as I do. I am somewhat hindered though.'

'In what way? You strike me as an astute and intelligent young man, and I too pride myself on my perception.'

'Talent is not the issue,' Mr Throckton replied. 'I may as well tell you, since it is common enough knowledge. I am the natural son of an aristocratic acquaintance of the Duke of Brockmore's. He cannot formally acknowledge me, but he does wish to assist me. This gathering is my opportunity to establish myself with our host.'

'So you have your heart set on a career in politics yourself, Mr Throckton?'

'I would be honoured if you would call me Edward. Yes, I do, but not for personal advancement. I wish most fervently to serve my country, though you'll probably think me an insufferable prig for putting it so. And I am aware,' he said, touching his flaming cheek, 'that aside from the misfortune of my birth, I must conquer this affliction.'

'I think your aspirations noble, and not at all priggish,' Drummond said, eyeing the young man with respect, 'though I recommend you have a care to whom you speak so frankly.'

'Perhaps,' Edward replied, with something approaching a grin, 'but though I may have mistaken your occupation, I did not mistake your character, Mr MacIntosh. You will not betray my trust.'

Drummond acknowledged this insight with a bark of laughter. 'You may continue to confide in me then. Share your thoughts on the group at the centre of the room.'

'The older gentleman is Lord Truesdale, a close friend of our hosts and another politician, so most certainly a guest I intend to cultivate. The pretty girl is Miss Burnham. I believe the man trying to charm her is Matthew Eaton, and the older man with the dark hair and rather stern countenance who looks as if he would rather be anywhere than here is Percival Martindale. According to Miss Canningvale, Mr Martindale has had a very tragic time of it lately, for his sister and her husband were killed in a coach crash, leaving him with the charge of his orphaned nephew and niece. I wonder where they are spending the Christmas period, for they are certainly not here. I believe there may be a grandmother.'

'I feel sure you will unearth both the location of the children and the precise nature of any gifts they receive before our stay is over. You really are a mine of information Mr—Edward. Please carry on.'

'The rather vivacious lady talking to our host is Lady Viola Hawthorne.' Edward pursed his lips as the object of his scrutiny burst into a peal of laughter. 'An extremely well-born young woman, her parents are the Duke and Duchess of Calton, but she has the reputation of being rather *high-spirited*, as they say.' The young man grimaced. 'It always strikes me as ironic that the more high born one is, the more society tolerates inappropriate behaviour.'

Edward was clearly referring to his natural father, but Drummond couldn't help thinking of society's reaction to his own transgression. Though Edward Throckton was entirely unaware of it, they were both outcasts in their own way, both attending this party as a first step towards joining or re-joining the fold.

'Forgive me,' Edward interrupted this melancholy train of thought. 'Again. I did not mean to sound bitter. I am in fact extremely grateful that the man who begat— that he facilitated my invitation here.'

'From what little I know of Brockmore, you wouldn't be here if he didn't think you could be of use to him,' Drummond said. 'Don't take that the wrong way, I meant it as a compliment. Now, why don't you finish what you've started, and then I think we must both mingle or we'll draw our hosts' ire.'

'Then it is as well that there are only the two wall-flowers gathered in the far corner to be identified. On the left of the group is Miss Pletcher, who is a cousin, and companion to Lady Anne. Beside her is Miss Sophia Creighton, whose father, a man of the cloth, rather shockingly died in a debtors' prison, from which one must deduce that Miss Creighton has been left in penurious circumstances. Our hostess is one of the patronesses of the prison, so I surmise this particular invitation is her doing. I hope Miss Creighton can be coaxed out of her shell enough to enjoy it. She has the look of a young lady who has not had great cause to laugh much of late.'

'Perhaps you are the very man to coax her,' Drummond said drily.

Edward blushed, but he did not dismiss the notion. 'And there we have it. Though the hour is advanced, we are lacking three of the guests from the list. I expect the worsening weather has detained them,' he said, glancing out at the now heavily falling snow. 'This is not one of the famous Brockmore Midsummer Matchmaking parties, but I wonder if our hosts have some other grand design? How many other guests have been invited, like me, for a purpose, do you think?'

The speculative look which accompanied this remark left Drummond in no doubt that the young man was fishing. He smiled blandly. 'We may find out as the party unfolds. Why don't you go over and join Miss Creighton, for I see Miss Pletcher is abandoning her to re-join Lady Anne. There, as you can see our hosts have also spotted that Miss Creighton is in need of company. This is your chance to make your mark.'

'You will join me, Mr MacIntosh? I would appreciate your support.'

'Directly, but I'd better circulate a bit first.'

Edward made his bow, and a beeline for Miss Creighton. Smiling to himself, Drummond contemplated joining the group at the fireplace, but a burst of laughter from the brassy Miss Canningvale stopped him. A moment's respite was what he needed.

Slipping as unobtrusively as he could out of the drawing room, he reached the expanse of the black and white tiled hallway, then hesitated. What he really wanted was to get outside and get some invigorating fresh air, but he had the absurd conviction that if he escaped the confines of the house, he'd find it difficult to make himself return.

One of the Duke's army of footmen, standing sentinel by the front door, looked at him enquiringly. Striding purposefully towards the room furthest from the drawing room, Drummond stepped inside, leaning back against the door. It was freezing in here, and the air smelled oddly fragrant, like a forest. The small room faced east, the fading light only visible through a single tall window. The source of the scent was obvious enough, for the table that took up most of the space was piled high with swathes of green spruce, stacks of pine cones, bundles of holly and mistletoe, obviously to be used as seasonal decorations. He picked up a wreath formed of pine. The distinctive resin-scented perfume of the needles caught him unawares, catapulting him back to the forests of his father's Highland estate, the earth soft as a mattress beneath his feet, carpeted with fallen needles, the canopy formed by the branches sheltering him from the elements. He had not been back there for so long, hadn't even allowed himself to miss it until now.

A rustle and a sigh made him drop the wreath. He had thought himself quite alone but there, in the darkest corner of the room, was a silhouetted figure. 'Who is that?' Drummond demanded, thinking himself spied upon. 'What are you doing, lurking there? Get up, man, and show yourself.'

'I am not lurking, I am not a man and I do not take kindly to having orders barked at me. I have as much right to be here as you do. Captain Milborne, I presume.'

'No, you may not presume,' Drummond snapped. 'Who the devil are you?'

The figure rose from the chair where she had been concealed in the gloom. 'I am Joanna Forsythe. I am at Brockmore as a guest of the Duke and Duchess, and I am in this room because I needed a moment of quiet contemplation before the ordeal of facing the assembled company.'

She was not tall. Her hair was brown, as was her gown. Her countenance was pretty enough. Sweet, some would call it. Unremarkable is how those less charitable would describe her. Yet her cool voice was very much at odds with such an assessment, and her clear, assessing scrutiny of his own countenance even more so. She continued to study him through eyes which were also brown. Big eyes, thickly lashed, and not plain brown at all, but more golden, and somehow, he couldn't explain how, giving the impression of acute intelligence.

'At first I thought it was simply your stance,' she said. 'Those shoulders, the straight back, the set of your head, that's what made me think you a military man, but it is not only that. It is in your eyes, now that I see you up close. You are a man accustomed to being obeyed. I confess, I am very much surprised that you are not Captain Milborne.'

It should not be surprising that his career had marked him indelibly, but it had never occurred to him that it should be so. 'Drummond MacIntosh,' he said, making a stiff bow. 'You are half-right, Miss Forsythe. I was an army major, but am no longer a soldier.'

'Ah.' Joanna Forsythe gave him a sympathetic look. 'Since Waterloo delivered peace to Europe, there are many men in a similar position. That is, I presume…'

'Aye,' he interrupted curtly, 'I left military service shortly after the battle.' It was not a lie, but the manner of his leaving was none of her business.

'We owe you and your comrades a huge debt of gratitude, Mr MacIntosh, but I can see the subject makes you uncomfortable. Tell me, what is a man who is brave enough to fight in battle doing lurking in here, to use your own phrase?'

'Like you, I came in search of solitude. Though unlike you, I've already had a surfeit of the company, while you have yet to sample it.'

She smiled crookedly. 'I am not weak-willed, not usually, but when I peered into the drawing room and saw everyone taking tea and looking so relaxed and at home…' Miss Forsythe straightened her shoulders, adjusted her paisley scarf, and forced another smile. 'But there, I know I must step into the breach at some point. A military term you will be familiar with, Mr MacIntosh. I will leave you to your solitude, while I head into battle.'

Which was exactly what she looked like she was about to do, Drummond thought, adding brave to her list of attributes. He extended his arm. 'Allow me to escort you. We will face the enemy together. A pincer move, if you will. Shall we?'

Could her fellow guests really be regarded as the enemy? Joanna Forsythe wondered as she sipped on her tea and made polite conversation. How would they react if they discovered they were mingling with a social pariah? She didn't recognise a single one of them, which was a considerable relief, since it made it highly unlikely that any were privy to her shameful reputation. Save her host and hostess.

Glancing over at the Duchess, Joanna felt that mix of excitement and nerves which made her feel sick and giddy at the same time.

The Duchess had written a letter in her elegant script, accompanying the invitation to Brockmore Manor.

*Now that she is aware of the painful truth, Lady Christina wishes to make amends and has desired me, as one of her oldest and—forgive my lack of modesty—most influential friends, to act as her intermediary.*

*There will be opportunity to discuss this further during the course of the party, but it is my sincere hope that you will be able to partake in and enjoy the festivities without allowing this most regrettable matter to prey on your mind.*

All very well for Her Grace to say, but despite the opulence of her surroundings, the fine food, the luxury of silk sheets and a roaring fire in her bedchamber, and the promise of a fun-filled holiday, Joanna's thoughts turned again and again to the question of how, precisely, her former employer proposed to make reparation for the damage she had inflicted. Clearly, the all-important discussion with the Duchess was not to be tonight. Then tomorrow was Christmas Day. Boxing Day? There were activities planned from dawn to dusk. How was she to contain herself in waiting?

A burst of laughter from the other side of the room drew her attention. Looking over, she settled her gaze on Drummond MacIntosh who, having handed her into the care of their hosts, had been conversing for the last half-hour with the group of men by the fire, but now he excused himself to make his way over to join her.

He unsettled her, but there was no doubting that he was by far the most attractive man in the room. Not the most handsome, that accolade must go to Aubrey Kenelm, but Mr Kenelm's golden-haired perfection held no appeal for Joanna. Drummond MacIntosh's features were more forceful: a strong nose, a most determined jaw, and an even more decided mouth. His skin was deeply tanned, despite the season, the colouring of a man who spent much of his life outdoors, and there were lines fanning out from his eyes. Etched by the elements, or by carousing, or by pain? He was a soldier, so most likely all three. His hair was the kind of glossy black that she would have attributed to artifice, were it not for the streaks of auburn in his curls.

'Now that you have entered the battlefield, Miss Forsythe, are you feeling more at ease?'

'The company seems most convivial,' Joanna replied. 'I am sure I will feel much more relaxed when we are better acquainted.'

'You must know our hosts in some capacity, surely, to have been invited?'

'I've never met them. In fact, I know you better than any other person in this room.'

He smiled at that. 'Then we are in the exact same situation, for I know not a soul here either.'

'Which begs the question, why are you here? Oh, heavens, I'm sorry, I didn't mean to sound so inquisitive. You will have your reasons, as I have. I'm a teacher,' she clarified, 'at a school for girls. A provincial institution, you will not have heard of it. The school is closed for the holidays, but unlike my pupils, I have no family to celebrate with. So you see...'

'...the Brockmores' generous offer was most timely. A very good reason, Miss Forsythe, but now I'm intrigued as to why they would do such a thing for a complete stranger.'

She would not lie, but the truth—no, she could not be telling someone she barely knew the whole truth, no matter how oddly tempting it was. 'I'm afraid you're going to be very disappointed,' Joanna said lightly, 'the reason is very mundane. My former employer is a great friend of Her Grace. It was she who facilitated this invitation, having learned of my currently straitened circumstances.'

Mr MacIntosh frowned at this but said nothing. He had a way with silence, Joanna was discovering, of making her want to fill it. She used it herself, to good effect, on her pupils. Usually they squirmed, then they confessed. Joanna bit her lip. Finally, he surrendered with a gruff little laugh. 'It would be unfair of me to press you further, especially since my case is remarkably similar.'

'What do you mean?'

'My invitation also came via a—a well-wisher who regrets my current circumstances, and wishes to change them for the better. For me, this party is something of an initiation test.'

'Then our cases are not so similar after all! I assure you, Mr MacIntosh, that I do not require to pass any sort of test. Whatever it is that the Duchess proposes—' She snapped her mouth closed, staring at him in dismay. 'If you will excuse me, Mr MacIntosh, I would not wish to monopolise your time.'

But he shook his head, detaining her by the lightest of touches on her arm. 'I would be delighted if you'd call me Drummond.'

'Drummond,' she repeated, 'a very Scottish name, though your accent is almost imperceptible.'

'I have been a long time away from the Highlands, Miss Forsythe,' he replied, his accent softening at the same time as his smile hardened.

'Joanna.'

'From the Greek?'

'Why, yes.'

'You look surprised, but not all Highlanders are heathens, Miss—Joanna. I was packed off to school in Edinburgh, and had Greek and Latin beaten into me along with any number of other useless subjects.'

'Education is never useless, Mr—Drummond— though it should never be beaten into anyone.'

'I did not mean to imply—I am sure that you do not subscribe to the view that to spare the rod is to spoil the child, and are an excellent teacher.'

'I love my profession. Even in my current situation, I cannot imagine another way of earning my living.'

'Then for your sake, I sincerely hope that this party is the route to securing a better living—if that is what you hope the Duchess will propose.'

Joanna laughed shortly. 'I'm not a charity case. I didn't come here in search of patronage, but justice. Now you have somehow managed to extract a great deal more from me than I intended.'

'Justice,' Drummond said, his mouth twisted. 'It is a noble aim. My motivations are a wee bit more prosaic. All I'm looking for is a fresh start and I'm afraid, unlike you, that the patronage of our hosts is a prerequisite for that. There, now you have also managed to extract a deal more from me than I intended.'

She shook her head, quite at a loss, for his tone had been so bitter. 'I did not mean to imply that there was anything wrong with patronage, Drummond.'

'Were it for anyone but myself I'd agree with you, but I'm like you, you see, I prefer my independence. However...' He forced a smile. 'There now, as I said, I've told you more than enough.'

And it had cost him, Joanna thought. Whatever he wanted or needed from the Duke of Brockmore, it hurt his pride to have to ask. She, who had been forced to beg and to plead, could understand that, though she suspected her sympathy would be very unwelcome. 'I don't know about you, but I truly am in dire need of some solitude,' she said, touching his arm lightly. 'I think I will retire to my chamber to rest before we green the house.'

Drummond nodded, but as she turned to go, he caught her hand. 'You will return though, won't you? You won't spend the whole evening hiding in your room?'

'Or even lurking in a dark corner,' she said, smiling weakly. 'Do not fear, whatever the outcome of my— my other business, I intend to forget all about the harsh realities of life, and enjoy these festivities to the full, while I can.'

His grim expression softened. 'A most commendable strategy,' Drummond said, with a lop-sided smile. 'With your permission, it's an approach I'd like to share with you.'

## Chapter Two

*Friday, 25th December 1818, Christmas Day*

Christmas morning began, as tradition dictated, with a church service, then an elaborate champagne breakfast followed by a stroll to the village green, now carpeted with a thick blanket of snow. The local children had gathered, and were crowding excitedly around the huge horse-drawn sleigh which accompanied the Brockmore party. On Boxing Day, food baskets would be delivered to tenants and those in need, but today was all about distributing treats to the children of the estate. The Duke and Duchess, aided by some of their guests, handed out wooden dolls and horses, lead soldiers, tin drums, skittles, balls, skipping ropes, hoops, spinning tops and penny whistles, and soon the air was filled with whoops of glee. The frenzied beating of tin drums was soon interspersed with the shrill sound of penny whistles being blown, as if some miniature marching band were tuning up.

Percival Martindale was making a terrible hash of the gift-giving, Drummond noticed as he watched from the sidelines. The poor man got it wrong every time, handing dolls to small boys, skipping ropes to toddlers, and a tin drum to the perplexed mother of a swaddled baby. Heaven knew how he would cope with his new wards. Perhaps he would find a wife to help him bring them up. Or hand them over to a governess. Martindale was smiling gratefully now at Joanna, who had tactfully intervened, swapping Martindale's choices for something more appropriate, earning herself a grateful smile and a pat on the arm.

For some reason, Drummond did not appreciate this over-familiarity. On impulse, he headed across the snow, waiting patiently until the last gift had been dispensed, then stepping quickly between Martindale and Joanna, offering his arm, and sweeping her away before the other man could protest.

'I was not in need of rescue, you know,' she said, as Drummond steered the pair of them away from the revelry. 'Mr Martindale seems a pleasant but rather melancholy gentleman.'

'I take it, then, that you are not aware that he has recently been obliged to take in his sister's two children? Both their parents were killed in a carriage accident, apparently.'

Joanna's smile faded. 'I had no idea. How very tragic. But what then, is Mr Martindale doing here at Brockmore? Surely his place is with his new charges, especially at this time of year?'

'According to Edward Throckton, who is a positive mine of information, the Brockmores were close friends of the deceased couple. They felt the chap desperately needed a break after all he has been through. Apparently, the children have been packed off to mutual friends who have a large brood of their own. They will be well cared for, I am sure, and most likely better able to cope with the loss than poor Martindale, for children, as you must know, are actually very resilient.'

Joanna's mouth tightened. 'I never knew my mama, she died giving birth to me, but I have known several children lose a parent, Drummond, and whether they are five years old or fifteen, what they need more than anything is security.'

'Martindale strikes me as someone who knows his duty. I am certain he will do his best by them—better, perhaps, when he's had this break to distance himself from his grief.'

'I hope so, for the poor mites deserve nothing less.'

'I've some experience in this field, you know. I've had lads—and I mean lads, Joanna, fifteen, sixteen, seventeen—lose a parent. Sometimes, when we were on campaign, word came months after the death, and often it would fall to me to break the news. I happen to agree with you, security is what they need the most. In such cases, it is the army routine which provides that.'

'And so as an officer, you also acted in loco parentis, just as a teacher does at times—though I do not mean for a moment to compare the two. For you, so far away from home, it must have been so much worse.' Joanna pressed his arm. 'Though not so bad as to have to inform a parent on the loss of a child.' She covered her mouth, aghast almost before the words were out. 'Oh, I'm so sorry, what a tactless thing to have said. I cannot imagine…'

But it was too late. 'No,' he said, his voice sounding hollow, as if it did not belong to him. 'No, you cannot.' So many such carefully crafted letters, full of kind words and platitudes, glossing over the terrible reality of death in battle. And that one, last letter he had not been permitted to write, despite it being the most important of all. Drummond squeezed his eyes shut, shaking his head to dispel the memory.

Joanna's face was pale, her expression horrified, but he felt as if he was looking at her from afar. It was the deafening silence he remembered most. The sudden, shocked silence like that which followed a cannon's roar. The disbelief writ large on the faces of his men, that must have been reflected in his. Followed by a blood-curdling roar of anguish. His own voice, emanating from the darkest, deepest recesses of his soul.

'Drummond?' Joanna gave him a little shake. 'Drummond?'

He dug his knuckles into his eyes, pushed his hair back from his brow. 'Forgive me,' he said.

'It is I who should apologise. I did not intend to evoke whatever terrible event it was you recalled. I am so very, very sorry.'

'I'm fine,' he said, relieved to hear that his words had a deal more conviction.

'Do you want to tell me...?'

'No!' he barked, making Joanna flinch. 'No,' he repeated, more mildly. 'Some things which happen during conflict are not for the ears of civilians—they would not understand.'

'I am truly sorry.'

'Forget it. We have talked enough about my occupation, tell me about yours. What is it you love so much about teaching?'

To his relief, though she hesitated, she accepted the crude change of subject. '*Not* beating Latin and Greek into my pupils, for one.'

'Men teaching boys, that is a very different thing.'

'Did they succeed?' she asked, eyeing him quizzically. 'Or might a gentler approach have been more effective?'

Drummond shrugged. 'It is simply how things were, and no doubt are still. Masters on one side, boys on the other, the one pushing, the other resisting.'

'You don't think that a little encouragement, some interest in the subject matter would have helped bridge the gap? How can one expect to imbue a child with enthusiasm for a subject when it is patently obvious to the child that their teacher does not share it?'

'A good point. Perhaps if my teachers had been more like you I wouldn't have been so eager to finish school.'

'I was lucky, I had an excellent example to follow. My father was a botanist as well as a tutor, and taught me to think of pupils as flowers, some blooming easily and showily, some needing to be gently coaxed. I have a weakness for those who need coaxed, I must confess,' Joanna said with a tender smile. 'There is nothing quite so rewarding as helping a child to find their own particular talent—and every child is gifted in some way, you know.'

'That has been my experience too,' Drummond said, 'though I'm not too sure any of my raw recruits would have taken to being likened to a flower. I take it, from the way you talk of him, that your father is no longer with us?'

'He died very peacefully, a few weeks after my twenty-first birthday, almost seven years ago.' Her eyes were misty with tears, but when Drummond made to apologise, she shook her head. 'No, you've not upset me, I have nothing but lovely memories of our time together.'

'May I take it that it was the loss of your father which required you to take up teaching for a living?'

'In a way, that is how I have always earned my crust, as they say, for latterly, I took over the youngest of Papa's pupils but, yes, his passing changed things. For a start, the house was only a life rent, and though I could have negotiated to take it on…' Joanna grimaced. 'A man can command a great deal more fees than a mere woman, no matter how well educated she is. I simply couldn't afford it.'

'That seems damned unfair.'

'So many women would agree with you, and so surprisingly few men,' Joanna said wryly. 'Right or wrong, it is how it is, there is no point in getting angry about it.'

'I'm not angry. Well, yes, I am. To be forced from your home and into—where did you go?'

'I found a good position as a private governess to two girls. My education and Papa's reputation made it astonishingly easy—not that my education was much called for. A smattering of French, literature, history, enough to make an adequate conversationalist, was all that was required along with the usual singing and sewing.' Joanna wrinkled her nose. 'Young girls who are destined to marry well care little for learning.' Her brow cleared, and she smiled. 'You know, I hadn't thought of my current position in a positive light until now, but there is a great deal to be said for being a school teacher, even when one is not being paid, and is treated as a drudge.'

'Then what on earth are you doing at such a school, when it is clear…'

'On the contrary, the situation is far from clear. It is a decidedly complicated matter, and one that I am not in a position to discuss until I have spoken to the Duchess.'

The cold air had brought a rosy flush to her cheeks. Her plain poke bonnet framed her face. Her countenance was heart-shaped, with a most decided chin. Her mouth was set, and her eyes met his unflinchingly. It was not only curiosity which made him want to press her further. He liked her. He had an absurd wish to help her, though what he could do—and besides, it seemed help was already on hand in the form of the Duchess. What's more, he could hardly press her to talk when he'd so steadfastly refused to confide in her himself.

Drummond sighed, holding up his hands in a gesture of mute acceptance. 'It is Christmas Day, and we agreed only last night, didn't we, to forget all about reality and to enjoy ourselves.'

'We did. We aren't doing very well are we?'

'Well, we must remedy that forthwith.'

She smiled with her eyes. A silly phrase, but in this case it was true, her eyes were smiling. The snow was falling thickly now, swirling around them. A snowflake fell on to her cheek. Drummond gently brushed it away. Joanna stood stock-still. Their eyes locked. There was a stillness in the air, a muffled silence enveloping them as the snow fell softly on to the existing carpet of white. He trailed his fingers down her cheek, to rest on the soft wool of her scarf. Her breath formed a wispy white cloud. Another snowflake landed on her cheek, and this time he used his lips to melt it. Her skin was cold, and so very soft. He wanted to kiss her. Her lips were parted so temptingly, and it had been so very long since he had wanted to kiss anyone.

But a gentleman did not go around kissing ladies he was barely acquainted with, no matter how much he wanted to. Making a show of brushing the snow from

Joanna's shoulder, Drummond looked up at the sky, blinking as a flake of icy snow landed on his eyelash. 'They'll be sending out a search party for us, if we do not make haste.'

'Yes,' Joanna said, making no move.

Her breath was rapid, her cheeks bright. 'When you look at me like that,' Drummond said, 'I find it very hard to think of anything but kissing you.'

'Only think? I thought you were a man of action.' She smiled at him, and that smile heated his blood beneath the icy cold of his exposed skin. 'There is nothing to think about, Drummond, for this is not real, and no one will ever know. Our paths have crossed for a few days, but when we leave Brockmore, we are very unlikely to meet again. Are you afraid I will slap your face?'

A laugh shook him. 'It would be what I deserved.'

'Are you prepared to take the risk?'

He wrapped his arms around her, sliding his hand under her scarf to the warm skin at the nape of her neck. 'I most certainly am,' he whispered, putting his lips to hers.

Joanna owned only one serviceable evening gown. Purchased ten years ago, in the days when she had a little spare cash, it had started life as a simple tea gown of pale blue satin. As a governess, she was occasionally required to accompany her charges to soirées, and with no funds to purchase a new gown had been obliged to adapt this one, shortening the sleeves and lowering the neckline. When the invitation to spend Christmas at Brockmore Manor had arrived, she had upgraded her evening dress for the third time, layering panels of sprigged muslin over the skirt, using the same material to put a new trim on the neckline and sleeves.

Standing in front of the long mirror in her bedchamber on Christmas night, she was pleased with the result, though she couldn't help wishing that she, like the other female guests, had brought a different gown for every night. Which was as silly a wish as ever could be made, for it was highly unlikely that she would ever have an opportunity to wear any of them ever again. Unless she was able, once again, to take up a governess position in another household similar to Lady Christina's, once her name had been cleared. Perhaps this was the form the *amends* the Duchess had referred to would take. Eighteen months ago, she would have given anything to be able to do so but now—the conversation with Drummond this afternoon made her question whether that was still what she wanted.

The Duchess had made no attempt to speak to her yet. Until she did, there was no point in her speculating, though she assumed that removing the terrible stain on Joanna's reputation would be a pre-requisite. Mind you, if the Duchess had seen her this afternoon, kissing Drummond with shocking abandon, she'd have another, very different blot on her copybook. One which, moreover, she'd been very, very careful to avoid, for whether governess or teacher, she could not afford to be branded a brazen hussy. Yet she'd behaved like a hussy this afternoon, and what's more she'd thoroughly enjoyed it.

The gilded shepherdess on the ornate ormolu clock on the mantel marked the half-hour by raising her crook to strike a goat bell. It was time to assemble for dinner but Joanna, who normally had a horror of being late, sat down on the footstool by the fire. She was not paired with Drummond for dinner tonight, the seating plan had placed him further down the table, between Lady Beatrice and Miss Burnham. Later, games were due to be played in the ballroom, and she would have the opportunity to speak to him then, if she wished to do so. That he might not welcome her company was a possibility she must consider, given her shockingly forward behaviour. She had practically demanded that he kiss her! Mind you, he had needed little encouragement, and he had seemed to enjoy kissing her every bit as much as she had enjoyed kissing him.

No, there was no denying it had been an extraordinarily nice kiss. Not a bit like Evan's kisses, and Evan's kisses were the only ones Joanna had for comparison. She hadn't seen Evan for seven years, but she most certainly didn't remember his kisses making her feel like she might melt. She had *liked* them, they had been *pleasant,* but she'd been content when they were over, and she didn't recall ever replaying any of them over in her mind, and ending up all hot and bothered and—and wanting. Yes that was the correct word, the teacher in her thought, *wanting.*

When Drummond had rubbed the snowflake from her cheek, kissing him was all she'd wanted, and when their lips had met, her only thought was that she didn't want it to end. Wrapping her arms around herself, she closed her eyes and indulged herself by remembering once more. The soft leather of his gloved hand on the nape of her neck, beneath her scarf. The slumberous look in his eyes. Close up, the hazel of his iris was tinged with green. Close up, she could see the faint slash of a scar slicing neatly through his right brow. Close up, he smelled of soap and wet wool and cold, crisp winter air.

He had not crushed her in his embrace, there were so many layers of warm clothing between them she could not feel the heat of his skin, but she could test the breadth of his shoulders with her hands. His lips had been warm, gentle, careful. It was an *amuse-bouche* of a kiss, Joanna thought, smiling at her own fancifulness. A tasting kiss, a foretaste, enough to tease, to tempt, to entice. It was a perfect kiss as the prelude to another kiss. The question was, whether there should be another.

The shepherdess chimed quarter to the hour with her crook. Startled, Joanna leapt to her feet. There was no time to be posing such questions, and no point either, for the answer was a very emphatic yes! Quickly threading the silk ribbon which matched her gown through her hair, she stabbed a few more pins randomly into her coiffure. Her turquoise necklace and matching earrings, her last gift from Papa, were the finishing touch to her *toilette*. Placing the guard in front of the fire and draping a shawl around her shoulders, Joanna gave her reflection a final check and, satisfied with what she saw, headed down to dinner.

After an elaborate meal of countless courses, the guests were invited to assemble in the ballroom, which was a grand affair, running the full length of the house from front to back, opening out on to the terrace and the south lawn, which could be glimpsed, glittering with frost, through long French windows. The ceiling, twice the height of the other reception rooms, was painted alabaster white, with only the ornate Adam cornicing to relieve its plainness. The pilasters running down one side would give the room the look of a Roman forum, were it not for the garlands which had been twisted around them. The greenery and mistletoe which they had so enthusiastically hung yesterday had been festooned with silver and gold paper formed into stars, lanterns and snowflakes, which caught the light from the three huge chandeliers which blazed down, their flames reflected in the highly polished wooden floor.

The striking of a gong announced the emergence of their hosts on to a small balcony set above the assembled guests dressed, as Joanna was beginning to realise was their custom, in co-ordinating evening wear of silver and dove-grey.

The skin on the nape of Joanna's neck prickled with awareness.

'They are fond of a little theatricality, are they not?' Drummond spoke softly, for her ears only. 'I've been waiting all day for the opportunity to speak to you.'

She bit back a smile of relief. 'I'm afraid you'll have to wait a little longer. Our hosts are about to address us.'

Which was no lie. 'Ladies and gentlemen,' the Duke of Brockmore began, 'as you can see, we have laid on some festive games. We hope that there will be something to suit everyone.'

Joanna listened distractedly as, between them, the Duke and Duchess explained the various activities laid out in the ballroom, all the time acutely aware of the man by her side. Drummond, like the rest of the gentlemen, was wearing country evening dress. A pale blue waistcoat almost the exact, original shade of her own gown. Dark blue pantaloons which clung to his legs. He had very long legs, and they were very nicely shaped too. Not many men looked so well in tightly knitted pantaloons, but Drummond's legs showed them to perfection. Not flabby, but certainly not too thin either. Muscled, she was willing to bet. Though who would take on such a wager, and how she could be so certain, when she had never seen a pair of well-muscled legs in the flesh before, she could not imagine. She dragged her eyes away from the perfect legs and her thoughts away from their shocking trend, only to discover that the owner of said legs was gazing at her quizzically. 'Your coat,' she said distractedly. 'I was just thinking how exactly it matched the panels of my gown.'

'We have inadvertently copied Their Graces,' he agreed, 'in co-ordinating our attire.'

Joanna laughed. ''Do you think they will be flattered by our imitating their style, or consider us presumptuous?' The Duke and Duchess, having concluded their little speech, were now descending from their Olympian heights to join their guests.

'I am inclined to think the former, in which case we should continue to co-ordinate each night, for their good opinion, as you know, is essential to my future happiness.'

His tone was light, but there was an underlying edge to his words that made her turn to face him. 'You do not sound overly enthusiastic about achieving that.'

'I am as enthusiastic about it as I am to bob for apples. Though perhaps you wish to have a go?'

It was the lightest of brush-offs, but it still stung. 'I have no intention of bobbing for apples,' Joanna said tartly. 'This is my only evening gown, and I cannot risk ruining it with water stains. Which means, I'm afraid, that unless you plan to wear that same coat and waistcoat every evening, you'll have to come up with some other method to impress our hosts. If you will excuse me.'

'Joanna, I did not mean…'

But she turned her back on him, making for the French windows at the furthest point in the ballroom from the laughing guests gathered around the huge copper bath of water where apples bobbed on the surface, beguiling the innocent into thinking them easy to capture between their teeth.

She was not, however, the only guest to seek this secluded spot. Lady Beatrice, dressed in a deceptively simple gown of puce figured silk with piped satin trimming, was standing in the shadow of the long curtains. 'A wise decision, Miss Forsythe,' she said coolly. 'If one is set upon eating an apple, there are plenty in the fruit bowl to be taken without destroying one's coiffure.'

'Or making one's gown virtually transparent.'

'Neither dilemma seems to have occurred to Miss Canningvale,' Lady Beatrice said, eyeing the flame-haired beauty disdainfully. 'Though if her objective is to draw the attention of every male in the company, she is succeeding. Just look at Aubrey Kenelm, he is positively mesmerised.'

'Perhaps he has made a wager on her success,' Joanna said drily.

'More likely he has made a wager on the probability of her bosom falling out of that dress, and if she leans over into the bath one inch further—oh, please, do not pretend to be shocked, Miss Forsythe.'

Joanna laughed. 'I am surprised, not shocked, and Mr Kenelm is about to lose his bet. Look, Captain Milborne has come to the rescue with a towel and an apple.'

'A practical man, and a thoughtful one,' Lady Beatrice said. 'Much underestimated qualities, don't you think? I can't imagine Captain Milborne lisping poetry and sending flowers, and treating one as if she were a feather-witted piece of Sèvres that might fracture in a summer zephyr. Why is it, do you think, that so many men believe beauty and brains are incompatible?'

Joanna laughed nervously. 'Clearly not in your case.'

Lady Beatrice shrugged. 'It would be much better for me if it were so. I am nearly thirty, Miss Forsythe, yet I cannot bring myself to play the vacuous ninny the men who court me desire in a wife.'

Joanna, who hadn't thought of Evan in years, now found herself thinking of him for the second time in a day. He had not thought her a vacuous ninny, but he had not been much interested in any of her thoughts. 'Perhaps you have not met the right man,' she said.

'Your words lack conviction, Miss Forsythe,' Lady Beatrice replied sardonically. 'I think you are as cynical as I. I wish I was a man,' she confessed with a heartfelt sigh. 'If I were a man, I could enter politics, and that is what I wish above all. The power to influence events, Miss Forsythe, not what passes for love, that is what would make me truly happy. Have I shocked you?'

'You have reminded me it is wrong to make assumptions based on first impressions.'

'Talking of which, I think the rather intimidating Mr MacIntosh assumed he would be spending what is left of this evening in your company. He has scarce taken his eyes off you. He is looking over at you again now. What did he say to you, may I ask, to make you seek refuge here by the window?'

'I asked him an impertinent question and he lightly slapped me down. I suspect I overreacted.'

In the centre of the room, a narrow wooden beam had been suspended from the roof by two lengths of rope. Aubrey Kenelm was removing his jacket and rolling up his sleeves, amidst much cheering from the other guests. Shoeing the wild mare, the game was called, the amateur farrier expected to mount the wooden horse and to hammer the underside on a marked spot, four times in eight blows. It did not look particularly difficult, but Mr Kenelm was struggling to get on to the beam, which swayed alarmingly, and was just far enough off the ground for his legs to be unable to gain purchase on the ballroom floor when he was positioned in the 'saddle'. Drummond had joined them now, standing next to young Mr Throckton.

'I kissed him,' Joanna confessed abruptly. 'Drummond—Mr MacIntosh—I kissed him, and now I think that he might think—I don't know what he thinks,' she admitted, her cheeks flaming.

'What do you think, Miss Forsythe? Did you enjoying kissing him?'

'This is becoming a very personal conversation. Yes, if you must know, I did enjoy it. Very much.'

Lady Beatrice raised her brows. 'I've always found kissing a rather insipid pastime.'

Joanna laughed, part scandalised, part in admiration. 'That has been my limited experience, until today.'

'Then you need a rapprochement with Mr MacIntosh, if you wish to experience more of it. If you do desire such a thing?'

Aubrey Kenelm, having finally succeeded in mounting the wild mare, was ignominiously thrown tumbling to the ground as he leaned over with his hammer.

'Your silence speaks volumes,' Lady Beatrice said. 'I rather think this game will provide much entertainment,' she added, with what in a lesser-bred person would surely be called glee. 'Let us go and enjoy the spectacle.'

\* \* \*

One male guest after another had dismally failed to 'shoe the wild mare'. Watching with trepidation, knowing he could not refuse his turn, Drummond was extremely relieved when Captain Milborne, exhorted by Miss Canningvale, finally achieved the feat.

'You do not feel the need to try to equal the Captain?'

Drummond turned to find Joanna at his shoulder. 'I have no wish to steal his thunder. Look, I shouldn't have brushed you off as I did.'

'There is no need to apologise. We have known each other for little more than a day. It was presumptuous of me to question you, and silly of me to take offence when you chose not to confide in me.'

'I would like to explain, all the same,' Drummond said sheepishly. 'Our acquaintance may be short, but I don't feel—I find that I would like you to understand. If you would like to…'

'I would.'

He saw his own relief reflected in her eyes. And something else too. Not only liking. She too thought them alike, he'd not misunderstood. Drummond looked around anxiously for a way to escape.

A game of Blind Man's Buff was getting underway. The majority of the guests were shouting out and running around while poor Miss Creighton as 'it', a silk cravat tied around her eyes, stumbled about in pursuit. At the other end of the ballroom, the Duke and Duchess were supervising the setting up of a huge shallow punch bowl filled with raisins. The Duke was pouring brandy from a decanter over the dried fruit. The Duchess was tugging at his sleeve, obviously concerned that he was utilising too much spirit. Later, the brandy-soaked raisins would be lit, the ballroom dimmed, and in the dark the foolhardy would try to snatch the 'snap dragons' from the hot punch. It had been a popular game in the Mess at Christmas. Drummond was very good at it, but he wasn't in the least bit interested, at this precise moment, in demonstrating his prowess.

A round of applause signalled Miss Creighton's success in handing over the mantle of 'it' to another. Drummond grabbed Joanna's arm and rushed the pair of them through the nearest door. It led to a small retiring room lit by a single lamp on a round table, two low-backed chairs set opposite each other by the grate. 'The Duke and Duchess's retreat, I suspect,' he said. 'I wonder if there's a spyhole into the ballroom? It wouldn't surprise me. His Grace has a reputation for being all-seeing and all-knowing.'

He waited for Joanna to seat herself, then took the other chair. 'When you asked me if I was in two minds about being here…' He smoothed his finger over his brow, feeling the tiny indent of the scar. 'Ach, the truth is that I am.'

'You sound very Scottish when you say that. Akk.'

'Ach,' he said, accentuating the accent for her benefit, enjoying the way she smiled at him, the soft curve of her breasts above the neckline of her gown, the flush in her cheeks, the glint of red that the firelight reflected in her hair. He leant over to touch her hand. 'Though I am glad I came, for if I had not I would not have met you, the reason I'm here in the first place is because the Duke of Wellington more or less commanded me to come.'

'Wellington! You do have friends in high places.'

'I wouldn't exactly call us friends,' Drummond said,

thinking of the deafening silence between them since Waterloo. 'He wants me to serve him as an aide, but unless I can persuade the Duke of Brockmore that I'm worthy of his support I'll be of no use to Wellington.'

It was a convoluted enough explanation. Judging by the frown on Joanna's face, it was no explanation at all. Her words proved him wrong. 'A word in the right ears from the Duke of Brockmore will establish you with the right people, you mean?'

*Re-establish* more accurately, but to admit that was to encourage questions he could never, ever answer. 'That's the gist of it.'

'But if you have the support of the Duke of Wellington, isn't that enough?'

Drummond's fingers strayed once more to the scar on his eyebrow. He jerked them away, knowing the habit betrayed his discomfort. 'Two dukes are better than one,' he said, unable to keep the sarcasm from his voice. 'When Wellington acts, he likes to be sure he will succeed.'

'He has cause to believe he will. He is a national hero. What a privilege to serve directly under him—what an opportunity for you though...' Her brow furrowed. 'Is the position not to your liking? Are you—I don't even know how you've been occupied in the period since you left the army. What have you been doing in the—what is it, three and a half years, since Waterloo? Or did you remain in the army for some time afterwards?'

Wednesday, the fifth of July, 1815, a mere two weeks since the battle had been fought, had seen his final day of military service dawn, preceded by what had seemed an endless night. A day that was over in a matter of minutes. Drummond hauled his thoughts back from that overcast parade ground, for Joanna was waiting patiently for an answer to her questions.

'I've been in the country,' he said, staring into the fire. 'I have a small estate in Shropshire. When I took out the lease, it was sadly run down, the tenanted farms in great need of modernisation, the house itself in a state of disrepair. But it is astonishing what one can achieve in a relatively short period, when one has no other occupation to distract one. And how little effort it takes, when things are in fine fettle, to keep them ticking over.'

'You mean you are bored?'

He gave a gruff little laugh. 'To distraction.'

'And so this offer of a post with the Duke of Wellington…'

'Is a godsend. So I ought to think.' Drummond winced. 'That sounds damned ungrateful, and I'm not. You can have no idea, Joanna, what this would mean to me.' He hunched forward on the chair, his fingers curled into his knees. 'I have served my country for most of my life. My father bought my first commission when I was fifteen. It was all I'd ever wanted.'

'Then it isn't surprising that you're finding life as a country squire frustrating,' Joanna said, leaning towards him, close enough to cover his hand with hers. 'Even if I did not have to earn my bread, I think I would still want to teach. It gives my life a purpose.'

Drummond nodded. 'A purpose. Aye, that is exactly what I need.'

'Yet you have mixed feelings about the one which is on offer?'

'It is not so much the position itself, it is…' He thumped his thigh with his other hand. 'One of the reasons I can't bring myself to talk of it is because I know

I'm being so contrary. I should be grateful that Wellington is willing to take a chance on me, that the Duke and Duchess of Brockmore are willing to open the right doors for me. It is more than I deserve, I know that.' He stared down at his clenched fist, slowly, deliberately unfurling it, his mouth set, his eyes narrowed. 'All the same, it sticks in my craw that I'm reduced to depending on others to do what I can't do myself. But I have no other options, I've proved that beyond doubt.' Drummond heaved a huge sigh, managed a very twisted smile. 'It just feels so *bloody* unfair, but there it is. If I wish to end my seclusion, I must do so on their terms. And so here I am.'

'Reluctantly willing,' Joanna said, with a twisted smile of her own.

He laughed softly, getting to his feet and pulling her with him. 'You've a way with words.'

'I should hope so.' She was still frowning. The wheels were turning furiously in that clever mind of hers. There were gaps, he supposed, in his explanation, and she'd find them quickly enough. He tried to smooth the furrow between his brows with his thumb.

She caught his hand, pressing a kiss to his knuckles. 'Don't worry, I can see you've had a surfeit of weighty talk for tonight. I only wish I could help.'

'Oh, there's nothing to be done, it is all being done for me, providing I behave like a good wee laddie. You must be thinking I'm a right misery guts.'

'I'm thinking no such thing.'

'What is it then, that's going on behind those big brown eyes of yours? Though they're not actually brown.' He trailed his fingers down her cheek to tangle in her hair, caught up loosely at the nape of her neck. 'They've a sort of golden light to them, did you know that?'

'No.'

She was staring, as one mesmerised, into his eyes. Was he imagining the passion smouldering there? 'And your hair,' Drummond said, gently easing her closer, sliding his arm around her waist. 'I thought that was brown too, when I saw you first, hiding yourself away in the gloom, but brown is far too dull a colour to describe it. Chestnut maybe, or chocolate.'

Her laugh sounded breathy. 'One cannot describe hair as chocolate.'

'Yet it is permissible to describe lips as cherries?'

She shivered as he caressed the back of her neck with his thumb, and her shiver set his pulses racing. 'Ridiculous,' Joanna said, twining her arm around his neck, closing the gap between them, her skirts brushing his legs.

'You're right,' Drummond said softly. 'Not cherries, but rose petals.' His lips touched hers. 'Soft pink, warmed by the sun, with a promise…' He groaned, pulling her tight up against him. 'With a promise I cannot resist.'

This kiss was just as delightful as the first one, only more so, for their mouths moulded to each other without hesitation. Not a tasting kiss, but something more raw, more sensual. He closed his eyes, a *frisson* of desire shooting through him as the tip of his tongue touched hers, and angled his head to deepen the kiss. With a soft moan, she leaned into him, her breasts brushing against his chest, sending the blood rushing to his shaft.

When they broke apart they stared at each other, eyes clouded, cheeks flushed, lips parted, astonished by the passion which had swept them up. From the ballroom, he could hear the Duke ordering the servants to dim the lights. 'Would you like to play with fire?'

'I thought we just had.'

He laughed. 'That is not what I meant. Come with me.'

Drummond opened the door, edging them both through the darkness to the crowd gathered by the flaming bowl of hot punch and raisins. He eased them to the front. 'Do you trust me?'

Joanna eyed the flaming bowl. 'Implicitly.'

'Good.' In the crush, no one noticed that he slid one hand around her waist, that she pressed herself back into his embrace, that he pressed his lips fleetingly to the delicate skin at the nape of her neck. 'Now take off your glove, and do exactly as I say, and I'll show you that it's possible to play with fire, without getting your fingers burnt.'

# Chapter Three

*Sunday, 27th December 1818*

Boxing Day had offered no opportunities for Joanna to be alone with Drummond, giving her ample time to reflect upon their conversation from the previous night. What she struggled to understand was why a man who had served his country with distinction had to wait for three years before being offered an opportunity to do so again? A second chance offered by Wellington, he had said, implying that he had erred. Had he left the army under a cloud? From what little she knew of him, she found that hard to believe.

Though her head buzzed with questions, when the man in question finally did find her alone in the breakfast parlour the next morning, suggesting a walk through the succession houses, she knew they would remain unasked. Let the past be. Weren't they both here to make a fresh start?

The Duchess's famous orchid collection was housed in a wooden-framed glass structure, comprised of a central block three storeys high, flanked by a low wing on

either side. As the door closed, a blast of hot humid air
hit them, followed by the sweet, earthy smell of the carpet of moss which acted as groundcover for the rare and
precious blooms, whose heady, perfumed scent hung in
the air like incense in a cathedral.

Steam rose from the damped-down floor. Drummond
unbuttoned his greatcoat and draped it over his arm. He
wore a pair of tight-fitting buckskin breeches tucked into
a pair of Hessian boots with brown tops which showed
off his long muscular legs to perfection, Joanna thought.
His navy-blue coat fitted tightly across the breadth of
his shoulders and had, like all his coats, a military cut to
it. His cravat was simply tied, his linen shirt dazzlingly
white. Hatless, his hair began to curl in the steamy air.
Her own would begin to frizz. Her fawn-striped wool-
len gown with long ruffled sleeves was one of her favourites, and least patched, but as she unfastened her
cloak, when compared with Drummond's immaculate
attire, she felt decidedly dowdy.

'I am thoroughly enjoying this break from routine,'
Joanna said, 'but I must confess I am unused to being
so idle.'

Drummond folded her cloak neatly and laid it on top
of his greatcoat, on a gilt-painted wrought-iron bench.
'Then salve your conscience by giving me a lesson in
botany,' he said with a teasing smile. 'Let us take a tour
of our hostess's spectacular collection.' She tucked her
hand into his arm and he pulled her closer, so that their
hips touched, their legs brushed as they moved.

In the central atrium, a selection of palm trees, exotic
ferns and succulents soared towards the glass ceiling like
a miniature patch of jungle, and some of what appeared
to be the more common orchid specimens were planted

in waist-high containers around this magnificent centrepiece. The two wings faced east and west, the latter, according to a helpful plaque, housing the rarer specimens, and so Joanna and Drummond headed through those doors. The orchids were artfully planted in beds built to resemble a mountainside, with streams burbling between the rocks, a shoal of tiny fish swimming in a pool. The colours of the blooms were breathtaking: delicate blushing-powder-pink; impossibly fragile pale lemon; tiny icing-sugar-white clusters like constellations in the night sky; huge single blooms on mossy mounds, ranging from pale blue to speckled green and poisonous purple.

'Latin name, origins, habitat, donor. The Duchess has been most meticulous,' Joanna said, peering down to read a label. 'You can educate yourself without any help from me.'

'Never mind that. Which ones do you like?' Drummond asked. 'Did your father grow orchids?'

'Oh, no, even a small succession house was quite beyond our humble means. His hobbyhorse was roses. He loved to experiment with them, to graft different varieties and create new colours and scents.'

'Did he name one after you?'

'He did. An English rose. Apricot, with a blush of pink. He called it Joanna Athena—after the Roman goddess...'

'Of learning—you see, they did manage to beat some Latin into me at school.'

Joanna led them over to a gilded bench set into a nook beside the waterfall. 'What about your family, Drummond? Are your parents still alive? Have you brothers and sisters?'

He sat down, stretching his long legs out in front of him. 'My father is still hale and hearty, to the best of my knowledge. I lost my mother about ten years ago. I am the bairn of the family. My eldest sister, Fiona, moved in with her brood to look after my father when my mother passed away. Eilidh and Catriona, the other two, are both married, and have a thriving clutch of weans apiece. In fact the county of Argyll is awash with my nieces and nephews, for none of my sisters has strayed far from the ancestral home.'

'Ancestral home? Good grief, do you mean a castle?'

Drummond laughed. 'Aye, though I reckon if you saw it, you'd likely be disappointed. It has turrets right enough, and battlements and even a section of dried-up moat. If your taste runs to crumbling ruins, it's romantic. I've often thought it would make a fine setting for a Gothic novel.'

Joanna chuckled. 'Are you aware that your accent broadens whenever you talk about your homeland?'

'Then it's going to be nigh on impenetrable on New Year's Eve—or Hogmanay, as we call it. His Grace asked me to brief him on all our Highland customs for the party. He has a piper coming, of all things, and has plans for us all to dance a few reels.'

'Will you be wearing the kilt?' Joanna asked, fascinated by the idea of him in such a garment, with those fine legs on display.

His smile faded. 'I've not worn the plaid since I was last home, which was a long time ago. Too long. When my appointment with Wellington is confirmed, I've promised myself I'll visit, for depending upon my posting, I may be abroad for the foreseeable future.'

And yet he had not returned in the last three years despite having ample opportunity to do so once he had left military service. His absence from the Highlands was deliberate then, but why? 'So, instead of returning to the Highlands you chose to settle in Shropshire,' Joana said, thinking to tackle the issue from another angle. 'You have friends there? Fellow officers, perhaps?'

'To my knowledge, there is not a single officer of the Scots Guards in that county or any neighbouring it. That was part of the attraction.'

Having no idea what to make of this, Joanna said nothing. It was an uncomfortable silence. Drummond had a habit, she'd noticed, of touching the scar which ran through his eyebrow, when he was discomfited. He was doing it now.

'I have never thought of Shropshire as my home,' he said finally. 'It was simply a place to—to bide my time. And soon enough I'll be posted abroad. Have you ever travelled to the Continent?'

'I've never even been to Scotland, though I would love to stay in a romantic castle such as the one you described. I have a secret weakness for Gothic romances, I am embarrassed to admit.'

To her relief, Drummond's harsh expression softened. 'The reality is such places are full of cobwebs and mice, and the walls are crumbling with damp, and there's always a gale howling down the fireplace. There's nothing romantic about that.'

'You've pretty much described my current abode,' Joanna said.

He took her hands between his. 'Is it really that bad?'

'Oh, I'm sure you've suffered much, much worse living conditions while on campaign.'

'Not always. I spent a winter in Seville, once. We officers were barracked in a palace, all tiled terraces and fountains, and marble courtyards. Oh, and orange trees, lots of orange and lemon trees. The scent in the morning, it was one of the most delightful aspects of staying there.'

'And were there delightful Spanish ladies to keep you company?'

'Oh, indeed,' Drummond said with a wicked look. 'One only had to pick one from the bunch, like plucking a ripe orange from a tree.'

'I don't doubt it.'

'You know I'm teasing you?' He caught her hands between his. 'I'm thirty-two years old, Joanna, I'm no virgin, but I'm not a rake. There have been women from time to time and I've had my share of amorous fun, but there has never been anyone serious.'

'Why not?'

'The army always came first with me, and the army is no place for a woman.'

'But there are army wives...'

'And a very rough time they have of it. No,' he said decidedly. 'I would never want a wife of mine to lead that life.'

'But since you left the army?'

'Since I left the army, my life has been—uncertain, as unsuited to marriage as life in the army. And so I have never allowed myself to become anywhere near fond enough of any woman to ask her to marry me.'

'Never allowed?' Joanna exclaimed. 'You find it so easy to place a leash on your emotions?'

Drummond gazed down at their hands, twining his fingers between hers, a frown furrowing his brow. 'Normally,' he said, looking up to meet her squarely, 'but you seem to be providing a sterner test.'

Her throat went dry. 'What are you saying?'

'I don't know, exactly. What about you, Joanna? Have you ever been in love?'

'Good heavens, no,' she exclaimed, thrown by his abrupt turn of the subject. 'That is, I have never swooned or palpitated or—or felt as if I would die for the want of some man. I am no Clarissa, nor indeed Madame de Tourvel. *Les Liaisons Dangereuses*,' she added, at Drummond's questioning look. 'Madame de Tourvel is seduced by Valmont and—oh, it doesn't matter. What I'm saying is…'

'That you have never been in love. But you have been kissed.'

She blushed. 'Yes, most expertly by you, several times now.'

'It is not like you to be coy. You know perfectly well I meant before.'

'Sorry.' She loosed her hands from his to try to cool her cheeks. 'It is really very hot in here.'

Drummond shook out a large kerchief and dipped it in a little waterfall, handing it to her, watching her silently while she dabbed it gratefully on her heated skin, aware all the time that he was biding his time, that he would not let the subject drop. So she sighed and nodded. 'There was a man. His name was Evan. We had known each other all our lives, and it was always assumed that we would marry, I suppose. He proposed to me on my eighteenth birthday, though there was no question of our marrying for some years, for Papa needed me. Then Papa died, and it made a great deal of sense for us to marry for I had no home, but I realised that I had never really—well, the truth is, I'd never really thought too much about it, and when I did think about it…'

'You didn't love him?'

'Well, no, but I never thought I did, and he never pretended—we were very *fond* of one another, it would have been a very *amicable* marriage, but—oh, dear, this sounds dreadful—but it would have been so frightfully tedious, Drummond. You probably think me a most unnatural female. Evan did, but I knew I would not have made him happy. I was twenty-one. I had never ventured more than ten miles from home, and though I loved Papa with all my heart, I cannot pretend that his passing—it felt like a release. I didn't want to swap one life of duty and devotion for another. As I said, you probably think that unnatural…'

'Actually, I think it perfectly natural, and admirable.'

She was feeling hot again, though it had nothing to do with the heated succession house. It was the look on Drummond's face. Desire warring with caution. 'You said I'm proving a stern test.'

'What I meant is that I fear we are playing a very dangerous game.'

'But that's exactly why it is not dangerous. It is a game, Drummond, it is not real. We both know that whatever happens between us will come to an abrupt end when we leave here.'

'Is that truly how you feel?'

'I cannot afford to feel anything else, and nor can you. We both have too much to lose. Despite your ambivalence, you need this post with Wellington, don't you? And for Wellington to appoint you, the Duke of Brockmore must first approve you and then continue to vouch for you,' she continued when he nodded reluctantly. 'He would not approve of your association with me, Drummond. Believe me, if he had an inkling…'

'I reckon the Silver Fox's reputation for being all-seeing and all-knowing is much overstated.'

'And I reckon we are making far too much of this—this attraction which exists between us,' Joanna said, as much for her own sake as his. 'I think our feelings have been exaggerated by the situation.'

'Because we know we've so little time, you mean?'

'Exactly,' Joanna said. That is exactly it, she told herself.

Drummond pulled them both to their feet. 'So you don't think this—this thing between us, has any real foundation?'

Though it shimmered between them, it was most likely the succession-house heat haze, Joanna thought. Did a heat haze have the power to draw one body to another, or was it the gentle pressure of Drummond's hands on her waist?

'I think it is—I don't know what it is,' she said, her own hand lifting of its own accord to curl her fingers into the silky, damp curls at the nape of his neck. The heat was affecting her breathing. And his. She stared mesmerised at his mouth. His lips were sinful. That was every bit as preposterous as saying that hers were like cherries, or rose petals, yet there was something inexplicably sultry in the contrast of his full bottom lip, the thinness of his upper that made sinful the perfect word to describe them.

'If we are playing with fire,' Drummond said, 'the sensible thing would be to extinguish the flame.'

There was barely an inch separating them now. One of his hands rested lightly on the base of her spine. One of hers lay flat on his chest, just at the point where his coat met his waistcoat. She could feel the dull, steady thud of his heart. Her own was hammering. 'Is that what you want?'

'No.'

'Perhaps it will fizzle out of its own accord,' Joanna said, aware she sounded unconvincing.

'If we indulge it, you mean?'

'Yes,' she said without hesitation. 'Do you want to indulge it?'

'You have no idea how much.'

This kiss was different. No tasting, no sampling, no pretence, this was a raw kiss. A hungry kiss. A kiss which was every bit as sultry as their surroundings. A passionate kiss, and a very adult one. Joanna clung to Drummond, for if she did not, she was sure her legs would not support her. All her energy went into that kiss. Their tongues tangled, their hands stroked and roamed. Hers on his back, sliding inside his waistcoat, flattening over the hard wall of his chest. His skin was heated, his shirt damp. His chest rose and fell rhythmically.

Their kiss deepened. She arched against him, pressing herself into him, shuddering as the evidence of his arousal pressed against her thigh, relishing the way her touch made him groan. Panting between kisses, she was drowsy with heat and with passion. His hand cupped her bottom. His other stroked up from her waist, brushing the side of her breast, drawing a sharp intake of breath from her, which he took for a protest. 'No,' Joanna said, 'don't stop.'

He kissed her again, and she kissed him back, matching him, kiss for kiss, touch for touch, eyes drifting shut, lost in the sensations he was rousing. His hand was on her breast now, carefully cupping, then his thumb, swirling circles round her nipple that made her ache for more, that made her want to tear off her clothing, for it was so tantalising, so delightful, and yet not nearly enough.

Who knew that passion could be as intense as this? she thought dimly as Drummond kissed her throat, the hollow of her neck, his tongue lingering on the fluttering pulse there. Positively aching for the feel of flesh on flesh, skin on skin, her clutching hands tugged at him, down his back, the sleek, taut muscles of his buttocks, pulling him closer. She was shockingly aware of his manhood, a hard ridge nudging against her belly, and felt her own throbbing response inside. Who knew that it could be like this? So urgent yet so sweet, kisses like cloying honey, her blood roaring in her veins. Dear God, who knew?

It was Drummond who brought them back down to earth. His kisses slowed, became less intense, his hands smoothing, easing her upright, creating space between them where there had been none. Joanna stood, eyes glazed. His hair was dishevelled. His eyes too were glazed. His cheeks slashed with colour. His cravat was askew. And his smile…

'Don't look at me like that,' Joanna said. 'You have a very, very sinful smile.'

He laughed. 'That is because I'm having very, very sinful thoughts.'

'I think I may be about to swoon or palpitate for the first time in my life. Does that mean my thoughts are sinful too?'

Drummond swore under his breath. 'I need a cold bath, not further encouragement. In fact, now I come to think of it…'

He pushed his damp hair back from his brow, picking up her cloak, draping it around her shoulders before shrugging into his greatcoat. His smile had become distinctly mischievous. 'What are you thinking?' Joanna asked. Drummond grinned. 'What are you…?' She squeaked as he caught her up in his arms, holding her high against his chest. 'Drummond!'

'We need to cool down,' he said, striding back through the succession house, out of the heavy door, carrying her as if she weighed no more than a sparrow. His boots crunched on the hard-packed snow which had become crusty as the temperature dropped.

Joanna clung, still laughing, feeling his laughter reverberating in his chest, until he stopped, just inside a high-walled garden, letting her slide to her feet, though keeping his arms around her waist. 'Are we cool enough now?' she asked. 'Has the danger passed?'

'Perhaps, but we better make doubly sure,' Drummond said, falling backwards into the deep snow, and taking her with him.

*Monday, 28th December 1818*

Drummond was reading the London papers in the library when Joanna found him. Fortunately he was alone, for one look at her face told him she was quite distraught. Casting *The Times* on to the floor, he hastened to her side. 'Don't say anything,' he said, putting his finger to her lips, before ushering her into the little room off the main reception area where they had first encountered each other on Christmas Eve. As he hoped, it was empty. The fire had been set but not lit, but the tinder box was lying conveniently by the grate. He settled Joanna in a sofa by the hearth, locked the door, and saw to the fire. 'Fear not, we won't be disturbed. What on earth has happened to overset you so badly? Do you want me to get you a medicinal brandy?'

She shook her head. She was quite pale, though there were two high spots of colour on her cheeks, and her eyes were bright with tears. Drummond sat down beside her, chafing her hands between his.

She stared at him in mute anguish, her throat working. A tear tracked down her cheek, and then another followed. A sob escaped, and she began to tremble. 'It is just so *bloody* unfair,' she said, throwing herself against Drummond's chest.

He wrapped his arms around her and held her as she sobbed. Such deep, shaking sobs that racked her, there could only be one explanation. The justice she had been anticipating was not forthcoming. Sickened, he tightened his hold around her, smoothing her hair with his palm.

Lying in the snow yesterday afternoon, her body pinned under his, the laughter in her eyes had turned to desire as he kissed her, abandoning restraint, his tongue sliding into her mouth, tangling with hers, his hands roaming over her curves. Rolling on to his back, pulling her on top of him, he had found the contrast of the freezing snow, the heat of her mouth, her body, intoxicating. And it had been the same for her. When their snowy kiss came to a lingering end, he had no doubt she wanted him as much as he wanted her.

It was one thing for them to agree that they were destined to follow separate paths, that this *affaire* or whatever the hell it was, had a very finite life, but it was quite another to act on this knowledge. He was not only playing with fire, he was playing with his very future, but he could find no appetite to halt the charade, no matter how many very sound reasons there were. Holding her now, soothing her violent sobs, he felt a fierce desire to protect her, to fight whatever battle it was she needed help fighting. It was not his battle though, and she would likely spurn his assistance for his own good. And hers. Whatever that may turn out to be.

Joanna had stopped crying. Her breathing had slowed. She sat up, and before he could offer his kerchief, had retrieved her own, a small, practical square of cotton, which she used ruthlessly on her red-rimmed eyes and nose. 'I've made your shirt damp, I'm afraid,' she said in a small voice.

'I've plenty other shirts.' He covered her hands with his. 'I take it that Her Grace did not offer you satisfactory terms?'

'Oh, she offered me extremely generous terms,' Joanna said bitterly, 'but the one thing she has not offered me is justice. She merely wishes to buy my silence and that is grossly unfair, no matter how generous the settlement. The problem is, I've no option but to accede, if I wish to prosper. There, we have that in common too, though I fervently wish we did not.'

Recovering her composure, she folded her kerchief away and pushed herself upright. 'The two people who owe me a grovelling apology are quite notable by their absence,' she said, her eyes sparkling, not with tears now, but with fire. 'Her Grace is merely the intermediary. I was so excited when the invitation to Brockmore came, I didn't think about the fact that it should have been preceded by a letter from another.' She pushed a damp tendril of hair back from her cheek and sighed. 'I didn't want to tell you the about the whole sordid episode until it was satisfactorily resolved, but now it can have no happy ending—or at least, not the happy ending I'd hoped for.'

'Then you better tell me now, for if you don't, how am I supposed to help?'

He was rewarded with a tremulous smile. 'That is very gallant of you, but I fear my situation is beyond rescuing, even by you.'

'I'll be the judge of that, once I know what we're dealing with.'

'It's a long story, Drummond.'

'The one thing I'm not currently short of is time. Fire away!'

'Well, if you are sure.' Joanna clasped her hands together, angling herself to face him. 'About three years ago, I was employed by Lady Christina Robertson to act as governess to her eldest daughter. Lottie was then sixteen, and due to make her debut the following year. Lady Christina is...'

'A doyenne of society,' Drummond said drily. 'I was introduced to her at the Richmond ball actually, on the eve of Waterloo. Her husband was at that time a bigwig in the Foreign Office. You were mixing in rarefied circles.'

Joanna snorted. 'A governess does not exactly mix but—yes, I had by any standards secured a prestigious position and Lottie was, unlike some of my previous charges, an excellent pupil. I was—am—very fond of her.' She bit her lip. 'That is why it hurt so much when she betrayed me.'

Drummond frowned. 'What did she do?'

'I trusted her. It was naïve of me, to think that such an excellent pupil would have maturity of judgement to match her intelligence. She was very pretty, indulged, popular, and where there are young girls like Lottie, there are always young men. I knew the signs to look for, having prevented just such foolishness with another of my charges, but with Lottie I was complacent. It didn't occur to me that she was capable of being deceitful, and she therefore found it easy enough to go behind my back.'

'To meet with a beau?'

Joanna nodded. 'I don't know how many times—I still can't quite believe she had the nerve. I was not in the habit of checking on her once she retired, she was sixteen years old after all, and eligible to be married within a year. But that particular night, for some reason I did. The Robertsons had intended to spend the night with friends, but his lordship took ill on the journey, and they came back about eleven. The noise woke me, I had this—this odd feeling, and went to Lottie's room and she wasn't there.'

She felt sick, remembering it. She'd slumped down on Lottie's bed. The girl hadn't even tried to make it look slept in. Her first thought had been to question the maid, but before she had reached for the bell, the signs she had been ignoring for weeks fell into place like the pieces of a puzzle.

'I didn't know what to do, save to wait up for her. It was an interminable night, Drummond. I have always thought that pacing the floor was something only characters in books do, but I paced and paced, until I began to worry about the floorboards squeaking. She eventually turned up at about three, and as you can imagine, just about leapt out of her skin to find me waiting. All I cared about at first was that she was safe. Such a little innocent, she could have been ruined before she was even out in society!'

'Little hussy, more like,' Drummond exclaimed. 'At sixteen, she should damned well have known better.'

'Precisely. As her governess, I should have made sure that she did, but I…'

'Joanna, you cannot possibly blame yourself.'

'But I was at fault, Drummond, and though I knew that I'd most likely be dismissed for my lack of vigilance, I also knew that I could not possibly keep Lottie's behaviour a secret from Lady Christina. I told her that unless she confessed to her mama first thing in the morning, I would tell her myself.' Joanna shuddered. 'She begged and she pleaded and she threatened, and she cried—how she cried, I'm surprised she did not wake the household. In the end, I thought I had persuaded her to do the right thing. I should have known better. The next day…'

'The next day?' Drummond prompted. 'Take a deep breath and tell me precisely what happened.'

She did as he bid, though her voice was shaky. 'Lottie had "borrowed" her mother's emerald necklace to impress her beau. I assumed she would hand it over when she confessed to her foolish behaviour, but in the event, she did neither. When the necklace was discovered to be missing the next day, it was found in my bedchamber when a search was made of the house.'

'And your employers duly accused you of theft,' Drummond said heavily. 'Why the devil didn't you tell them the truth?'

She flinched at the anger in his tone, though she couldn't blame him. 'I tried to, but Lottie flatly denied everything, and Lady Christina accused me of trying to ruin her daughter's character in order to save my own skin.'

'When in fact the opposite was the case?'

'Yes. It was a nightmare. I kept thinking that Lottie would eventually speak up and take responsibility, but she wouldn't even look at me. I should have—no, not expected it, but I shouldn't have been so surprised. A young person of Lottie's age, in Lottie's position, was bound to think only of saving her own skin. She was young and spoilt and selfish, and she had her back to the wall. So she acted both rashly and wrongly.'

'That, I do understand,' Drummond said. His expression darkened. His hand, which was resting on his knee, clenched into such a tight fist that his knuckles turned white. 'I understand that better than anyone.'

The bleakness in his eyes made her shiver, but before Joanna could ask what he was thinking, he gave himself a shake. 'I think I can guess the outcome.'

'It is sadly predictable. I was dismissed on the spot. They informed me that, thanks to my otherwise un-sullied reputation, they had decided not to involve the authorities, though upon reflection, I suspect they had their own reputation to consider, not wishing to become embroiled in a court case,' Joanna said bitterly. 'I left, thinking that Lottie would be bound to confess sooner or later, and in the blithe assumption that I'd easily find another position, for despite a lack of a character reference from Lady Christina, I had many other letters of recommendation. But Lady Christina had other intentions, and is, as you said yourself, a doyenne of society with influence almost as far-reaching as her very good friend, the Duchess of Brockmore. She branded me a thief, and she made sure that everyone knew it. Door after door was slammed in my face, and no respectable school would employ me, which is how I come to be in my current position, employed for no more than my bed and board, and expected to act the drudge when I am not teaching.'

Drummond swore. He raked his fingers through his hair. He swore again. He jumped up from the seat, dug his hands into his pockets, took a rapid turn around the room, then sat down and cursed again.

'My thoughts entirely,' Joanna said, with a poor attempt at humour.

'What changed?' he demanded. 'You said you came here expecting justice to be finally served.'

'Lottie belatedly found her conscience a few months ago,' Joanna said wearily. 'She wanted to write to me but could not establish my whereabouts. She turned to her mama's best friend, our hostess, whose reach is long, and when she discovered the depth of my plight, Lottie was horrified and told her mother the true story. Her mama also felt guilty, but not guilty enough to do something about it herself, and so asked Her Grace to intercede—what is it you said about the Brockmores? Where they lead, and all that.'

'But where it won't lead, I take it, is to the clearing of your name?'

'Precisely. My name, so the Duchess implied, is not as important as Lady Christina's. Having gone to immense efforts to brand me a thief, she must be spared the social embarrassment of retracting her accusations, and instead branding her daughter a coward, and herself a fool for believing her,' Joanna said, her lip curling. 'So you can be sure that even if I did choose to speak out, it would be pointless, for she would deny it all. But Lady Christina will pay me a financial recompense for the harm done to my reputation, if you please, or I may, if *I* please, be offered the position as governess to poor Mr Martindale's wards—you see, Mr Martindale's presence here is not only to give him a respite from his grief, but to give him the opportunity to size me up! But both so-called amends are dependant upon my continued silence.'

Drummond's fists were clenched again. 'Which means that, as far as respectable society is concerned, you will be branded a thief for ever. That is outrageous.'

'I heartily agree, but there is nothing I can do about it. Lottie is apparently to be married shortly, and though she is most contrite, she is even more terrified that the story may come to the ears of her betrothed, and you see how it could unravel? Once the question is asked, why did she take the necklace, then her foolish indiscretion could come to light.'

'And her utterly selfish act in framing you.'

'Yes.' Tears welled, but she forced them back. 'So I am to have no clean slate, but I must not lose sight of the fact that I am being offered a second chance.'

'Aye, on someone else's terms.'

'Worse than that. I am being offered payment for a silence I had already resolved to maintain, until Lottie—but now there is no chance of that. None at all. It is grossly unfair, but there we have it.' Joanna slumped back on the sofa, completely drained. 'I believe our conversation has come full circle.'

'And you are exhausted,' Drummond said. 'Best not to make any rash decisions. Let it settle in your mind, and we can...'

'This is my problem, Drummond.'

'I want to help.'

She didn't doubt his sincerity, but instead of reassuring her, it set alarm bells ringing in her head. She could not embroil him in this. He needed to keep his nose clean or he might jeopardise his own chances. Getting to her feet, she shook out her dress and picked up her cloak. 'I don't need help. Now I know the terms, I must make a simple decision, and that is the end of it. In the meantime, do you think we can turn our attention to enjoying the festivities?'

He hesitated only a moment before following her lead, taking her hand, turning it over to kiss her palm. 'I warn you, you will regret asking me to hurl myself into the wassailing this evening.'

She was not fooled. In four days, she had learned enough of him to know that he would not drop the subject for ever. At the moment, she was exhausted, disappointed and disillusioned, and she also knew he wouldn't press her further until she was restored. She smiled weakly, making for the door. 'You are a fine figure of a man, Drummond MacIntosh. I refuse to countenance that you do not have a fine singing voice to match.'

The pianoforte had been moved to the centre of the music room, with two semicircles of chairs set around it. In comparison to the other state rooms of Brockmore Manor, this was an intimate space, the walls and ceiling plain white, the cornicing embellished with lyres, trumpets and harps. The rose-coloured curtains, which matched the damask of the seating, were pulled shut, a large fire burned brightly, and a multitude of holly-adorned candles were lit, giving the room a cosy, festive air.

Drummond sat at the end of the second row next to the door, with Joanna beside him. She looked quite restored to good humour, and determined to enjoy herself.

His resolution to give her a respite from her problems was, he was sure, the right thing. 'I've reserved the best seats in the house from which to escape,' he whispered to her, 'should the assault on our ears prove intolerable.'

'Are you persisting with the pretence that you can't hold a note in order to surprise me? You will have competition you know, there are some other very fine voices present,' Joanna said. 'Lady Viola for one,' she said, nodding over at the beauty, who was tonight dressed in a red gown that left very little to the imagination. 'I believe her voice is as pleasing to the ear as her figure is to the eye.'

'Yet her figure seems not to please the one man in the room she has set her cap at,' Drummond said sardonically. 'The Duke's heir,' he added, in response to Joanna's questioning brow. 'Haven't you noticed, how very pointedly he's ignoring her?'

'I had not. Do you think…?'

'I think His Grace would have something to say, if the case were otherwise. The heir to as great a dukedom as this one would never be permitted to align himself with a woman with such a reputation as Lady Viola has amassed, no matter how well born she is. I suspect that Brockmore has other plans for his nephew.'

Joanna pursed her lips. 'But if Mr Penrith desires…'

Drummond laughed shortly. 'Vale Penrith's wants or desires have naught to do with the case. It is what the Duke wishes, and what a duke wants, a duke gets.' He had been thinking of his Duke, not Brockmore, and was irked at the note of bitterness in his voice. Of course Joanna noticed. She noticed everything. Fortunately, the arrival of their hosts prevented her commenting. They had chosen to feature moss-green as their co-ordinating shade for tonight. 'Most festive,' he muttered for Joanna's ears only, and was rewarded with a complicit smile.

'Ladies and gentlemen,' said His Grace, leaning on the pianoforte, his other arm encircling his wife's slim waist, 'welcome to our little musical soirée. Now, we all know that wassailing is traditionally performed by tenants and villagers, singing for their supper, so to speak, but here at Brockmore, our people have no requirement to go a-begging.' The Duke paused, and his guests laughed politely. 'In the West Country, I believe, they sing to their apple trees in the belief that a few songs will produce a better yield, and more importantly, consequently will produce more cider. We're not expecting you to go out and chant incantations in our orchard, but Alicia and I thought it would be rather nice for us all to have a bit of a sing-song, something to bring us all together. And for those of you who need a little encouragement, we've some West Country cider mixed with a few other special ingredients, to lubricate the vocal cords. Now, if you all have a charged glass…'

The Duke waited, while his stately butler ensured that all the guests were served. The potent mixture was warm, served in little crystal cups. Joanna's nose wrinkled as she sniffed it. 'Rum,' Drummond informed her, taking a sly sip, 'and nutmeg, I think, cinnamon, some brandy. One cup of this, we'll not only be singing, but we'll be convinced that we're in tune.'

'Then I had better try it.'

They clinked glasses, but Joanna's cautious sip became a splutter as the Duke of Brockmore burst into song. *'Wassail! wassail! all over the town!'* His Grace boomed in mellifluous tones. *'Our toast it is white and our ale it is brown,'* he continued, and Drummond felt a rumble of totally inappropriate laughter.

It was the accent, he realised. Brockmore was attempting a West Country accent, and though he was perfectly in tune, an excellent baritone in fact, he sounded as if he had a mouth full of the apples from which the cider was made.

*'Our bowl it is made of the white maple tree,'* he trilled, and Drummond felt himself begin to tremble.

He was not the only one. Beside him Joanna, her hands laced tightly together in her lap, her eyes downcast, was biting her lip. He could feel her thigh shaking, distracting him for a moment from the Duke's performance, but His Grace's crescendo put all thoughts of Joanna's trembling flesh from his mind.

*'With the wassailing bowl, we'll drink unto thee.'*

The Duchess of Brockmore kissed her husband. The guests rose to their feet applauding and shouting bravo, bravo. Drummond met Joanna's eyes, and was almost overset. She covered her mouth, turning an escaped giggle into a cough. Drummond took a large gulp of the wassail, felt the strong liquor burn its way down his throat into his belly. 'I can recommend this,' he whispered, urging Joanna to do the same.

She did as he bid her, and her laughter turned into a real spluttering cough. 'Dear lord,' she said, fanning her cheeks and draining her glass, 'this has gone straight to my head.'

'I suspect you'll be glad of it,' Drummond said, as the butler refilled the glasses and handed out music sheets, and Miss Canningvale sat down at the pianoforte with a flourish of her cherry-pink gown.

'A song in the round,' she said. 'Captain Milborne,

I rely upon you to divide the room into three. On my count...' She struck up a chord.

Drummond threw back his second wassail, noticing that Joanna followed suit. He cleared his throat. They were in the first group. *'As I strode out one morning with my sweetheart by my side...'* he sang, with punch-fuelled abandon.

Drummond and Joanna stood by the tall windows of the empty ballroom, gazing out at the vast expanse of pure white snow which covered the south lawn and glittered in the inky darkness. It was late. Most of the guests, exhausted by the wassailing and tipsy from imbibing the wassail, had retired to their bedchambers, though Lady Viola and several of her court were playing billiards.

'Poor Miss Creighton,' Joanna said, 'how mortified she will be tomorrow when she discovers that she was carried up the stairs by two strapping footmen.'

Drummond laughed. 'I doubt she'll remember it, and I hope no one will be so unkind as to remind her. She had only one glass of that stuff too. Obviously she is not a drinker.'

'I would have limited myself to one, had you not joined in the singing with such gusto.' Joanna chuckled. 'I have to say, you are an absolutely atrocious singer, Drummond MacIntosh.'

He laughed. 'I did warn you that a fine figure did not predicate a fine singing voice.' He put his arm around her waist, turning her to face him. 'So you think I have a fine figure, do you, Miss Forsythe?'

It was not embarrassment which coloured her cheeks in the cool air, but the nearness of that very fine figure just inches from her. The light touch of his fingers, resting on the flare of her hip through the silk of her gown, the heat in his eyes as he looked down at her, the shadow their silhouette made on the window pane. 'I am sure I'm not the first female to compliment you on it.'

Drummond laughed. 'You overestimate my charms.' His other hand slid up her arm to rest on the nape of her neck, his fingers feathering little spirals on to her skin, which sent shivers down her spine. He caught her wrist, pressing a kiss to her palm. 'Does that mean you don't want to hear more of my caterwauling?'

'I sincerely hope that you have not promised to regale us with a wee Highland lament on New Year's Eve.'

'Hogmanay. It's not just my off-key singing that you need to worry about. Have you ever heard the bagpipes being played, Joanna?' When she shook her head, Drummond grinned. 'Like a cat being squeezed, some say, though I reckon they're more like the wailing of a banshee.'

'Then I will be sure to stuff cotton in my ears before I come down to dinner.'

'Oh, that won't do. You can't dance a reel with cotton in your ears, and I'm looking forward very much to dancing a reel with you. I dance much better than I sing, I promise.'

Over at the window, the last of the candles flickered out, leaving them in the eerie light of the moon reflecting on the snow outside. 'That's not much of a boast,' Joanna teased.

'Then I'll prove it.'

He swept her into his arms and began to waltz with her, humming tunelessly but in time. 'You are trying to lead,' he said.

'I am accustomed to playing the gentleman's role with my charges,' she answered, stumbling laughingly to a halt.

He pulled her closer, tightening his arm around her waist. 'I could never mistake you for anything but a woman. Follow my lead, Joanna. I won't let you fall.'

She could not see his face in the dim light. She had already fallen just about as far as she could. She was to be rescued from the mire, but she was not to be restored.

'Joanna? Shall we?'

Enough. There would be time enough to come to terms with all that the Duchess had said later. She smiled up at him. 'Yes, please,' she said, and surrendered to the strange magic of a midnight waltz in a ghostly ballroom with the man of her dreams.

## Chapter Four

*Tuesday, 29th December 1818*

Thick snow clouds meant the morning light was murky and gloomy, reflecting Drummond's mood as he tramped through frozen and rutted country lanes. His breath was a billowing white cloud. He'd forgotten his gloves, but he was too deep in thought to be aware of the cold. He needed to put some distance between himself and Brockmore Manor. He needed to decide whether his growing conviction that he should tell Joanna the real story behind his visit here was one of those crazy middle-of-the-night thoughts, or the right thing to do.

Walking had always been Drummond's way of clearing his head. When he was a lad he'd wandered the network of drovers' tracks which meandered over moors, through glens, and up mountainsides in his native Argyll. During his long career in the army he had tramped the hot dusty plains of Spain's heartland, traversed the wild beauty of the Ardèche, and trod the stark white paths along the limestone cliffs they called *calanques* in the south of France. He'd followed a good part of the

Camino, the ancient pilgrims' route to Santiago de Compostela, and in Lisbon, Cadiz, Grenada and Toledo he'd walked the ramparts.

He paused beside a frozen pond, dug his frozen fingers into the deep pockets of his greatcoat, and tried to order his thoughts. Wellington prized Drummond's eye for detail, his talent for resolving the most complicated of logistical problems in a structured way. But this tangle—he wasn't at all sure there was a clear path out of it. Not any path he cared to take, anyway. Which was the nub of it. The fact was that in the space of less than a week he'd come to care more for Joanna Forsythe than he'd ever thought it possible to care for any woman. And Joanna Forsythe was about the most unsuitable woman he could possibly have set his sights on. Not that he'd set his sights on her. No, it had not come to that, not yet. But if he was not careful—aye, he could easily fall in love with her.

Groaning, Drummond squeezed his eyes shut. That would teach him to boast about keeping a leash on his feelings! What's more, there was no point in telling himself that the number of hours he'd spent in her company amounted to less than zero. With time at a premium, it seemed the essence of something important could be distilled far more quickly, every moment made to count. Every minute he spent with Joanna, he came to know her better, and to like her better, and to desire her more. Oh, Lord, he wanted her, and that had nothing to do with the fact that he'd not had a woman in his bed since…

Since that life-changing event. He realised he had to tell her. It was only fair that she know the truth. She had to see, as he did, that the pair of them had no prospect of any sort of future together—even if she wanted that, which actually, he was far from certain about.

Drummond pondered this intriguing, if utterly irrelevant question. She did like him. She did want him. She was every bit as taken aback as he by this force of attraction, the invisible cord which drew them to each other. That much was obvious. And she was every bit as wary of it too. How many times had she asserted her desire for independence? An unnatural sort of woman, she'd called herself, for not wanting a boring marriage, but he couldn't imagine life being boring, living with Joanna.

His smile faded abruptly. How exactly would they live? Inhabit some fairy-tale land where the scandal of the crime she was accused of, and the crime he had committed, no longer clung to them? He had not come here to dream, he'd come here to face reality, and the reality was that he needed Wellington's patronage, and Joanna needed a post befitting her talents, and neither of them would get anywhere without the helping hand of Their Graces of Brockmore. Yes, he'd better come clean. That way they could both see, in stark terms, that they were risking not just failure but personal heartache.

But it was not only that, he acknowledged, beginning the long walk back. He wanted Joanna to reassure him he'd done the right thing. Absolution? Understanding? Whatever, after all this time, he was pretty sure he'd found the one person who could provide both.

A Frost Fair was being held on the village green today. A selection of booths strung with seasonal greenery were set up on the perimeter with a variety of goods for sale: fine wines; ribbons; sugared sweets; carved wooden toys; and a vast selection of elaborately iced gingerbread. The air was scented with spices and pine, the vendors of each little shop encouraging the crowd to sample mulled wines, barley sugar, baked apples, and a variety of cakes.

The ladies and gentlemen from Brockmore had set out in separate groups, but as they walked towards the fair some had paired up, the ladies' hands tucked into the arms of the gentlemen. Lady Beatrice Landry had fallen into step with Joanna. 'I think Miss Pletcher and Lord Truesdale may make a match of it, what do you think?' she asked.

She wore a cloak of emerald-green velvet which perfectly matched the simple but beautifully cut gown of fine worsted which she had worn at breakfast. The wide hood of her cloak was trimmed with fur which matched the huge muff into which she tucked her hands. Her boots and gloves were plain brown leather, practical but beautifully tooled. 'I think what I think every time I stand next to you,' Joanna said with a wry smile, 'that I look like a complete dowd. My boots are brown like yours, and my gloves, but so too are my cloak and my gown. I suppose you could argue that I am perfectly co-ordinated but...'

'Oh, stuff and nonsense. You have excellent taste, Miss Forsythe. Your gown is not brown but russet, and your cloak is not brown but chestnut. No doubt you'll be telling me that your hair is also brown...'

'No, I have it on good authority that it is chocolate,' Joanna said, laughing.

'Ah. It's not difficult to guess who paid you that compliment. Where is Mr MacIntosh? He was not at breakfast.'

'I don't know, I do not keep track of his whereabouts,' Joanna said, flustered.

Lady Beatrice raised a beautifully plucked brow but said nothing, guiding them towards a neglected stall where everything, it seemed to Joanna, was either broken or missing an essential part. There were saucers without teacups, and a sugar bowl with no matching cream jug. There was a rusty horseshoe, a china doll lacking an arm, and a garden hoe bereft of a handle. Lady Beatrice picked up a perfectly hideous china cow with only three legs and held it up to the sky, where the sun would have been had it not been covered by heavy grey clouds presaging more snow. 'How lovely,' she said, with a warm smile at the young woman behind the counter. 'A perfect gift for my great-aunt. How much do you want for it?'

'A shilling, ma'am,' the young woman said, looking every bit as astonished as Joanna felt.

'Oh, I have only a crown,' Lady Beatrice said, pressing the coin worth five times what the woman had asked for into her hands. 'Don't trouble yourself fishing for change.'

'That was most generous of you,' Joanna observed as they walked away.

'A mere trifle. The world is full of iniquities, I only wish I could do more.'

'It is a pity that you cannot achieve your ambition of being a politician.'

'Oh, there are other ways to exert influence. Madame de Staël, the famous French salonist, is a perfect example,' Lady Beatrice said with a conspiratorial smile. 'You are not the only one to have been cultivating one gentleman in particular. You need not deny it, Miss Forsythe, nor concern yourself overmuch either. You have been very discreet, but I am a most acute observer, and Mr Throckton even more so.'

'Edward Throckton! You have set your cap at him of all people.'

'Looks are no measure of a person, as I know only too well. He is eight years younger than I, and he was born on the wrong side of the blanket, but—hmmm. I hear he made a fool of himself in the billiard room last night, playing for a kiss from Lady Viola, if you please, but he was not the only one, and one must forgive the vagaries of youth. A very ambitious man, a most acute observer, and not at all averse to the notion of a politically ambitious wife, I do believe Mr Throckton would do very well for me. Are you shocked, Miss Forsythe?'

'You would like me to be, wouldn't you?' Joanna countered, which made her companion laugh.

'Mr Throckton and I certainly make a most unlikely couple in most people's eyes, but we can be of great mutual benefit. While you and Mr MacIntosh—I understand that he is destined to be one of the Duke of Wellington's aides? I am very sorry to have to say this, for I like you very well, but I am, sadly, much more practised in the ways of the world than you. I have the pedigree and the money and the connections to carry off marriage to an illegitimate man, and to help him prosper. I apologise for being blunt, but you, while clearly gently bred, have nothing to recommend you to the Duke of Wellington, I fear. Mr MacIntosh will need a wife who can help him climb the political ladder. A woman who can form part of Wellington's coterie—his inner sanctum of comrades and ladies of beauty and influence—and birth. You would not be an asset to Mr

MacIntosh, no matter how much Mr MacIntosh himself may think you are.'

'I know that,' Joanna said, though she felt slightly sick. If Lady Beatrice already thought her a barrier to Drummond's success without even knowing her blackened reputation… 'I know that very well,' she said with a forced smile. 'You are quite mistaken, if you think that either of us have any thoughts—there is nothing between us, nothing of a permanent nature, that is. I am grateful for the warning, but it was unnecessary.'

She sounded not in the least convincing, but Lady Beatrice had already proved herself the soul of tact. 'Indeed,' she said, pressing her arm. 'I am sure you will do what is right. Now, if you will excuse me, I must have a word with Lady Viola. And if I am not mistaken, there is a gentleman over there, wishing to have a word with you. I have discovered that the boating house is an excellent location for a private tryst. You will find the key conveniently located on the lintel.'

'Drummond.'

He took her hands in his, a familiar clasp. 'Joanna.'

'What is it, you are looking troubled?'

'I've been walking. Thinking. I need to talk to you.'

He had come to tell her it was over. 'Have you been— has Mr Throckton spoken to you?' Joanna asked, thinking that a well-intentioned two-pronged attack had been launched.

But Drummond looked at her blankly. 'I haven't seen him today. Why?'

'Nothing. I thought—I've been speaking to Lady Beatrice. She said…'

'Joanna.' He gave her a little shake. 'I've no interest

in what Lady Beatrice has to say for herself, but I have been thinking a great deal about what you told me yesterday, and…'

'And you think we must call a halt to this. Whatever it is. Not that it is anything, because we agreed…'

'Joanna!' Casting a quick look around to ensure that all attention was elsewhere, Drummond put his arm around her and ushered her away from the Frost Fair. 'I don't want to call a halt to this. Whatever it is. I don't want it to end, and that's the problem, because it must.'

'I know. Oh, Drummond, I know that.'

He smiled at her, a crooked little smile edged with tenderness that made her heart ache, for it reflected everything that she felt herself.

'But you don't know why,' he said slowly, 'and that's what I want to remedy.'

She took him to the boating house as Lady Beatrice had suggested. It was a pagoda-style pavilion, with a little jetty running out to a frozen lake, which had a small island at its centre, the leafless trees standing stark against the winter sky. Two days ago, there had been an ice-skating party here, but today it was deserted.

'Lady Beatrice has been having secret assignations with Edward Throckton here,' Joanna explained when he asked how she knew where to find the key.

Once inside, Drummond busied himself setting light to another of Brockmore Manor's thoughtfully pre-laid fires. 'He told me at that opening tea party—oh, centuries ago it seems, that he had a fondness for marble statues, and I thought it a highly unlikely ambition, but mayhap I was wrong.'

'Yet it is not as unlikely as the match with poor Captain Milborne which Philippa Canningvale seems determined to pursue,' Joanna said, pulling two rustic wooden chairs towards the hearth. 'What ails him, Drummond? I have twice seen him forced to retire with the most debilitating headache, and at dinner last night, when the servant dropped that silver salver with a clatter, he turned the most dreadful colour, and his hands were shaking so much he could scarce hold his cutlery. I saw you speaking to him afterwards. Are his headaches the result of an injury sustained in combat?'

'It is highly likely, but not all battle scars are physical, Joanna. There are some which never heal.' Drummond was leaning forward in his chair, his hand resting on his knees, a slight frown knitting his brow. 'Yesterday,' he began, after a painful pause, 'you told me that it stuck in your throat, to be offered a fresh start and no clean slate. Not justice, but reparation, and on someone else's terms. It struck a chord with me. A dirty big chord, if there's such a thing. Like you, I did what I knew to be right, and was punished for it. Like you, I've been offered a second chance, and I'm painfully aware...' His voice faltered. He swallowed hard, then coughed. 'There is someone who cannot be given a second chance, and it is he—that story, that is what I need to recount to you.'

She could see that he was steeling himself. She could tell by the way his mouth thinned, by the way his finger strayed to the scar in his eyebrow, that this would be painful, and though she desperately wanted to know, she hated what it would cost him to tell her. 'Drummond, you don't need to...'

'I do,' he said firmly. 'I've thought about it long and hard, and I want you to know. And though it will—I've never spoken of it before—it's better for both of us that you know the full circumstances.'

'Then I am honoured,' Joanna said, bracing herself for what was to come.

'I told you that I left the army after Waterloo. You've no doubt wondered why I spent the last three years or so rusticating in Shropshire, when it is clear I'm not cut out to play the country squire.'

'And when you said yourself that your only desire is to serve your country,' Joanna added. 'It struck me as odd, yes. I also don't understand why you need the approval of the Duke of Brockmore. It is obvious to me that you must have been a most excellent officer, Drummond. Why would you need the Duke's patronage?'

She could see a pulse beating in his throat. His hands, resting on his thighs, were clenched into fists. He cleared his throat. 'I didn't contradict your assumption that I voluntarily resigned my commission after Waterloo, like many others did. The truth is that I—my commission was stripped from me. I was cashiered from the army, Joanna. On Wednesday the fifth of July, while the dead were still being buried and the wounded still suffering, I was frogmarched out into a courtyard in front of my entire regiment. My epaulettes were ripped from my shoulders, my medals were torn from my chest and my sword was broken. You can't understand what it meant, how could you, a civilian, but it was—the shame, the humiliation—I can't explain it.'

'You don't need to, it is writ large in your expression,' Joanna exclaimed, quite stunned. 'But why? What on earth did you do to deserve to be treated in such a way?'

'Oh, I deserved it all right. I have never disputed that.

But as to what I did—it is a rather a case of what I didn't do. I refused to kill a man.'

'But—is it such a heinous crime to show mercy to the enemy?'

'It was not an enemy soldier. It was one of my own men. And what's more, I'd do the same again. No matter that Wellington and all of my comrades would violently disagree, I know I did the right thing.'

'Oh, Drummond!' Utterly stunned and completely confused by what he had just told her, Joanna's first instinct was to comfort him, but when she made to do so, he shook his head.

'No, otherwise I won't be able to—I have to finish this,' he said, waving her back to her seat.

And so she did as he bid her, though it cost her, watching him struggling to get his emotions under control, his fists clenching and unclenching, his eyes staring off into some bleak landscape she could not picture. Finally, he drew a ragged breath and began to speak, the words spilling out in a rush.

'Ensign Alick Patterson was just seventeen. You learn to spot the ones that won't cope, and from the start I had my worries about the lad. Too much bravado, not enough gumption. He was not cut out for army life, but he was a second son, and in the Patterson family, the second son traditionally joined the Scots Guards. To cut a long story short, on the day we went into battle at Waterloo he took fright, ignored a direct order to advance and turned tail in full view of the troops, dropping our regimental flag into the bargain. If only he'd run off before the lines were drawn it might have been easier to ask for clemency, but the rules are very clear, Joanna. An officer must lead the way, and that way is forward, not back.'

'But he was just a boy. Seventeen years old…'

'It makes no difference. He deserted his comrades under fire, and by lowering our flag, he virtually signed his own death warrant. I acted as advocate for him at his court-martial, but the problem was that the facts were indisputable, and there were hundreds of witnesses. Men who had stayed to fight while Alick Patterson fled, men who proceeded to lose many comrades. Waterloo was sheer carnage, I've never seen the like in all my years of campaigning. Who could deny them the right to see Patterson face the music, but at the same time…'

Drummond drew a shuddering breath. 'I don't know. Something about this particular case moved me in a way that previous ones had not. We'd just won the bloodiest battle in living memory and secured peace for Europe. It was a momentous and glorious moment in Britain's history. A time for forgiveness and magnanimity. It seemed both futile and senseless for any more blood to be shed, for one more young life to be cut short, simply because he had panicked and acted rashly. I said as much in the letter I wrote to Wellington. I thought it so obvious, Joanna, I couldn't believe that he would view it differently.'

'But he did?'

'He did, and he did not take kindly to my persistent challenging of his decision. I remember…' Drummond blanched. '"Cowardice cannot be tolerated," he said. "I will not have my officers' hard-won reputation for bravery compromised by anyone, not even a callow youth."'

'What sentence was handed down?' The question was no more than a whisper, for Joanna had already guessed the answer, and it made her feel sick to the pit of her stomach.

'Execution,' Drummond said through gritted teeth. 'Francis Larpent, Wellington's Judge Advocate General who reads all appeals for clemency, is a just and fair man, or so I had always thought. I pushed hard for the sentence to be commuted, but the only concession I secured was for the method to be changed to facing a firing squad, for it is considered more honourable to be shot than hanged.'

His expression became even more grim. 'I tried to reconcile myself to it, but something in me rebelled. It was plain wrong, and no amount of military reasoning could make me believe otherwise. Eventually, Wellington grew weary of what he saw as my insubordination in questioning his decision, and in an effort to bring me to heel, ordered that I attend the execution. It would not be the first I had witnessed but it would be the last.'

'How unspeakably awful for you!'

'The Colonel in charge of proceedings and the firing squad itself were drawn from other regiments. All the same, half the men turned up blind drunk, knowing full well it was the only way they could blunt their own feelings sufficiently to obey an order to fire on one of their own. Young Patterson was brought in and blindfolded. I've seen men begging for mercy, crying like babies in such situations, but he did neither. Alick Patterson had found courage from somewhere that he hadn't displayed in the heat of battle. Only it was too late—'

Drummond broke off, swearing under his breath. His eyes were glazed, lost in the memory. Watching him, Joanna felt heartsick, dreading what was to come.

'I stood there, rooted to the spot, and I kept thinking, it won't happen, there will be a last-minute intervention, someone somewhere will see sense, show some mercy. But it was a vain hope. So I was forced to stand and watch.'

Sweat gleamed on his brow. Beneath his tan, he had turned a sickly grey. 'When the Colonel gave the order, some of the squad fired into the air or fired to deliberately miss. That always happens, though not usually to such a degree. It is no easy thing for a man to shoot a comrade, no matter what his crime. Alick was still standing, not one bullet had hit him. A second round was called for, but with the same result. The lad was on his knees by then, only lightly wounded, and I—I thought that maybe now, the Colonel would call a halt to the grisly proceedings. But he clearly liked to do things by the book.'

'What did he do?'

'He ordered me, as the senior officer present, to complete the task, as required by military law.'

Joanna had never seen such stark misery on a man's face before. Sweat tracked down his temples, tears tracked down his cheeks, though he seemed quite oblivious. She could taste her own tears, but she was quite incapable of moving, even to reach for her kerchief.

'I drew my pistol,' Drummond said. 'I walked up to him. I knew he couldn't see me, but somehow that made it worse. I simply couldn't do it. Wouldn't do it. I couldn't even lift my arm to aim. I could feel them, the firing squad, the Colonel, all watching me. Silence, that's what I remember, this deafening silence as I stood there for what seemed like an age. I knew that there would be no going back if I didn't follow orders. None the less, I turned to tell the Colonel I refused to carry out his order but he was already marching towards me. To arrest me, I thought. Stupidly. That came later. First, he dispensed summary military justice. Afterwards, all I remember is my own voice, crying out over and over. No. No. No.'

He dropped his head on to his hands. His shoulders shook with the effort of containing his sobs, and Joanna could no longer restrain herself. She threw her arms around him, holding him awkwardly, aghast, appalled, utterly horrified at what he had told her. Words seemed trivial. The picture Drummond had painted was shockingly real, yet quite beyond her ken. She supposed she must have been aware that such things happened, but it was one thing to read a report in a newspaper of an execution for—what did they call it, gross neglect of duty? But to hear the detail, to be able to picture the scene—it was not only one man's life, but the life of every other man present which was changed for ever.

Drummond's shoulders had stopped heaving. She loosened her hold on him, but his head remained in his hands. Reluctantly, she let him go, sensing that he'd want a few moments to himself. 'I'll go and check if the Duke has a secret cache of brandy hidden somewhere. I think we could both do with a snifter,' Joanna said with false brightness, making for a door on the side wall. She found herself in a storeroom, filled with boating paraphernalia, ropes and hooks and rowlocks and oars, a clutch of fishing rods, some nets. If there was any brandy, it would not be here, but she waited, counting to a hundred, before returning to the other room.

Drummond was standing by the fire. 'I appreciate your little charade but there's no need, I'm fine,' he said, holding out his hand to her.

'Are you sure?'

He was pale, but his eyes were no longer glazed with grief. When she reached up to smooth his hair back, he managed a faltering smile. 'I was not fine, not by a long chalk, and not for a long time, but I am now.' He kissed her brow then let her go, sitting back down. 'I'll try to make the rest brief. I spent a year in the country trying to come to terms with what had happened, and then I decided that feeling sorry for myself wasn't serving any purpose, and I wasn't going to let that day ruin my life as well as Ensign Patterson's. So I set about finding myself a new career. But every door was slammed in my face.'

'That is absolutely outrageous! And so unfair!' Joanna exclaimed.

Drummond gave a ghostly laugh. 'Society judges mutineers harshly.'

'To act as you did, in front of all those men—men who had themselves found a way to avoid carrying out the order—that takes a unique kind of bravery, as far as I am concerned.'

'It was a futile gesture in the end.'

'It was far from futile.'

'How can you say that? Alick Patterson is still dead.'

'Yes, he is, poor lad. Would you have been able to live with your conscience if you had acted any differently?'

His smile was ghostly, but it was a smile. 'You know the answer to that.'

'And that is why there was nothing futile about it. Drummond, you couldn't save Alick but you did save yourself. To have acted counter to years of instilled discipline and military training, to do what you believed was right knowing the price you would pay, is testimony to your integrity. Your actions were noble, even if they were technically wrong. I cannot tell you how very, very, very much I admire you.'

'Thank you.' Drummond squeezed her hand. 'I knew you would understand. Unfortunately you are in a minority of one.'

'But surely your family...?'

He shifted uncomfortably, crossing one ankle over the other, then uncrossing it. 'I wrote to my father. Informed him that I'd been cashiered, though not the circumstance. He was always so proud of me—I didn't tell you that before. I find it so difficult to think of him. Cashiering is very rare and consequently very shameful. I felt I'd let him down.' He winced. 'I knew my father would be mortified, so I told him that I'd not make matters worse by darkening his door with my presence.'

'You cut yourself off?' Joanna exclaimed in dismay.

'He wrote back, saying that I would always be welcome, and that I was his son no matter what.'

'It sounds as though your father is as fine a man as his son—his only son. You said your father is hale and hearty, but if anything were to happen to him, think how much you would regret this self-imposed estrangement.'

'Of course I've thought about that, dammit!' Drummond jumped to his feet. 'It's one of the reasons I'm so keen on securing this posting. It is important to me to be able to look my father in the eye again.'

'From a position of legitimate status you mean?'

'I'm not sure you appreciate how bloody unusual it is, to be offered the opportunity to come back into the fold. Wellington never reverses a decision. He told me that I'd paid the price for my actions, but perhaps the truth is, he has a conscience after all.'

Joanna snorted. 'More likely it is simply that he needs you. This new position he is to take up, he will want to make his mark in it, for he is a man who revels in glory.

If the Duke of Wellington did not think you indispensable, he would have continued to dispense with you, I think.'

'Aye, you may well be right at that,' Drummond said sardonically, 'but he made it crystal-clear there would be no room for latitude. "You displayed insubordination and a lack of judgement. Any repeat will have dire consequences. There must be no bending, never mind breaking of rules," he said to me. He didn't actually ask me to aspire to be a saint, but it's what he meant. "I require my inner circle's reputation to be beyond reproach." Do you understand what I am saying?'

'You're warning me off. Associating with a woman branded a thief would be fatal to your chances with Wellington.'

Drummond pulled her into his arms, tilting her chin, forcing her to meet his gaze. 'I'm warning us both off. We mustn't jeopardise our opportunity to be rehabilitated into society. At the start that seemed an easy task. We took the opportunity to enjoy each other's company, nothing more. I confess that I am finding it increasingly difficult to limit it to that. But then anything else is impossible.'

He pulled her closer, kissing her softly. 'The truth is, you matter more than you should to me, despite the fact that I've tried to put a leash on my feelings. You've got under my skin, and I dare not let you in any further.'

'Well, if it is any consolation, you've managed to get well and truly under my skin too,' Joanna said.

He feathered his fingers over the nape of her neck, sending little shivers of delight rippling down her spine, 'A consolation or a curse, I'm damned if I know which.'

'Obviously we must heed the warning bells,' Joanna

said, twining her arms around his neck, 'but it does not mean we cannot enjoy each other's company. Especially since there is such little time left.'

'Then we should make the most of them,' Drummond whispered, kissing her, 'provided we are discreet and very, very careful,' he said, kissing her again.

And then there were no more words, only kisses.

# Chapter Five

*Wednesday, 30th December 1818—Brockmore Manor*

The sleigh race, which involved the gentlemen competing to pull a small sleigh on which perched the lady of their choice round a marked-out circuit of the south lawn, was the sort of event Drummond would normally have avoided like the plague, but he wanted to exploit every opportunity to spend time with Joanna. Though it came at a cost to his dignity, for he slipped on a patch of ice after taking the first corner too fast, skidded, regained his balance, then skidded again before landing unceremoniously on his backside.

Joanna, still seated on the little sledge, was clutching her sides laughing, so he caught the leather straps and whirled her around in a huge circle until she fell into the snow. Almost forgetting that they were not alone, and recalling their kiss in the snow in the walled garden, he sank to his knees beside her before the cries of encouragement for the front runners, which were coming from those spectating from the terrace, brought him to his senses. He made an elaborate show of helping her up and brushing the snow from her cloak, just for the delight of physical contact. Her nose was pink with the cold. Her smile made his heart dance. Not that hearts danced. Though that's how it felt. Out of the corner of his eye, he saw Brockmore, swathed in furs, watching them. Drummond bowed solemnly, a gesture he feared he would probably come to regret.

Fortunately, the Duke's attentions were diverted by the climax of the race, as Lady Beatrice's sled, being pulled by Edward Throckton, whose weedy frame clearly belied a steely determination, vied for first place with a scarlet-faced but dogged Percival Martindale pulling the sleigh upon which Sophia Creighton clung, a look of terror upon her countenance. As they entered the home straight and the small clutch of guests cheered excitedly from the terrace, Drummond grabbed Joanna's hand and took off in the opposite direction.

'What are you doing? Where are we going?' she asked, panting, her breath forming little puffy clouds in front of her.

'We are going where we can have some privacy while remaining in clear view of our fellow guests and our hosts.'

Drummond brought them to a halt by the boathouse. 'Wait here.'

He entered the boathouse, noting as he passed through the little room where he had poured out his heart and soul to Joanna only yesterday, that the fire had been freshly laid. Would its use be reported back by a housemaid to her mistress? Were the servants part of the Brockmores' network of spies? If so, then the Duke would already be aware that someone had used this room for clandestine purposes. Recalling that Lady Beatrice had tipped

Joanna off about its suitability for a tryst, Drummond smiled wryly to himself. What other couple might venture along, primed by Lady Beatrice? 'Good luck to them,' he muttered, heading into the store room and quickly retrieving what he had come for.

Joanna was sitting on one of the little wooden bollards that were used for mooring the pleasure boats in the summer, looking out over the lake, but she turned when she heard his footfall on the jetty.

Drummond held up two pairs of skates. 'To anyone casting a glance at the lake, we are simply enjoying a little gentle outing on the ice,' he said, kneeling down to tie the wooden patten with sharp blades attached, to Joanna's boots. 'Perfectly understandable, especially since we missed the official skating party last Sunday.'

Joanna blushed adorably. 'Only because we were both obliged to retire to our chambers to dry off and change out of our sodden clothes.'

'Ah, yes, we had discovered an alternative winter pastime,' Drummond said, enjoying the way her blush deepened at the memory. Yet when he looked up from attending to his own skates and their eyes met, there was a *frisson* in the air, like the premonition of an electrical storm.

'I am not sure that kissing in the snow can be referred to as a winter pastime,' Joanna said.

He got to his feet, holding out his hand to help her. Their fingers twined together automatically. His free hand had settled on her waist. Her face was tilted invitingly to his. He could almost taste her. He had never in his life wanted to kiss someone as much as he wanted to kiss Joanna here, right now. 'No, not a pastime, more a dangerous game,' Drummond murmured, easing her closer. Most likely Brockmore was watching them from the terrace. If not him, someone else surely would be. 'Far too dangerous for us to play in full view.'

Sweeping her off her feet, he stepped down on to the ice and set her down. Joanna wobbled, clinging to his arm, laughing. 'Drummond, I've never been on a set of ice skates in my life.'

'Perfect,' he said, wrapping his arm tightly around her waist and anchoring her to his side. 'Now you may truthfully tell anyone who asks that I have been giving you lessons.'

'You have taught me a lot about many things. I sometimes wonder which one of us is the teacher.'

He laughed. 'I'm sure you are an exceptional teacher but you are also an excellent pupil. As you are about to demonstrate. Now, just relax and follow me. Trust me, I won't let you fall.'

The words were redolent with more meaning than he had intended but luckily Joanna was concentrating so hard on not falling over that she did not pick up on it.

Acutely conscious that they were being watched and at the same time, unable to deny herself the thrill of being so close to him, Joanna's first steps on the ice were timid, like those of a newborn lamb. The curling tip of her blade caught in the ice, making her stumble forward, but Drummond kept her upright. Her ankle gave way and she would have fallen sideways, but he straightened her before she had time to cry out. She took tiny, tentative steps, tottering forward faster and faster in an effort not to fall.

'You have to glide,' Drummond said, catching her again. 'Here, I'll show you. You'll be fine once you get the hang of it.' He held both her hands and began to pull her, skating backwards with a rhythm and dexterity that spoke of many years of practice.

'The loch back at home froze solid every winter,' he explained, when she asked. 'Though we had not these contraptions on our feet. We polished the soles of our boots to make them slippery, and that served just as well. We also played curling in rinks, which is a bit like English bowls, only with stones that you slide across the ice, and not so polite a game either. We Scots are a right competitive lot, and a violent race too. Have you ever heard of the game of shinty—or *camanachd* as it is in the Gaelic? Two teams with sticks hitting a ball made of wood or bone—and knocking lumps out of each other into the bargain,' Drummond said, laughing at the memory. 'There now, you're coming on a treat. No, don't look down, keep looking ahead.'

Startled, Joanna realised that while Drummond had been, quite deliberately she realised now, distracting her with tales of his Highland childhood, her body had fallen into a natural rhythm and she was now gliding rather than tottering, and they had completed a full circuit of the lake.

'There,' he said, sliding his arm around her waist again, 'now we can skate as a pair.'

They struck out over the ice together, left leg then right, left leg then right, their bodies attuned as they gained momentum. The skies cleared, a pale lemon sun appeared above them, throwing shadows from the trees which grew on the small island at the centre of the lake into their path, so that they glided from dazzling light to dark, light to dark, for one circuit and then two and then another, the only sound the swish of their skates, the ruffle of the breeze, the flap of Joanna's cloak as it flew out behind her.

On the fourth circuit they slowed of one accord by the island, where a path led from the shingle beach at the frozen water's edge. 'I wonder where that leads?' Joanna said.

Drummond glanced up at the terrace, which was now empty as the party had retired inside to the warmth. 'Since we are not being observed, why don't we take the opportunity to find out?'

They left their skates on the shingle and followed the path under the canopy of the leafless trees. To their astonishment, right in the centre of the island was a tiny stone cottage. 'How charming,' Joanna said, 'like something from a fairy tale—save that is not constructed of cake and the windows made of clear sugar.'

The cottage comprised of a single room. There was a table and two chairs, a cupboard, and a bed. 'How very odd,' Joanna said, stepping over the threshold. The floor was clean-swept, the bed covered in a thick quilt. 'There is a fire laid in the hearth. Who on earth do the Duke and Duchess imagine would venture out here?'

'Perhaps it's their own secret trysting place.'

'Drummond!'

'Why not?' he asked, with a wicked smile. 'Theirs is clearly a love match. I can picture them slipping away from their guests and their many servants. Perhaps taking separate boats to get here.' Drummond pulled her into his arms. 'Don't you think it would be romantic? Not to say exciting, for there is something innately exciting in behaving illicitly, isn't there? Even if, in the Brockmores' case, it is pure artifice.'

He had taken off his gloves, and put them with his

hat on the bed. Now he pushed back the hood of her cloak, his fingers stroking the nape of her neck which was making her shiver, and not with the cold. Joanna leaned into him, unbuttoning his greatcoat, sliding her hands under the skirts of his jacket to cup the delightfully taut muscles of his buttocks. 'Certainly,' she said in her best schoolmarm voice, 'there is something arousing in the forbidden.'

Drummond kissed the skin behind her earlobe. He kissed his way along her jaw. And then he kissed his way along her bottom lip. Little sipping kisses. 'Indeed,' he said softly, 'we are contrary creatures, for the more we tell ourselves we must not do something...'

'...the more we want to do it.'

'Precisely,' Drummond said, and covered her mouth with his.

There were flowers which grew in the heat of the African desert, Joanna had read, which lurked under the dry sand for months on end, waiting for rainfall. As the first drops of moisture hit the ground they pushed their way up, blooming almost instantly at a speed which defied nature, yet was required by nature in order for them to survive. Her desire for Drummond was like those desert flowers, lying latent, just below the surface, ready to come into full bloom at the first kiss, with no time to spare, no time to pretend. As his tongue touched hers, as she pressed herself wantonly against him, the hard ridge of his arousal pressed into her thigh. Her hands roamed over his back, his chest, his shoulders, clutching at his hair. Her nipples ached for his touch, and as if he could read her body as well as her mind, he cupped her breasts, stroked her through her gown, her undergarments, and instead of releasing the tension growing inside her, it tautened it. She moaned, a strange urgent sound that drew an answering response from him.

He pulled her tighter against him, falling back on to the bed, taking her with him. Their kisses became ravening, famished kisses that could only be slaked by more and more and more. She lay on her back, half-covered by him, one of his legs pressed between hers. He was saying her name over and over between kisses, and she was murmuring his, both a plea and a caress, not knowing what she wanted, save that she did. More of his kisses. More of his touch. More.

It happened so quickly. His hand covered her breast, his fingers stroked her nipple. Arching under him, she could feel his hardness brushing at the apex between her thighs, and the sweet knot of tension which had been slowly building tightened and unravelled in a rush she could not control. She cried out, tumbling into a shuddering climax she could not disguise, and which left her completely mortified.

Joanna burrowed her face in the quilt. 'I'm so sorry. I have never—that has never…'

'There is nothing to apologise for,' Drummond said, kissing her forehead.

'I'm not sorry, just extremely embarrassed. You must think me…'

'Extremely desirable. Extremely, flatteringly, delightfully responsive and equally delightfully without guile.' He kissed her again, gently forcing her to look up. 'You can be under no illusions about how much I want you, and now I know how much you want me. What is there to be embarrassed about?'

'Unlike you, I lack control.'

Drummond's shoulders shook with laughter. 'Your

lack of control is utterly delightful, but you give me too much credit. Watching you—no, don't go burying your head again—witnessing that was a very serious test of my self-control, I assure you.'

'Really?'

He kissed her slowly. 'Really.'

Her shame gave way very quickly to a new wave of desire. Joanna wrapped her arms around his neck and kissed him again, letting her tongue run along his sensual lower lip. 'Truly?'

Drummond groaned. 'Truly.'

Their kiss deepened, but just as Joanna began to lose herself once more, he let her go, extracting himself from her embrace and sitting up on the bed. 'I do, unfortunately, have my limits and if we continue I cannot promise anything. Have you any idea how tempting you look lying there?' Drummond said, pulling her to her feet. 'Besides, the light is failing. We should get back to change for dinner.'

Joanna groaned as she began to tidy herself. 'Another meal. Breakfast, luncheon, tea, dinner, supper, every one several courses long, and each course more elaborate than the other. And as if that was not enough, every table in every room is set with fruit and sweetmeats that are almost impossible to ignore. I have eaten enough to sustain me for a year since I arrived here. I'm not in the least bit hungry.'

'We'll skate another couple of fast circuits of the lake.' Drummond ushered her through the cottage door. 'That way, you can work up an appetite and we'll both have an explanation for the rosiness of our cheeks,' he said with a wicked smile.

'Is it so obvious?'

Her did not answer, but took her hand, leading her back down the path to the shore, where they retied their skates. Resuming the ice, Joanna found her calf muscles had stiffened, and it took some effort of concentration to find her rhythm again. The silence around them had a different quality now in the late afternoon light. The air was colder, crisper under the clear sky, the sun dropping over the horizon on the far side of the lake, streaking the western sky with a pale palate of pinks and oranges.

To the north, across the white expanse of the south lawn, a sole figure with a distinctive mane of silver hair stood on the terrace of Brockmore Manor. A thin wisp of smoke rose from the cigar he was smoking. It was not fair. The Duke of Brockmore had it all, Joanna thought. Bloodline. Love. Power. He held their lives in those perfectly manicured hands. But for now, the only hands she cared about were the ones twined in hers. So few precious moments left to them. She would not let anyone, not even one of the most powerful men in the land, spoil them.

*Thursday, 31st December 1818, New Year's Eve
—Hogmanay*

The Duke and Duchess of Brockmore had gone to great lengths to add some Scottish flavour to the Hogmanay celebrations. Joanna knew that Drummond had been instructing their French chef in the various regional delicacies which were to be offered. At dinner, she was seated once more next to Mr Martindale, no doubt a deliberate ploy on the Duchess's part, eager to allow Joanna every opportunity to impress, and to allow her potential employer to continue his delicately tactful enquiries into her teaching methods and accomplishments. Haggis, the famous minced offal and oatmeal pudding, had been served, and Drummond had been right, it was actually very tasty, if one did not dwell on the ingredients. Some of the more fastidious guests had been less adventurous, nibbling the accompanying dishes of neeps and tatties, but opting for roast goose over haggis.

And Their Graces did not stop at the food. As the guests assembled after dinner for what they were promised would be a 'true Scots Hogmanay', they were serenaded by the bagpipes. Though serenaded, Joanna thought, was hardly the word. Drummond had been right about this particular aspect of Scottish culture too. She'd never heard a banshee wailing, but she was willing to wager that it would sound exactly like this.

He was not in the ballroom to share this thought with her. He had been well down the table from her at dinner, and when they had risen, he had disappeared, along with their hosts. Just as Joanna was beginning to wonder what was afoot, the bagpipes came to a skirling screeching end, and the double doors of the ballroom were thrown wide.

The Duchess of Brockmore wore a ballgown made of red plaid. Her husband wore a short jacket and a kilt in the same matching tartan. The kilt stopped above his knees, his long stockings stopped just below, leaving an expanse of pale knobbly flesh that made His Grace look oddly vulnerable.

The Duke, however, seemed quite oblivious of this, beaming proudly, making a little flourishing bow when his guests broke into a smattering of applause. 'Ladies and gentlemen,' he proclaimed. 'I had hoped to make this little speech in the Scots dialect, but I am afraid I found it impossible to get my English tongue around the words. And so instead, I will hand over to a man who has perfect command of that language. A man whose name will become very familiar to those of us interested in matters of state,' said His Grace with a knowing look. 'A man who is destined, in the coming year, to make a well-deserved name for himself. Ladies and gentlemen, I give you Mr Drummond MacIntosh.'

The Duke of Brockmore had a gravitas that would have prevented him from looking ridiculous in the most outlandish garb and a reputation which would inhibit any mockery, even if he did. In the kilt, he looked, as he always did, like a well-preserved thoroughbred, but Drummond, in his national dress, looked like a wild Highland warrior.

He spoke softly in the musical lilt of Gaelic. Joanna had no idea what he was saying, but she hung on every word. As did every other guest in the ballroom, she saw, dragging her eyes briefly away from the magnificent vision, the men with a mixture of admiration and envy, the women with something much more—goodness, lascivious really was the only description for the expression on timid Miss Creighton's face. No doubt it described her own expression too.

Unlike the Duke, Drummond wore no jacket, but a pristine white shirt with wide, pleated sleeves, and a neatly tied stock. An expanse of dark green plaid was pleated in a complicated manner and worn like a broad sash across his chest, fixed at the shoulder with a large pin in the shape of a shield. His kilt, formed from the same tartan, was held in place at his waist by a simple broad leather belt. Where the Duke sported a furred and tasselled purse-like accessory strung across his front,

Drummond wore only a long dagger in a leather hilt. His legs were every bit as fine as Joanna had imagined. Muscled and tanned, a shapely calf and a neat ankle shown to perfection by his knitted stockings.

'…a traditional toast which in your own language means good health, wealth and happiness,' Drummond concluded, reverting to English.

The glasses of whisky which had been distributed during his brief speech were raised. As Joanna took a tentative sip of her own, her eyes met his, and he smiled. It was a complicit smile that warmed her even more than the smooth, peaty taste of the whisky.

'My goodness, but that man positively oozes virility,' Lady Beatrice whispered. 'One can all too easily imagine him throwing one over his shoulder and carrying one off to his cave.'

'I believe they have castles and cottages, just as we do in England.'

Lady Beatrice chuckled. 'I know that, but don't you find the idea of a cave much more romantic? One would be laid back on furs, and—and tended to,' she said, her eyes dancing with mischief.

'Tended to?' Joanna exclaimed, raising her eyebrows, succumbing to a little mischief-making of her own. 'Your ladyship has changed her tune. I seem to recall a conversation on Christmas Day when you described kissing as a rather insipid pastime.'

'And I seem to recall that you informed me I had not met the right man. It seems that you were right, Miss Forsythe.'

Lady Beatrice spoke in her customary lightly ironic tone, but the faint trace of colour in her high cheekbones betrayed her. 'Mr Throckton has more to offer then, than political nous, may I assume?' Joanna enquired.

'You may. And as for Mr MacIntosh?'

But Joanna, watching Drummond in conversation with the Duke and Duchess, could not match her ladyship's tone. In just a few hours, the bells would chime to herald the new year, a new beginning. But also heralding a necessary ending.

'Oh, dear,' Lady Beatrice said, turning her back on the other guests in order to cover Joanna's obvious distress. 'You did not heed my warning, then,' she said, handing her a beautiful lace kerchief.

'Oh, I assure you I did,' Joanna replied, dabbing at her eyes. 'I am very much aware of how impossible it is—you heard His Grace's introduction. Drummond—Mr MacIntosh is destined for a world well beyond my ken.'

'But you have not, if you will forgive me, managed to make your heart chime with your head, Miss Forsythe. You are normally a woman of excellent judgement, and much to my liking,' Lady Beatrice said. 'When this party is over, I do hope that you will permit me to keep in touch.'

'Thank you, I am honoured,' Joanna said, colouring painfully, 'but I fear if you knew me better—knew more of my—I fear that an acquaintance with me would do your ladyship's ambitions no favours.'

'My only ambition was to form a friendship with a like-minded woman,' Lady Beatrice remarked drily. 'It is still my ambition, Miss Forsythe, regardless of whether you have been indiscreet or scandalous. Now, before you feel obliged to confess whatever dark secret you are hiding, let us go and join in the festivities. I do believe that is a broom the Duchess is wielding. I am most intrigued to find out why.'

'It is to sweep out the old year,' Drummond said, finally escaping from the Duke's company and taking the chance to join Joanna before someone else decided to monopolise her. 'The idea is to have a spotless house when the bells ring at midnight, so that there's no cobwebs or dusty corners for the faeries to hide in.'

Joanna had a throaty laugh that did something to his insides. 'Faeries?' she said, and her smile did something to his insides too.

'Oh, aye,' Drummond replied, deliberately broadening his accent. 'We Scots are terrible feart of the wee people. The measures that are taken to make sure a new babe cannot be replaced with a changeling—you would not believe them.'

'No, I would not. I must say, you look very dashing in your kilt.'

'I seem to remember a certain person expressing a wish to see me in it.'

Her smile faded. 'You told me that the last time you'd worn the plaid...'

'Was the last time I was home,' Drummond said. 'A new year is about to dawn. I reckoned it was time to reclaim that part of my heritage.'

'Well, I'm very glad you did. You look magnificent.'

'Ach now you're just being kind.'

'I am being honest. What's more, every other lady in this room shares my opinion.'

'I'm only interested in this particular lady.'

'Oh, Drummond, I...'

'I know.' He touched her hand. Her gloved fingers

curled briefly around his. 'I know,' he said, and it was all that needed to be said, for what was the point in articulating what they would not allow themselves—could not allow themselves—to feel.

As if she read his thoughts, something he was becoming convinced she might actually be able to do, Joanna released him, fixing her smile back into place. 'So tell me then,' she said, 'what other traditions have you in store for us tonight?'

'Well, there's still some work to be done to keep the faeries at bay,' Drummond said, following her lead to join the rest of the party, who had abandoned their brooms and were now gathered round a table bedecked with greenery. 'Hazel does that, and rowan brings us good luck.'

He handed her a sprig of both, then reluctantly abandoned her to assist Miss Creighton. Miss Burnham then begged his help, and then Miss Canningvale, and he was just being accosted by Miss Pletcher when the Duke clapped his hands and announced it was but a minute to midnight.

The French windows of the ballroom were thrown wide as the new year was counted in, and the church bells announced its arrival. Joanna was not by his side, but engaged once more in conversation with Percival Martindale. When the First Foot arrived, Drummond sought her out to share his amusement, for the Duke had far exceeded his specifications, which was that traditionally the first visitor over the threshold had to be tall and dark. The man who entered was a veritable giant with a shock of coal-black hair, carrying the requisite black bun which Monsieur Salois had baked. 'One thing about Brockmore, he never does things by halves.'

The skirl of the pipes made them both turn towards the balcony. The piper had been joined by two fiddlers. 'Oh, the dancing is starting,' Joanna said, looking at him expectantly.

'The ceilidh, if you please. Will you do me the honour of bestowing your hand for the first reel, Miss Forsythe?'

But Joanna's smile had become rigid as she looked in the direction of their hosts. 'I think the Duchess expects her guest of honour...'

He did not give a damn what the Duchess wished, but he ought to. 'Aye, you're in the right of it,' Drummond said with a sigh. 'But you'll save me the next one, won't you?'

'With pleasure.'

But the new year was four hours old, the ceilidh over, and the guests retired to their bedchambers before Drummond found her again, sitting by the embers of the fire in the little snug off the ballroom, telling herself not to expect that he would seek her out, and telling herself she was a silly fool when her heart leapt as he opened the door.

'I'm sorry.'

'It was not your fault. The Duchess had your next partner lined up before you'd barely finished dancing with the current one,' Joanna said. 'If I was of a suspicious nature, I'd say she was doing her very best to keep us apart.'

'That thought occurred to me. But we're here together now, and there's no one to disturb us,' he said, turning the key in the lock. 'Would you care to dance, Miss Forsythe?'

She stepped into his arms. He wrapped his around

her, cradling her against him, nuzzling her neck. 'A new year,' he said, leading her in a slow turn around the room. 'A time for new resolutions, new beginnings.'

'What is it they say—out with the old, and in with the new.'

'That is indeed what they say.' He spoke softly, his tone was weary. 'A fresh start for both of us,' he said, 'that is what we should be focusing on.'

'Yes,' Joanna said, 'we should.' He had removed the sash-like plaid. She burrowed her face into his chest, the fine linen of his shirt the only barrier to the flesh below. He'd taken off his stock too. At his throat, there was a fine smattering of hair. 'That is what Lady Beatrice and Mr Throckton will be thinking. I would not be surprised if they announced their betrothal before the end of the party.'

'I doubt it. Edward Throckton is a cautious man. He'll want to be sure of her father's consent before announcing anything.'

'But he'll have it, won't he?'

'I reckon Lady Beatrice will make sure of it.'

'In the years to come, they will look back on this party and say to each other, that was the start of it all.'

'Och, Joanna, don't. What is the use of being envious or bitter because they have what we cannot? Better to wish them well and all the happiness in the world.'

'You're quite right.' They had stopped dancing. Joanna lifted her head, smiling up at him. 'Do you know, I have not been kissed since last year?'

'That is a most strange coincidence, for I have not been kissed since last year either. That is a terribly long time. High time, in fact, it was remedied.'

Once again, their kisses seemed to start where they

had left off, the touch of his lips on hers, of his tongue to hers, setting off that sweet, shuddering tension deep inside her. Kissing, they knelt down on the hearth rug together. Kissing, they touched, stroked, cupped as they sank back on to the rug until they lay side by side, thigh to thigh, breast to breast.

Drummond rolled her on to her back, kissing her throat, the swell of her breasts above the décolleté of her evening gown. She kissed his hot, bare skin at the vee of his shirt. He loosened her gown, tasting and licking the newly revealed skin, sucking her nipple through the flimsy layer of her undergarments. She yanked his shirt free from his belt and ran her hands over his skin, relishing the responsive rippling of his muscles, the ragged sound of his breath.

He slipped his hand under her petticoats, his skin warm on the soft flesh of her thighs, smoothing, stroking, sending her to new heights of need. 'Yes,' she said, 'yes,' she urged, and 'yes,' she panted, when he hesitated, 'please.'

With a groan, he slid his finger inside her, and with a groan she opened for him, heedless now of anything but that touch, that heat, the unbearable anticipation of her climax, craving only more of his touch and more as his finger slipped and slid over her and into her, until she was so elevated that her fall was tumultuous, making her pulse and shudder, moan and clutch, kissing with passionate abandon, wanting only to sweep him away with her in a roiling sea of passion.

It was not so very difficult to believe that his desire matched her own, for the evidence—good lord, the evidence! His kilt had ridden up. His tan stopped short just above the knee, she saw, and his thighs were every bit as muscled as she'd imagined. But she could never have imagined—instinctively, she reached out to touch him, feeling his responsive shudder, and then his hand over her wrist, stilling her, muttering a strangled curse as he sat up, covering himself with his plaid. 'We said we'd be careful. You might say it's a bit late in the day, but we must try to hold to that.'

'I know,' Joanna said, 'it's just that at moments like this I couldn't care less.'

# Chapter Six

*Friday, 1st January 1819, New Year's Day*

New Year's day at Brockmore House started with a late breakfast, allowing the guests the opportunity to recuperate after the Hogmanay celebrations, which had gone on well into the small hours. Joanna, however, had not slept a wink. *We said we'd be careful. You might say it's a bit late in the day, but we must try to hold to that.* Drummond's words played over and over in her head. She'd been so certain that with everything to lose, the one thing she would not lose was her head. Now it seemed she was very close to losing not just her head, but her heart too.

It was one of those bright, deceptively sunlit winter days. Outside, the pale sun was a hazy orb in the celestial blue sky. Pulling on her cloak and boots, Joanna headed quickly through the sleeping household and out into the grounds. There was what she took to be a formal rose garden immediately outside the drawing room. In the summer, the perfume from the blooms would be heady, but for now, all that was visible were the little nubs of the clipped bushes.

Next to the rose garden was the maze. What was the

trick, always to turn to the right or to the left? Joanna entered, turning right and then left willy-nilly. She cared naught. If she became hopelessly lost, she could see through the denuded yew sufficient to extricate herself.

She was not in love. A person did not fall in love in a matter of days, and if they did, they would presumably fall out of love just as quickly. No, she was not in love with Drummond. But one more step, just one, and she could be.

*We said we'd be careful. You might say it's a bit late in the day, but we must try to hold to that.* In the cold— actually, bitterly cold—light of day, she was glad that he had been sensible enough to call a halt last night. And yet she couldn't help but wonder what it would have been like had he not. She realised with a start that, more by luck than judgement, she had reached the centre of the maze, where an almost-naked statue of Atlas was holding up the world. Joanna studied the bronze god, and found him, compared to Drummond, somewhat lacking.

She was being quite ridiculous! And most contrary, for no sooner had she finished reminding herself to keep a watch over her heart, than her heart was drifting off down that forbidden path. Utterly ridiculous. All she had to do was to get through the next five days without falling any further. Really, was that such a lot to ask?

Trying very hard to persuade herself that it was not, Joanna headed back, so intent on retracing her footsteps in the snow that she did not notice the man waiting patiently at the maze entrance until she quite literally walked into him.

Drummond was in the library disinterestedly flicking through yesterday's *Times*. In the middle of the night, he'd tried to convince himself that it was lust, frustration, the wakening of his long-latent desire that made Joanna so difficult to resist, but he knew in his gut that it was not that simple. He'd desired women before. He'd regularly been starved of female company, thanks to the vagaries of war. But he'd never felt anything like this, and he'd known it, he'd bloody well known it, right from the start.

He got up and wandered over to the window. Footsteps criss-crossed in the snow over the south lawn. There had been no fresh falls. The sleigh tracks from the race two days ago were still visible. Was Joanna still asleep, as it seemed the rest of the house party were? He'd been the solitary diner at breakfast. If they could negotiate five more days of this party without compromising themselves, their individual futures would be secured. A cloud scudded across the sun, casting a long shadow over the white lawn. Only five more days. The thought should bolster him but instead it made him feel unaccountably depressed.

He was about to resume his futile attempt to interest himself in the content of *The Times,* when a flutter of brown cloak emerging from the rose garden drew his attention. Opening the window, he leaned out and called her name.

Joanna sipped gratefully at the hot chocolate which Drummond had called for. 'Though Mr Martindale was at pains to assure me it was as much an opportunity for me to ask questions about the post and the children, since he had already learnt enough about me during our previous conversation, he didn't mean it, he still had a great many questions, and I can't help but respect him for that. It shows he takes his duty of care towards those two little mites very seriously.'

The library where they sat had been a male bastion for the reading of the London papers, but was this morning quite empty. Drummond was in morning dress, biscuit-coloured pantaloons, polished boots, a blue cutaway coat. His hair was still damp from his ablutions, his chin raw from his shave. He looked tired. Had he too spent a restless night? Don't ask, Joanna thought. Better to keep the conversation on more neutral ground.

'They are aged six and eight, the little girl the elder, but Mr Martindale wishes them to be educated together, at home, which means my tenure would be secure for some years.'

'And is it a position that interests you?' Drummond asked.

'It ought to. He raised the issue of my character—or lack of,' Joanna replied, colouring at the memory. 'With great sensitivity, I may add. Despite my being branded a thief, the fact that Her Grace is willing to vouch for me is sufficient for him. That is to Mr Martindale's credit. And yet, I find myself in two minds about accepting his generous offer. And for that, I'm afraid,' Joanna said with a small smile, 'you must take some of the blame.'

Drummond raised a brow. 'Must I?'

'Yes, you must. Talking to you has made me realise how much I love teaching—not just one or two children, children who have the privilege of choosing or discarding learning, but disadvantaged children who have a hunger to learn. Lots of them. I'm not convinced I want to be a governess.'

'By the sounds of it, what you really want is to teach in a charity school.'

'Whatever I do, I'm not going to accept Mr Martindale's offer,' Joanna said decidedly. 'Thank you, Drummond, you have once again helped clarify my thinking.'

'Don't be daft, you've a very sharp mind and would have got there on your own.'

'Not as quickly.'

'That's as may be, but where does that leave you?'

'I don't know. Education is changing,' Joanna said. 'There are new National Schools being established, though they too, being under the umbrella of the church, would never employ anyone whose character was less than spotless. And even the so-called British Schools which claim to be non-denominational, are actually simply non-conformist, and so I doubt I'd fit there either.'

'So what you really need is your own school.'

'I know you're teasing me, but that is exactly what I would like,' Joanna said ruefully. 'Then I could try out my own methods of education, and I'd be accountable to no one other than my pupils and their parents. You see, that is something else you have taught me, Drummond, I am a radical at heart.'

'If you mean a forward thinker, then I completely agree. Would you really like to pursue such a path?'

'I really would. Though I'm also a realist. I know it is little more than a pipe dream.' Joanna set aside her cold cup of chocolate and with it, resolutely, her desire to extend this interlude with Drummond. 'We are due to assemble in the drawing room in order to exchange gifts this afternoon, and I am afraid I haven't even decided what I'm going to give Mr Throckton, whose name I was given, so if you will excuse me…'

He got to his feet, but made no attempt to touch her.

The atmosphere between them changed to something expectant, awkward. 'About last night…'

'Last night, you prevented us both from making a very big mistake.'

Though he looked torn, he did not disagree, which made her feel very wretched indeed, for part of her had, she now realised, been hoping he would contradict her. Even though she knew he was right. 'So it is for the best,' Joanna said brusquely, 'if we avoid all circumstances which might encourage any further foolish behaviour.'

Drummond dug his hands deep into his coat pockets. 'Yes,' he said heavily.

'There are only five—no, four and a half days left of this party. Surely we can negotiate such a short period safely.'

'Aye. We must, we have no choice.'

'Precisely,' Joanna said. She waited, but he had nothing more to add. Telling herself sternly that she had acquitted herself very well got her out of the library and up to her bedchamber. But the moment she closed the door behind her a wave of sorrow hit her. She had done the right thing, and it felt as if she had thrown away something precious. Hurling herself upon her bed, she gave way to a much-needed and long-overdue bout of crying.

*Saturday, 2nd January 1819*

The Prime Minister, Lord Liverpool, had announced the Duke of Wellington's appointment as Master-General of the Ordnance on the last day of the old year. The Duke of Brockmore had waited until the second day of the new year to seek Drummond out in the library where, since his last private conversation with Joanna, he had spent increasing amounts of time. It should have been a relief at the very least, to be informed that he had impressed, that His Grace would have no hesitation in supporting his appointment as Wellington's aide and would ensure the necessary doors were opened subsequently. But Drummond had not been relieved, he'd been irked, and he had singularly failed to show the appropriate gratitude to his host, which was most ungracious of him, because it was not the Duke of Brockmore's fault that Drummond found himself in this dammed uncomfortable position.

There were winter games on the lake today. Ice racing and archery, and a demonstration of ice carving for the ladies. Though he had little inclination for company, the thought of seeing Joanna lured him to the scene, but she was not there. He'd seen briefly her at dinner last night, though once again his place had been far from hers, and she had retired early.

The flicker of rebellion which had sparked into life on his arrival had become a burning flame. Joanna was right, Wellington would not be welcoming him back into the fold if Wellington didn't need him. His rehabilitation had nothing to do with his having paid the price for his insubordinate actions, and everything to do with furthering Wellington's career.

And his own, Drummond reminded himself. They needed each other, he and Wellington, but still, he resented it. He resented the terms that were being offered. He resented being told what company he could keep, and he resented the implication that he'd be permanently on probation. If he had truly paid the price, then wasn't he entitled to a clean slate? But it seemed this was no more on offer to him than to Joanna.

A smattering of admiring applause from the assembled guests greeted Jonas Milborne's unsurprisingly excellent performance with the arrows. Watching as the captain instructed Philippa Canningvale in the basics of archery, Drummond felt a twinge of jealousy of which he was immediately ashamed. Milborne deserved to be happy, and if this most unlikely match was what the man wanted, then good luck to him. Drummond didn't envy him Miss Canningvale, but by God, he envied the man his freedom to have her.

Brockmore's parting words had made it very clear that Drummond had no such freedom, and equally clear that the Silver Fox's reputation for seeing and knowing all was not after all undeserved. 'You let your heart rule your head once before, at great personal cost, surely you wouldn't be foolish enough to do it again?' His Grace had said. 'My wife has gone to a great deal of trouble to ensure that Miss Forsythe's future is secured. As I am sure you are aware, that young woman, like yourself, is being given a second chance, and like yourself, must ensure that her reputation in the future is quite spotless. I am not the only one to have observed your—let us call it a dalliance. Gossip is a most corrosive force, Mr MacIntosh. If you care at all about Miss Forsythe, you will ensure that the scandalmongers are starved of ammunition.'

The warning was very clear, and indisputably fair, though Drummond's first reaction was to resent his relationship with Joanna being labelled anything so trivial as a dalliance. What he felt for Joanna was…

Drummond cursed under his breath. What was the point in putting a name to it? It made him heartsick, knowing that their time together was drawing to a close.

Why had Brockmore seen fit to point out what he already knew? And if he already knew it, why was it proving so damned difficult to accept! The problem was, he hadn't a clue what it was he did want, save that he didn't want what he could have, and he couldn't have...

Ach, he was going round in circles. He needed some mindless diversion to stop him thinking. Since he was damned if it was going to involve carving ice, Drummond took himself off to the billiard room.

*Sunday, 3rd January 1819*

'Ah, Miss Forsythe, I'm so glad you could join me. Please, do sit down. Tea? Milk or lemon?'

'Lemon,' Joanna answered, seating herself on the other side of the tea table. The service was Sèvres, the tea pot and the hot-water pot which sat on the little burner were chased silver, the caddy black lacquer. The Duchess of Brockmore's private parlour was, like its owner, both elegant and refined. Her Grace, Joanna noted wryly, was dressed in a gown of cream and straw-coloured silk which matched the window hangings. If she bought a new dress did she have to change the curtains?

'Tell me, Miss Forsythe, are you enjoying your stay here with us at Brockmore?'

Joanna made suitably polite noises. The Duchess made equally polite ones in return. The art of carrying on one conversation, while having quite another with oneself was surprisingly easy, Joanna discovered. Since her last conversation with Drummond two days ago, her decision not to take the post with Mr Martindale had hardened, but she had not moved much further forward in her thinking. Though she had been expecting this summons and had rehearsed various responses, she had not expected to feel this slow-burning resentment. This rich, privileged, beautiful and annoyingly likeable woman held her future in her hands. Last night, Miss Pletcher and Lord Truesdale had announced their betrothal, and the Duchess had bestowed her blessing. Aubrey Kenelm and Lady Anne Lowell looked certain to make a similar announcement, which would be equally well received. Joanna could imagine the reaction if she and Drummond…

She brought this train of thought to a sickening stop. Over and over, these last few days, she'd tried to congratulate herself that at least she had not taken that last fateful step towards heartbreak. She had been foolish, but not *that* foolish, she reminded herself.

'…and you have made an excellent impression on Mr Martindale,' Her Grace concluded with a warm smile.

'Thankfully my qualities as an excellent teacher cannot be besmirched.'

Her Grace looked quite taken aback, but she quickly recovered. 'Indeed. I am sure that Lottie's, admittedly belated, confession is due in no small part to the values you inculcated in her.'

'Sadly, her mother does not share them.'

'I beg your pardon?' The Duchess eyed her haughtily. 'Lady Christina's recognition of, and gratitude for, your discretion is the reason you are here.'

'I am here to be paid for my continued silence, and compensated for the disservice she has done me!'

Silence, marked out by the loud ticking of a clock, greeted this remark. Almost a minute passed before the Duchess spoke again in measured tones. 'You believe that Lottie's guilt should be made public in order to clear your name?'

'Is my reputation less valuable than Lottie's?' Joanna demanded, unleashing her pent-up feelings. 'Is it my lack of a pedigree which makes me less worthy of protection, or my lack of status?'

Another silence was her answer. When the Duchess spoke again, her voice shook. 'What you say is—I confess, I had not thought of the matter from your perspective. You are quite correct, you are being punished most unfairly for Lottie's crime. To your eternal credit, you have maintained a silence which has protected Lottie's reputation, even though it has cost you dearly, but what is to be done? You gave me the strong impression that you would not speak out of your own accord…'

'And I meant it. To accuse Lottie would not only ruin her prospects, it would be pointless. My word against that of your friend, Lady Christina—who do you think would be believed, Your Grace? When I first came here, I believed that the amends you referred to in your invitation must include the clearing of my name. But it seems my idea of justice is not yours. Or your friend's.'

The Duchess winced. 'Harsh words, but I cannot deny the truth of them. You have been placed in an impossible position. I must say, your strength of character and integrity are very much to be admired. Mr Martindale's wards will be in very safe hands.'

'As to that, Your Grace, I have thought long and hard about it, but I must reject his generous offer. Believe me when I say I have a good reason for doing so.'

To Joanna's surprise, the Duchess flinched. 'I had hoped not to have to broach such a very personal subject.'

'I don't understand,' Joanna replied, though the ominous fluttering of butterflies in her tummy told her differently.

'Miss Forsythe.' Her Grace quite clearly braced herself. 'Does this good reason go by the name of Drummond MacIntosh? Because if it does, I must inform you that any form of future relationship between you is completely out of the question.'

Though it was gently said, Joanna flinched as if she had been struck. 'Do you think I don't know that?'

'My husband suspects that Mr MacIntosh is on the brink of—frankly, that despite his words of warning, Mr MacIntosh's feelings for you run so deep that he will permit his heart to rule his head, for a second, fatal time. Trust me, Marcus and I have a wealth of experience between us in matters of the heart. You would, albeit unwittingly, be his downfall.'

'You are saying nothing that I'm not aware of,' Joanna said, though that was a lie. She knew Drummond cared, but to care that much…

'If that is the case,' the Duchess said crisply, 'then you will not, as I feared, take my husband's suggestion amiss. You must leave Brockmore as soon as possible, thus preventing Mr MacIntosh from making a terrible mistake. If he will not save himself, then you must do it for him.'

'I don't understand.'

'My dear, if he asked for your hand, would you truly be able to refuse him?'

'I haven't even permitted myself to imagine that he might.' But now she did, and her heart soared, and she knew with a horrible certainty that the Duchess was right. Mutely, Joanna shook her head.

'There, you see,' Her Grace said, and the sympathy

in her eyes almost set Joanna over the edge. 'It is best to ensure that he has no opportunity to do so. I will make the arrangements for first thing tomorrow. If Mr Martindale is agreeable, perhaps you could travel...'

'No.' Joanna got to her feet again, her tears dissipated by anger. 'I will do as you ask, not because you ask, but for Drummond. I don't want to be rewarded, Your Grace, not for my silence on Lottie's behalf, and even less for doing what I know is best for Drummond. You may thank Mr Martindale for his generous offer, but I must decline.'

'Then I beg you to at least accept the payment being offered by Lady Christina as recompense. It is scant compensation for what you have had to endure but I am sure you could put it to good use.'

'Absolutely not,' Joanna said scornfully. 'I will forge my own future, thank you very much, on my own terms, whatever that may mean. In the meantime, I will return to the school in which I am currently employed. Now, if you will excuse me.'

Joanna's bravado evaporated the minute she was back in her own bedchamber and reality began to hit home. What had she done? Throwing herself on to the window seat, she stared morosely out. Her chamber faced north over the front of the house, and the sky was already darkening. Was it really only ten days since she had arrived here, so filled with excitement about her prospects for a clean slate and a fresh start? But the slate had not been wiped clean, and as for her fresh start, she was back at square one.

Though at this moment, none of that felt important. Joanna leant her cheek against the cool of the casement window and closed her eyes. The Duke of Brockmore was worried enough about Drummond's state of mind to have warned him off. And when that had not succeeded, he'd enlisted his wife to warn Joanna off. The arrogance of the pair of them! Little did they know that they were wasting their time. Little did they realise that both Drummond and Joanna had known from the start how impossible—wildly, utterly impossible—their feelings for each other were. The Duke thought Drummond's feelings were such—but the Duke was mistaken. Oh, she knew he cared—but not that much. He did not love her, not as she loved him.

Joanna's eyes flew wide open. Love? She could not be in love, though when Drummond kissed her, she did feel as if she was melting and flying and the knowledge that he would never kiss her again was enough to make her think—though just for a few moments—that she might never eat again.

Did she love Drummond? She wanted to be with him all the time. When she was with him, she felt so much more alive, so much more—herself. And then there was that odd thing, the invisible thread between them that made her so acutely aware of him. Was this love? The oddest sensation, as if her heart was heating and expanding inside her, was her answer. Of course she did! 'I love Drummond MacIntosh,' Joanna said, feeling foolish but testing the words, and finding them filled with certainty. She loved him so much.

So very much, yet tomorrow she must leave without saying goodbye. A tear leaked out of the corner of her eye. She owed the Duchess nothing, not even the keeping of her promise, but she knew she would keep it all the same, because that was what love truly was. She wanted Drummond to be happy, no matter what the cost to her.

Another tear trickled down her cheek. Not to say goodbye, to walk away without explaining, seemed like the worst punishment in the world. He would never know why she had left. He would never know that she loved him, and oh, how she loved him!

The gilded shepherdess on the ornate ormolu clock on the mantel struck the goat bell with her stick five times. Startled, Joanna realised that the room had grown quite dark. It was time to dress for dinner. Another rich meal, no doubt with herself and Drummond positioned at opposite ends of the table, and then an evening spent helping with the preparations for tomorrow's theatricals, which would be taking place while she was far from Brockmore. Was this how she would spend her last night with him?

No! She wanted something more memorable. A slow smile dawned, as the most outrageous idea formed. She could not say the words, I love you. She could not say the words, goodbye. But there were ways of speaking without resorting to words.

# Chapter Seven

*Monday, 4th January 1819*

It had been a tedious evening, made interminable by Joanna's absence. She had sent her apologies at dinner, claiming the headache. Was she really ill, or was this simply another, more effective way of avoiding him? Now in the wee small hours of the next morning, Drummond surveyed the ballroom, where the stage had been set out, the costumes and props ranged and ready for the day's theatrical performance. Neither he nor Joanna had a part. Perhaps when everyone else was on stage, they could—what? Make the pending goodbye even more unbearable by stealing more kisses? No, it was better this way, the ending already begun, though *dammit to hell*, wasn't it better to have as many kisses as they could possibly steal, when soon there would be no more?

He was sick of doing as he was bid. Brockmore's words of warning had left a very bitter aftertaste. In the army, until that fateful day, though Drummond had questioned orders, occasionally challenged them, it had never occurred to him to disobey them. He was a sol-

dier, that's what soldiers did. But his mutiny had created a rebel, and that rebel did not take at all kindly to
the notion of dancing to another man's tune ever again.
Not even if it were a duke setting the music. Actually,
two dukes.

Was he being thrawn? What difference did it make
that he had no other options, wasn't he still getting what
he wanted? Drummond heaved a huge sigh. Right now,
all he wanted was Joanna. It was far too late now, the
entire household was abed, but tomorrow, he decided,
he'd seek her out. Enough of this sacrifice, what the pair
of them needed was succour. Just a wee bit. Just enough
to get them by.

Snuffing the candles, he quit the ballroom and headed
for his bedchamber, though sleep was far from his mind,
which was already racing ahead to the morning, to Joanna's smile and Joanna's kisses and Joanna's touch. His
room was warm, the fire banked up. He thought for a
moment that his cravings had conjured her up, but when
she rose from the wing-back chair and said his name, he
knew this was no apparition.

'Joanna!' Heedless of anything other than his overwhelming need to hold her, he swept her into his arms
and kissed her. And kissed her again. She twined her
arms around his neck, pressing her body against his,
and his senses reeled with the scent of her, and the feel
of her, and the taste of her.

Her hair was unpinned, hanging thick and lustrous
down her back. Only when he realised that he could feel
soft, warm flesh unconstrained by any corsets through
her attire, did he realise she was wearing a nightgown.
It was agony to tear his mouth from hers, but he did it.
'What on earth are you doing here?'

'Isn't it obvious? I want us to make love.'

Drummond groaned. 'Joanna, you know we cannot.'

'Why not? I want to. You want to. It is not as if my innocence is of any value to anyone else, and if you are careful—will you be careful?'

'Of course, but...'

'Don't you want me, Drummond?'

He cupped her face, wondering how he could ever have thought her anything but beautiful. 'You know I do.'

'And I want you. No,' she said, kissing his lips briefly when he would have protested, 'listen to me. This will be our only opportunity. Why shouldn't we grasp it, why shouldn't we have a brief taste what so many people are determined to deprive us of? No one will ever know. It will be our secret. Don't you want to, Drummond? Don't you?'

She kissed him again, and he knew he was lost. 'I want to,' he said, kissing her back. 'I want to so much.'

'I want you, Drummond,' Joanna whispered. I love you, Drummond, she thought, shuddering as he kissed her and stroked her hair. Her heart was beating so fast she could scarcely breathe. She dare not let herself think beyond one moment at a time, for fear her courage would desert her, for fear that if she faltered, Drummond's conscience would intervene. 'I want you,' she whispered, running her hands up his back under his coat, down to his buttocks, pulling him tighter against her.

He kissed her mouth. He kissed her throat. His hands shaped her breasts through the cotton of her nightgown, making her nipples peak, making her moan softly. He shrugged off his coat and waistcoat. She tugged his shirt free of his pantaloons, seeking flesh, warm skin, rough hair, feeling the hard nubs of his nipples tighten in response to her touch. His shirt fell to the floor. She pressed her mouth to his chest, kissing, licking, revelling in the resulting shudder, in the fast rasp of his breathing.

'So lovely,' he muttered, 'you are so very lovely.' He lifted her on to the bed, tugging at the fastenings of her nightgown, pulling it down over her shoulders, her arms, to reveal her breasts.

She fought the urge to cover herself, warmed by the blaze of passion in his eyes. Drummond eased her on to her back and took one of her nipples in his mouth. A surge of heat jolted through her, setting all of her senses on fire as she surrendered to the sweet, aching sensation of his tongue, his lips, his hands, stroking and licking and cupping. Restless with desire now, hot and damp with it, she moaned his name, arching under him, shameless in her wanting, wanting only this, and more of this.

'Take these off,' she muttered, her fingers flailing at the buttoned fall of his pantaloons.

'Joanna…'

'Yes, yes, yes, I'm sure. Take them off.'

He laughed, hauling off his boots, undoing the buttons, and she sat up to watch, gazing blatantly at the delightful sight of him, naked and muscled and fully aroused. She reached for him.

'Patience,' he said, catching her wrist, kissing her fingers one by one.

'I don't want to be patient.'

He kissed her again. 'Trust me,' he said, 'your patience will be rewarded.'

He eased her on to her back again, and slipped her nightgown off. His sharp intake of breath as he looked at her, just as she had looked at him, gazing with naked desire, made her forget any inhibition. When he lay over her, naked skin to naked skin, she could feel the thick, hard length of his arousal pressing into her belly. Their kisses became darker, deeper. Her own arousal was a tingling ache, throbbing, pulsing, longing, urgent, but still Drummond kissed her and kissed her, her mouth, her throat, her breasts, her belly. Only when he eased open her legs and kissed the flesh at the top of her thighs did she protest, and only then momentarily, for when he licked in between her legs, making love to her with his tongue, Joanna unravelled.

This climax was so much more intense than the last that she struggled to muffle her cries. Over and over again, it pulsed through her, but even as it began to ebb, she knew instinctively it was not over, that it was merely a prelude, and when he would have soothed her, held her, she would have none of it, reclaiming his mouth, her hands feverish on the heat of his flesh.

'Joanna, are you…?'

'Sure,' she said, utterly sure, relying utterly on her instincts, and trusting him utterly.

'I promise I will have a care,' he said, 'I promise.'

'Yes,' she said, and when she felt the tip of him sliding into her, 'oh, yes!'

He claimed her slowly, easing himself carefully inside her, though she was so ready, so wet and tight with wanting, that he had no need. Slow kisses, then slow thrusts, and with each one, the strangest, most delightfully unimaginable sensations. She clung to him, and then she opened for him. He slid his hands under her bottom, and she opened more, he thrust higher, and she felt herself waver. 'I want you,' she said. I love you, she thought, gazing into his eyes, dark with passion, before his next thrust sent her over and she was lost once more, and Drummond let out a low cry, pulling himself free as his own climax shuddered through him, mumbling something in his native Gaelic.

For long, blissful moments they lay together afterwards. They shared pillow-like kisses, the softest of touches, as if they were afraid to wake from a dream. But she knew she must stay awake, and that she must be gone at first light, so she slipped from his arms, slid out of the bed and pulled on her nightgown.

'Joanna, in the morning we must talk. You know that this changes...'

'I must go,' she said hurriedly, for it changed nothing, and she couldn't bear to tell him so. The Duchess had been right. Whether motivated by chivalry or true love, she would not be able to refuse a proposal, and so she would not let him propose. 'Goodnight,' Joanna said, reaching down to kiss him one last time. Her lips clung. His arms snaked around her waist, pulling her tightly to him. The temptation to stay was unbearable.

'Goodnight,' she said again, dragging herself free, and, slipping quickly out into the corridor, made her way swiftly along to the chambers set aside for the female guests on the opposite side of the house. She did not look back. She did not let the tears clogging her throat fall until she had closed the door of her own bedchamber and locked it behind her.

'Goodbye, my love,' she said to herself. And then the tears fell in torrents, and continued to fall through what was left of the night as she packed her trunk, and made her way out of the house to the waiting carriage, just before the first guests made their way to the breakfast parlour.

\* \* \*

Drummond did not sleep. Once Joanna had gone, he sat at the window, watching the stars peep between the scudding clouds, watching the sky change from indigo to grey, and becoming more certain with every passing moment. He loved that woman! He loved her with all his heart, and with his very bones he knew that whatever else happened, he'd move heaven and earth to find a way to be with her.

He knew himself too well. If it had felt wrong to make love to her, he wouldn't have gone through with it, no matter how strongly tempted he was. He had known in his heart that he was in love with her for days now, but he'd simply not been able to admit it, because the consequences...

Oh, to hell with the consequences, Drummond thought, and felt his heart lighten. To hell with the Duke of Brockmore and the Duke of Wellington and their terms and conditions. If Wellington really needed him, Wellington could take Drummond on his own terms. Though actually, Drummond wasn't at all sure that he wanted any truck with Wellington. He was weary of taking orders. Recalling Joanna saying more or less the same thing, he smiled. Aye, it was time for him to be his own man, whatever the hell that meant.

What he needed was a plan. First, and most important, he'd find Joanna and he'd find out if her feelings matched his. He was pretty confident they did, since their lovemaking had felt so right and she was no more likely than he to do such a thing if she were not utterly certain. But still. He wanted to say the words. He wanted to hear them.

Second step. Thank Brockmore for his efforts and inform him that he no longer needed his support.

Third step. Now that was a tricky one. He had no posting. Joanna had turned the one offered to her down. How the devil were they to live? Drummond smiled to himself. If they were to live together, the means was a problem he'd be delighted for the pair of them to tackle. Together.

Arriving early to breakfast, intent upon executing stage one of his plan as soon as Joanna appeared, Drummond was wondering whether he dared risk have a maidservant summon her from her bedchamber, when he received a summons himself. And so I'll deal with stage two first, he thought to himself as the door to His Grace's study was held open, and his name announced and he made his bow to his host and hostess.

'MacIntosh,' the Duke said, smiling genially. 'I wanted to let you know I've just received word from Wellington. We are to be honoured by his presence at our ball tomorrow, though you should know, the honour is largely yours. His Grace is most eager to have you on his staff as soon as practicable.'

'That is indeed very flattering, but I fear His Grace is about to be sorely disappointed,' Drummond said. 'I regret I cannot accept the position.'

Brockmore's distinguished jaw dropped like a stone. 'Cannot—may I ask…?'

'To put it bluntly, I find it not to my liking,' Drummond replied, unable to repress a smile. Really, this was most liberating.

'Not to your liking?' the Duke spluttered. 'Do you

understand what you are saying? Have you any idea how fortunate you are to be presented with this opportunity?'

'Oh, I'm very much aware of it, thank you very much, and I very much appreciate the role you've played, Your Grace, and your good lady wife, in helping with my rehabilitation. But I've come to realise, since I came here to Brockmore, that I don't actually require rehabilitation, because I didn't do anything wrong.'

'You were cashiered from the army, man!'

Drummond's smile faltered. 'I was indeed. And I've spent the years since hanging my head in shame as a result. I've cut myself off from my family too, thinking my shame was somehow contagious. The invitation to Brockmore has proved to be a turning point in my life, but not in the way either of us envisaged. I've discovered that I'm not ashamed of my actions. I'd go further, and state that I would do exactly the same again, if required. I won't apologise for them, and I won't allow anyone to dictate how I behave in future either, because of them.'

'But the problem is,' the Duke of Brockmore said, recovering after a stunned moment of silence, 'you have just effectively destroyed any prospect of a meaningful future.'

'I beg to differ. I intend to have both a meaningful and very happy future. Now if you'll excuse me, I'd like to take the first step on that path.' Drummond got to his feet. 'You'll wish me luck, I hope? I know that you consider it a misalliance, but it is the only alliance for me.'

'Mr MacIntosh, one moment.' The Duchess of Brockmore exchanged a worried look with her husband. 'Do you mean—are you absolutely intent upon offering for Miss Forsythe, regardless of the consequences for your future career?'

'I love her. My career is meaningless if the price I've to pay for it is Joanna.'

Her Grace clasped her hands together, looking extremely distressed. 'Then I am very sorry to tell you this, but Miss Forsythe has already left Brockmore. I feel quite dreadful, for it was my husband and I who suggested that drastic course of action. We were trying to save you from yourselves. But we should have learned by now, my dear,' she said, turning to her husband, 'that love is no respecter of authority or even common sense. One cannot stage-manage emotions.'

His Grace sighed. 'My wife, as so often, is in the right of it. Though I fear that Wellington will be most—but that is my problem. Your problem is rather more urgent,' the Duke said, pulling the bell rope. 'I'll have my fastest horse saddled. The carriage is headed north, and has about an hour's start.'

They had stopped at a coaching inn to change horses, and Joanna was taking a cup of coffee in a private room when Drummond strode in. He was mud-smattered, his complexion ruddy from the cold wind, and there was something in his eyes that made her heart stop then start to hammer.

'I had to leave,' she said, launching into speech. 'It was the best way. I couldn't bear to say goodbye, and I knew that after last night—Drummond, there's no need for you to do this. I don't want you to feel obliged...'

'My only obligation is to listen to my heart,' he said, taking her hands. 'Joanna, I love you.'

'Oh, Drummond. You should not have—I wish you had not.'

'Why not, my darling? Don't you love me?'

'Oh, I do, you know I do, how can you doubt that, but…'

He smiled tenderly. 'After last night, I have no more doubts. It is you I want more than anything. You I love. You I need. Will you be my wife, Joanna?'

'Oh, how can I! Do not ask me, the cost to you is too high.'

'Trivial, compared to the cost of losing you,' he answered, his expression becoming serious. 'I love you, Joanna. I can think of no higher honour than being able to call you my wife. Will you marry me?'

'But what will we do? How will we survive? You should know that I have not only turned down the position with Mr Martindale, but I have refused the money which Lady Christina offered.'

'I would expect no less of you, my love. What do you say to setting up our own school? A school for ragamuffins, a school where pupils are taught and not beaten, whose parents don't give a damn about their teacher's past reputation, provided their children get the best start in life?'

Joanna shook her head, smiling, dazzled, but trying very hard to keep her feet on the ground. 'It sounds wonderful. Just like a dream.'

'I admit it is very much a dream. In fact I've only just thought of it, but I reckon we could make it work,' Drummond said, warming to his theme. 'You could see to their minds, and I could see to their well-being. I could teach riding, drill, how to pitch a tent, how to survive off the land, all manner of practical skills. Now I come to think of it,' he said laughing, 'the only thing I couldn't teach them is how to follow orders! What do you say?'

'What about funds?'

'There's no denying that is an issue. Though I reckon there might just be a very rich patroness with a very high opinion of you and a guilty conscience to assuage who may wish to assist us.'

'The Duchess? Do you think…?'

'There's no harm in asking. But before we do, may I remind you, my love, that I've already asked you a question twice, and you've still not given me an answer.'

'Drummond, the life you are suggesting is a far cry from the one you have been offered.'

'A very far cry, which is a small part of its appeal. I know it won't be plain sailing, my love. We won't ever be rich. We'll always be on the fringes of society. I can't promise this idea of mine will work, but I can promise I'll do everything in my power to make it work, and though you might think me a fanciful eejit, I can't help but feeling absolutely sure that together we can do anything we want. Say you'll marry me, Joanna.'

Looking into his eyes, she believed him. Lock, stock and barrel, she believed him. 'I will,' she said. 'I love you so much, Drummond, I will be your wife.'

With a shout of joy, he pulled her into his arms and kissed her thoroughly. And then he kissed her tenderly. And then their kisses heated.

'One of the carriage wheels has inexplicably come off,' Drummond said, with a wicked smile. 'It will take some time to repair and so we will have to pass the time here. Have you any suggestions?'

'Yes,' Joanna said, with a wicked smile of her own. 'Lock the door.'

\* \* \* \* \*

*If you enjoyed this story,
you won't want to miss these other stories
from Marguerite Kaye!*

*CLAIMING HIS DESERT PRINCESS
THE HARLOT AND THE SHEIKH
SHEIKH'S MAIL-ORDER BRIDE
THE WIDOW AND THE SHEIKH*

# Dancing with the Duke's Heir

*Bronwyn Scott*

For Drum and Daphne and the girls. Thanks for opening your house to us and all the good meals over the past years. You are all great fun!

# Chapter One

~~~~~~~~~~~~~~~~~~~~

*Thursday, 24th December 1818, Christmas Eve*

Christmas. Again. The fourth without his father, without his brother. Vale Penrith drew a deep breath and stepped down from the warm carriage into the bracing cold of winter, the soles of his boots crunching on the crisp, thin layer of newly falling snow. *Lumi*, the Sami people of Lapland, his latest anthropological study, would call it. Perhaps later it would turn to *viti*, powdery snow, or if they were less lucky, *iljanne*—snow that was only a thin layer atop ice. Vale cast a glance towards the grey clouds, sending a prayer skywards. He just had to get through the next twelve days. At least, he wasn't doing it alone.

Vale reached into the carriage, offering a hand to his mother. Margot Penrith descended, a fragile, beautiful snow queen, delicate and elegant, swathed in expensive furs. The look in her pale blue eyes mirrored the thoughts of his mind: they weren't supposed to be here. Not like this, a broken family of two mourning the loss of their other halves: a beloved husband, an adored brother; a widow and an unlooked-for heir. He'd never thought to be at Brockmore as the heir to his uncle's legacy, a legacy he felt ill suited to assume. He was a politician by conscience when the occasion demanded it, an anthropologist by choice. He was *not* a duke.

He took his mother's arm and together they climbed the entry stairs to the imposing double doors already swagged with greenery. An invitation to some, Vale supposed. A note of caution to others like himself. Either way the message of the greenery was the same: Christmas began the moment one passed beyond these doors. Guests could expect the Duke and Duchess of Brockmore to engage the holiday fully. His aunt and uncle did nothing by halves.

Inside, the hall was warm. The sound of happy voices drifted from the drawing room along with welcoming scents of spiced tea and fresh baked cakes. The butler had barely taken their coats and furs when Uncle Marcus appeared, silver hair thick, clothes immaculate, his carriage hale and perfect as he strode forward, his arms held out wide, a broad smile on his face, his voice booming in welcome. He took Vale's mother in a full embrace. 'Margot, my dear sister-in-law! You're here and just in time. We'll start the greening in an hour or so. Alicia will be so glad you made it. One never knows with the roads this time of year.' He turned to Vale, studying him for a moment, the keen blue Brockmore eyes sweeping him from top to bottom in approval. 'My boy, it is good to see you,' he said simply before wrapping him in his arms. Vale hugged him back. For just a minute, he wasn't the heir, but simply a beloved nephew and this man was not the mighty Brockmore, powerful duke, but his uncle, his father's older brother, a living link to the man he'd lost. And Vale savoured it.

Aunt Alicia materialised beside him, tall and regal in a fashionable gown of dark blue, just as Vale remembered her. She looped her arm through his mother's, taking the delicate Margot under her hostess's wing and ushering her into the heart of the party in Brockmore's famed blue receiving room, already drawing her in with chatter and news of the guests. Uncle Marcus clapped a firm hand on his shoulder. 'Come, there's some people I want you to meet.'

Brockmore toured him about the room. He met the golden, blue-eyed Aubrey Kenelm, heir to the Marquess of Durham, the poised brunette, Lady Anne Lowell, daughter of the Earl of Blackton, whom the Duke introduced with a certain sparkle in his eye. That sparkle sent a *frisson* of caution through Vale. His uncle was notorious for his matchmaking at these parties. He had no wish to be his uncle's next project. Vale nodded politely to each woman, careful not to be too polite to Lady Anne, while smiling warmly at her subdued companion, Marianne Pletcher, who by nature of her situation posed no danger to him as a potential match.

These were the sorts of people he expected to meet. They were the sorts who ran in his uncle's circles. Well-bred, well-moneyed people with marital hopes. But, he noted, there was another set of guests that populated the drawing room—in fact, made up the majority of the guests in attendance. There was Miss Rose Burnham, a decidedly pretty girl of good family whose father had fallen on hard times, leaving her with nothing than her looks as a dowry; Matthew Eaton, son of the local baron, who never quite made it up to London but was charming and handsome despite the lack of any other true prospects to offer. With the exception of Kenelm and Lady Anne, these were *not* the typical guests one usually encountered at Brockmore. Finally, his uncle brought him to a man of later middle years sitting by himself in the corner.

The man rose to greet them, his uncle putting a hand on the man's shoulder in affection. 'Silas Arthur, Lord Truesdale, this is my nephew, Vale Penrith.'

Vale watched the man's tired eyes register with recognition. 'Ah, Penrith. The heir.' Vale was coming to hate the title, a constant symbol of all that had transpired in order for that label to come to him.

They made small talk briefly before his uncle excused them, his voice quiet at his ear as they moved away. 'Silas lost his wife two years ago.' Uncle Marcus squeezed his shoulder, drawing Vale's gaze. 'You are not the only one here who mourns.' There was a fleeting sadness in his uncle's gaze, a reminder that his uncle had lost a brother the same way he'd lost R.J. when his father had died. And yet, one would never know except in these unguarded moments. He envied his uncle that ability to go on. He had not mastered that quality yet. Perhaps he didn't want to. Perhaps he wanted the clock to stop on the twenty-first of April 1814, then both his father and R.J. would still be alive.

His uncle steered him towards the small cluster of gentlemen at the fireplace, the momentary sadness gone from his gaze. 'You'll want to get to know the other young men,' he instructed. 'They're all very nice. I think you will enjoy Kenelm and Eaton, especially. Others will be joining us before long.' He winked and gave him a final clap on the back. 'Be happy, Vale.'

His eyes sparked with mischief. 'Don't think I don't know you'd prefer to stay hidden away in London in your library with your anthropology, trying to ignore the world. Life goes on whether you want it to or not. You might as well enjoy it. Consider it my Christmas gift to you.'

Not just to him, Vale thought as Kenelm moved over to make room for him in their circle at the fireplace. It explained the mix of guests; the lonely widower in the corner, the pretty, desperate debutante, the country-bound baron's son who for all his potential would never escape the country without a boost from a high-placed mentor. The list went on. His uncle's gift to them was a chance: a chance to marry well if you were Rose Burnham, a chance to rebuild your life if you were Lord Truesdale; a chance to rise beyond the limits of the countryside on the merits of your own wit if you were Matthew Eaton. A chance to be happy and alive, if you were Vale Penrith and you'd been dead inside already for nearly four years.

At the entrance to the drawing room, his uncle clapped his hands, demanding attention. 'Everyone! A moment, please!' He waited for the room to silence. Aunt Alicia took her place next to her husband, smiling her own greeting. 'We want to welcome you to Brockmore for the holidays. We have festivities planned from skating parties to a gingerbread fair, and masquerade ball for Twelfth Night. It will be a Christmastide to remember!' Swift murmurs of excitement undulated around the room. Brockmore called for silence once more. 'The footmen have returned with the boughs, freshly cut from Brockmore pine. Let the greening commence! Let Christmas begin!'

Applause and cheers went up, filling the drawing room. Beside Vale, Aubrey Kenelm was good naturedly stripping out of his coat, ready to work. 'The ladies will need us for the heavy lifting.' He grinned and nudged Matthew Eaton with his elbow as if they were the best of friends even though they'd only met an hour ago. He grabbed Vale's arm with his other hand. 'Come on. I'll take the doorways, you and Matthew take the staircase.' Just like that, Vale found himself in charge of draping the banister with no chance to slink off to his room to unpack his books. He had a report to write for the board of the British Museum concerning Lapland and the mysteries of the north. His uncle was right. He'd rather be tucked away in his library where no one could bother him instead of being in the thick of the festivities. But it was too late to turn back now. The museum report would have to wait.

Just another half an inch and she'd have it. She couldn't turn back now, not when she was nearly there. Lady Viola Hawthorne stretched on the tips of her toes atop a ladder in Brockmore's hall, a mistletoe ball hanging from her fingers as she reached for the fire-polished crystal drop hanging from the chandelier's centre. Almost…there…

The ladder swayed precariously as she adjusted her position. A good sixteen feet below her a crowd of young people greening the hall began to gather around the base of the ladder, intrigued by her antics. On her periphery, she caught sight of a tall figure moving rapidly down the stairs. She felt firmer hands on the ladder a moment later, followed by an even firmer admonition. 'Come down at once! Do you want to break your neck?' She didn't dare look to see who it was below her or she'd lose her nerve. Did the Scold really think she hadn't already come to the same conclusion? She'd simply chosen to ignore the danger. Playing it cautious didn't fit her plans. Cautious girls weren't expelled from house parties.

Lady Viola laughed, loud and brave. 'Never!' The Scold's reproach served to spur her on, urging her up on to one toe like a ballerina, her gown drawn tight against her breasts as she stretched upwards, her hem lifting to reveal her ankles and quite a bit more. One could indeed be enormously scandalous atop a ladder, which was precisely what she intended, precisely *why* she'd worn silk stockings, red garters and nothing more beneath her gown. But at the moment, she cared less what the local lads might sneak a peek at and more about the challenge at hand. She was fully extended. There wasn't a fraction of an inch left to be had. Unless…

She couldn't be closer to the chandelier, but the chandelier could be closer to her. Viola's fingertips could just reach the nearest arm, just enough to give it a push. She set the great chandelier to swaying, a little at first and then more when it gained momentum, but not too much. It was delicate work. She didn't want the chandelier to mow her down like a wrecking ball. Now, all she had to do was time the in-swing, and… *Voila!*

'Got it!' she exclaimed, hooking the mistletoe on to the dangling crystal drop as the chandelier made its third pass.

The guests beneath her broke into applause and cheers, all except one—her disapproving ladder holder. Never mind him. She had no time for spoilsports. She climbed halfway down, stopping to sweep her adoring audience a gallant bow, before launching herself. 'Catch me!'

She let go of the ladder and fell. There was a collective gasp, a moment's chaos, others rushing forward to steady the ladder and then she was in his arms: strong arms, angry arms. He was not nearly as amused by her finale as everyone else. His blue eyes were thunderous when he set her down. 'You little fool! Have you no care? Do you value yourself so cheaply as to throw your life away over a tawdry trick? Or the lives of your fellow guests? You put them at risk as well. What do you suppose happens to them if the ladder falls, or the chandelier crashes without warning?' He did not bother to lower his voice and his tone froze the levity she'd conjured.

'Who the hell are you to tell me what I can and cannot do?' She looked him up and down, from steely blue eyes to long legs, her hands on hips in outrage. How dare he publicly reprimand her as if she were a naughty child? Worse than that, how dare he steal *her* attention?

'I'm Vale Penrith, Brockmore's nephew. This is my home as much as it is my uncle's. I will not see it used as a staging grounds for imprudent behaviour.'

*The heir.* Oh, well done. This was a record even for her. She'd been here less than two hours and she'd managed to give Brockmore's heir a peek up her skirts. This would not do. She knew a moment of uncharacteristic panic. Her parents, when they arrived, would be furious *if* they found out. True, she wanted them furious enough to send her home, away from the dangers of matchmaking, but not too furious—if they thought they could use a scandal to compromise someone as enticing as Brockmore's heir to the altar, her plans would have backfired in the extreme. The altar was what she was trying to avoid.

Diversion! She needed something to top the ladder escapade, something everyone would talk about instead. She flashed a challenge at tall, imposing Penrith with his angry eyes and strong arms before turning to the others. 'We're standing under a mistletoe ball and you all know what that means!' Viola pulled the nearest young man to her, Matthew Eaton, and kissed him hard on the mouth, a glorious, open-mouthed kiss that lingered long enough for everyone to take note. This was no chaste peck on the cheek, or a polite, dry buss on the lips.

Viola stepped back and raised her arms in pronouncement. 'The first kiss of Christmas!' The guests whooped with delight. Just like that, she had the crowd back. She tossed Penrith a victorious grin over her shoulder, but he was already gone, back up the stairs to fasten the last of the bows on the garland at maddeningly even, precise intervals, thanks, no doubt, to the measuring stick he probably carried in his…head.

# Chapter Two

Whoever said rank had its privileges didn't have to go in to dinner with Vale Penrith and all of his perfection. He stood before her in the drawing room punctually at seven o'clock with a bow and the offer of his arm, immaculately turned out in dark evening clothes and crisp white linen, cravat impeccably tied and accented with a ruby stick pin in the dead centre. He probably had a mental measuring stick for that, too. Even his hair, a dark blond and arguably his only break with convention since it was surprisingly longer than most men's, was tied back in a black ribbon, also perfect. Not a literal hair out of place.

She wanted to mess him up. Just a little. Perhaps pull a stray hair loose, or bump that stick pin a fraction so it was off centre. Or maybe she wanted to do something more devastating like spill her red wine on his white shirt at dinner. Except now she couldn't because of the 'hall incident'. He would think a little spilled wine was her idea of revenge instead of an out-and-out rebellion against his perfection. No, wine would look petty. She'd have to think of something else.

All she could do for the present was take his arm and

try to behave as blandly as he, as if they hadn't sparred earlier in the hall, as if one of them—not her—hadn't attempted to belittle the other in public. Surely, if he could pretend the hall incident had not happened, she could manage it, too. On the surface, at least. She was willing to *pretend*. She wasn't willing to forget.

They joined the parade into supper, the third couple behind the Duke and her mother and the Duchess and her father. Anne Lowell and Aubrey Kenelm were behind her. There was that to be thankful for at least. She'd have Kenelm on her other side to break up the monotony of conversing with Penrith. Good heavens, what *would* they talk about for two hours? If ladder safety in halls was of primary importance, she could imagine his concerns over the dangers of dining; The safety of knives, perhaps? The perils of open-flame candles and hot wax? They stepped into the dining room and all thought of conversation fled. Brockmore knew how to serve a supper and it was breathtaking in its subtle luxury.

Viola was used to opulence. Her father, the Duke of Calton, had wealth aplenty, but even a familiarity with luxury did not dim the elegance of Brockmore's formal dining room decked with all the pomp demanded of a ducal Christmas Eve dinner. The long, polished table featured three eight-armed candelabra done in heavy silver and set at intervals down the length of the table, the thick white tapers shining their light on thin-stemmed crystal goblets and beautiful china plates trimmed with a cranberry and gold rim.

The room even *smelled* lovely, like winter and Christmas combined, thanks to arrangements of rosemary and bay placed artfully about the room. While she'd been climbing atop the ladder in the hall in a blatant display of festivity, risking life and limb for a kissing bough, someone had seen to a discreet greening of the dining room. Probably some of the older ladies.

Subtle was not something Viola aspired to, but in this instance she approved. Her gown complemented the setting ideally in style and in tone. She was even glad her mother had insisted she wear the ivory gown with the elaborately worked net slip and its complicated draping, the overskirt edged in a detailed lace. Even the hem of the net over-slip was done in a heavier, pointed lace to give it weight. The gown was exquisite, the kind of fashion only a duke's daughter could afford.

Wearing such an advertisement always made her wary, however. Her mother suggested gowns for a reason. Viola cast a sideways glance at Penrith as he held out her chair, seeing him through her parents' desperate eyes: tall, perhaps handsome in their estimation, the candlelight favouring him, showing off the sharp planes of his face, the high cheekbones with their slight, aristocratic hollows beneath, the long straight slant of his nose. But that didn't change the fact he had the personality of a stump, or that marriage was for ever.

Just the thought of 'for ever' made her shudder. For ever with a stump? Well, that was absolutely *unthinkable* no matter how much money he had. It validated for her all the reasons she had for avoiding marriage so heartily. She would not give her life over to the whim of a man. It would mean the end of her dreams: of travelling the Continent, of studying music in Vienna, where she heard a woman could enjoy greater freedoms. To her, marriage was nothing more than a woman's enslavement. Enslavement to a *stump*.

Viola sat, careful of her skirts, and gave Penrith a polite smile for his efforts. She didn't dare anything more, not without raising her parents' hopes. Girls who won the hands of ducal heirs were *not* expelled from parties. She could imagine what was going through her parents' minds. She had no doubt they were covertly watching, and rejoicing. Their daughter had gone into dinner with Brockmore's heir, a most fortuitous event. One they could not have controlled, but certainly had hoped for.

Viola knew very well the only reason they'd been invited was because they'd *begged* Brockmore for the invitation. She was twenty-one and, in their estimation, running out of options, after having run off the most eligible men of the ton for the last three years. Dukes' daughters were never in dearth of suitors. Viola surveyed the table, taking stock of the guests assembled all in one place at one time, and took note. There were a lot of desperate people here. She did not count herself among them. She was not desperate for marriage. She was desperate for freedom.

Things were turning out *exactly* as she'd planned three years ago when she'd made her debut. Another year of living outrageously, and she'd be considered unmarriageable. She could get on with her life and not worry about the encumbrances of a husband and keeping up appearances. If she could get politely 'excused' from the party by New Year's she could be back home celebrating Twelfth Night with her friends in the village, performing her new musical composition.

'Lady Viola,' Penrith's baritone murmured on her left as partridge soup was placed in front of them. Brockmore had chosen to serve the meal *à la Russe*. 'So, you're the girl who swings from chandeliers.' The frosty disapproval was still there in the hyperbole.

'Yes,' She graced him with a wide, teasing smile, letting her eyes spark with a little flirtation because it would annoy him no end. 'And you're the man who brought her in to dinner. How do *you* feel about that?' It was probably quite disturbing to him that all of his perfection should be linked to such a madcap even for the span of a dinner. Disturbing or not, he gave no sign of it.

He gave a neutral shrug. She suspected he did a lot of that—embracing neutrality. It saved from having opinions, feelings. 'It is out of my control. The social gods preordain who takes who in to dinner.'

His reaction was disappointing. He was infuriatingly proper, infuriatingly unflappable. Infuriatingly *empty*. At least silly men had *something* in their heads even if it was inane. That decided it. She would get a rise out of him before dinner was over. It would be payback for the hall. 'Are you sure? Isn't it "who takes whom"?'

Something flickered in his blue eyes, his voice striving to convey patience while not being condescending, a battle his tone only partially won. 'I am sure. "Who" is used for subjects, and "whom" is used for objects. Furthermore, "whom" is reserved for use in subordinate clauses in most cases.' Oh, he did not like her. His disdain was evident.

She gave a sly smile and fluttered her eyelashes in her best impression of a simpering debutante. 'That is *most* scintillating, indeed. Perhaps it is *I* who am in the company of a celebrity. I had no idea someone actually *listened* to grammar lessons.'

'*You* are mocking me, Lady Viola. Please do not.' He wiped his mouth quite decisively with his napkin, signalling he was done with his soup and ready to have it removed, perhaps a metaphor for what he'd like to do with her. Or maybe she gave herself too much credit. Wanting to have her removed assumed she'd got to him.

He surprised her, leaning close to her ear, his voice low as if imparting intimacies, which was how it would look to the rest of the table. The table would be wrong. There was nothing intimate or even friendly about his words. 'I know all about you. I know what they call you in town—London's Shocking Beauty. While I'm sure you endeavour to live up to the epitaph, if you want to get a rise out of me, you'll have to do more than question my use of English grammar. I have far weightier considerations to spend my time on than forward young women who risk themselves needlessly on high ladders in order to give the local lads a peek up their skirts.'

'*I* was hanging mistletoe!' Viola hissed defensively, furious he'd seen through her so easily. 'How dare you make it into something lurid.'

'*I* didn't,' he replied blandly, leaning back so the footman could set down the second course, a hot raised pie of winter game that smelled divine. 'You did that all on your own when you decided to climb the ladder, or perhaps even as early as this morning when you decided to forgo wearing certain undergarments.' He gave her a piercing look that would have withered a less intrepid soul. It nearly worked anyway.

'So you did look?' She infused a sense of victory into her whispered response, but there was little victory. She could protest all she liked, but somehow he *knew* she'd known very well how she looked on the ladder, that it had been artfully arranged.

'How could I not? I had to balance the ladder, it

required I assume a certain posture. Had there been another way, rest assured I would have taken it. Your red-ribboned garters hold no charm for me.'

Viola felt her cheeks burn. He was calling her 'easy' and he wasn't done yet. 'It was a cheap trick you pulled today. I was not impressed. Foolhardy risk never impresses me.'

'And stiff propriety doesn't impress me.' She shot the innuendo back hotly, her temper getting the better of discretion. She wanted to shock him, to say something outrageous. 'How dare you sit there and scold me for having a little fun. It's the holidays and the Puritans have been out of style for centuries now, in case you didn't know. It's no wonder you've been invited, no wonder you need your uncle's help in finding a wife. No one would have a prig like you in their beds without the title and the money.'

For a moment his eyes blazed, a brilliant sapphire flame that was extinguished as quickly as it had been lit, so quickly it might have been only a trick of the candlelight. A cool, triumphant smile took his mouth and for an instant it occurred to her how truly handsome he could be if he would only try. He leaned close again and she smelled the vanilla-bay undertones of his soap— a winter scent for a wintry man. 'I think the question is, who got a rise out of whom? Now, if you'll excuse me?' He turned away, devoting himself to Anne Lowell as the Duchess of Brockmore initiated the turn of the table, leaving her beaten at her own game. She had meant to annoy him, but just the opposite had occurred.

The pie smelled delicious. Unfortunately, Penrith's comment ruined it. Damn him. Game pie was one of her favourites. Viola gave it a petulant stab with her fork.

Fine. She didn't want his stuffy company anyway. He could talk to Anne Lowell about grammar all night if he preferred and who knew? Maybe Anne Lowell was well born enough to know her duty and listen.

With a huff, Viola threw herself into flirting outrageously with Kenelm on her left and engaging him in a personal conversation that left no doubt she found his company preferable to Penrith's. She was Viola Hawthorne, London's Shocking Beauty, the life of the party, not some cheap trick, but when it came time to remove the game pie, hers was still untouched.

That did it. It was no longer enough to try to get a dinner rise from him. He'd scolded her twice now *and* he'd ruined her favourite dish. This was not over, not by a long shot. Whether Penrith knew it or not, he'd just declared war.

# Chapter Three

'Lady Viola, I need your help,' Lady Anne Lowell whispered in rushed undertones as they took their seats in the chapel for Brockmore's midnight service. 'I need you to do something for me.' Anne's hushed excitement was at odds with the serenity of their surroundings, candles illuminating the rich stained-glass windows that lined either side of the little church as midnight approached.

Intrigued, Viola leaned towards Anne, making sure her mother couldn't hear. 'What is it?' Anything to cause a little trouble.

'I need you to distract Penrith.' Anne leaned near, offering words of encouragement, trying to avoid the censorious glance of her cousin, Marianne, who sat beside her on the aisle. 'It shouldn't be difficult. I am only asking because you seem to be the logical choice. He was interested in you at dinner. Your heads were close together.'

Viola stifled a snort. If Anne only knew what had been said. Her friend might be less impressed with her abilities to 'distract' Penrith. 'Distract him? Whatever for? I don't know that Penrith finds me very compelling.'

'*Whoever* for,' Anne corrected. 'For me.'

Viola raised an eyebrow in enquiry, not quite sure she understood Anne's concern. 'You've only been seated by each other for a single dinner. It's hardly a proposal.'

'Don't you see it?' Anne argued swiftly. 'Conventional wisdom suggests Brockmore wants to find him a wife. He's thirty and its time for him to set up his nursery in earnest, especially after all the bad Brockmore luck these past four years. He really dare not wait.' She blushed and looked down modestly at her hands. 'I suspect that's why I'm here. In fact, I know it. My father and Brockmore have it all worked out.'

'You're to be the virgin sacrifice?' Viola said frankly, tossing Penrith a more assessing glance past Anne's shoulder, considering Penrith's suitability for Anne. 'I suppose he's handsome enough.' Penrith would be considered a catch by many, just not by her.

'He's certainly rich enough.' Anne answered practically, 'but I'm not interested.' She looked at her hands again, preparing to dissemble. 'I have fixed my attentions elsewhere, some time ago,' she confessed shyly before adding, 'with Kenelm. Please?'

Viola's instincts were on alert now. She gave Anne a sly look, taking in Anne with a new level of respect. Perhaps she wasn't such a virgin sacrifice, after all, like so many other young women too afraid to stand up for what they wanted. 'You and Kenelm? You know each other from before?' Perhaps more than knew each other if she considered Anne's words. Anne blushed again and Viola waited for the secret to come out. The vicar was ascending the steps to the pulpit. She hoped

Anne would hurry or else she'd have to wait until the service was over.

'You can't tell anyone. Nothing is official. His father...' Anne's voice dropped off decorously, a sure signal there were secrets for the probing if Viola was willing. 'Will you do it for me?'

'If I do,' Viola said slowly, 'you have to do something for me.' An idea was taking shape as her gaze darted past Anne once more to the pew across the aisle.

'Yes, anything!' Anne breathed in relief as the vicar opened his Bible and shuffled the pages of his sermon in the pulpit. 'What shall it be?'

Viola grinned. 'Anything. Just like you said. Anything I need, any time I need it. No questions asked. Do we have a deal?' But of course they did. Anne wouldn't have asked otherwise. It was settled. She would distract Penrith. Now the question was how to do it?

The vicar began to speak, welcoming them to Brockmore. He had a deep, sonorous but commanding voice, very pleasing to listen to, and Viola did listen. For a while. Viola fingered the pearl pendant at her neck, running her hand over the smooth nacre ball as she thought—sermons were good for that, plenty of time to be alone with one's thoughts. She had some of her best ideas in church, like the time she'd come up with the plot to ride a horse into a tavern dressed as the Ghost of Cawdor Castle in a blue-velvet gown to protest the innkeeper's poor quality of meat. That had been at a relative's in Nairn. She'd not been invited back, but she had heard the innkeeper's menu improved after that.

Ghosts wouldn't work with Penrith. He would be a challenge, perhaps her greatest challenge up until now.

Somewhere in the middle of the Christmas story, after Caesar Augustus had sent out his decree, and before an angel of the Lord appeared to shepherds, she came up with a plan. She'd start with getting Penrith's attention. Once she had it, she'd make him betray himself: She'd drive him wild. He'd like it, but he'd hate himself for it afterwards.

Her gaze slid to Penrith. He sat straight and tall, the candlelight doing the planes of his profile all nature of favours. It was a pity really, that a man who had so much going for him was so empty. It raised the question: how did a man with so much promise become so empty? Were some people simply born with no interest in the world around them? With no passion for living? Had he never felt a flicker for anything, good English grammar excluded?

Her mother elbowed her and gave her a reproachful look. Around her, everyone had stood up to sing 'While Shepherds Watched their Flocks by Night', decidedly *not* one of her favourite Christmas hymns. She didn't mind tonight. She was too busy plotting. She could use her arrangement with Anne to put herself in Penrith's path, while furthering her own agenda, which was two-fold: ruin Penrith's control *and* get excused from the party. This was working out splendidly. Even though it was early days yet, she felt confident she could check this house party off as a 'success'. She'd escape again with no husband in tow.

The vicar's pretty service concluded not long after the hymn, Baby Jesus safely swaddled in his manger and the angels returned to heaven as Brockmore's congregation rose once more and sang 'Adeste Fidelis', a hymn far more to her liking with its robust chorus, the ending punctuated by the first peal of the Christmas bells.

*The bells.* Her favourite part of Christmas Eve.

The small crowd of guests filed outside, hushed and respectful of the occasion, to hear the bells ring in the night. Viola closed her eyes and drew a deep breath of cold night air. This was one of her favourite moments of the year, perhaps *the* best moment of the year. She gave herself over to it—the deep pealing timbre of the bells, the ice of the falling snow on her face, the warmth of her body wrapped in the folds of her fur-lined cloak. She knew what peace on earth was. It was this. It was now. Throughout the year she tried to recreate this moment, recreate the intense peace of it, where she set aside her frantic, fast-paced life of frivolity, and she was never successful. This moment alone was unique among all the moments that peopled her year.

If she listened carefully, she could hear the bells in the village adding their song to the night. Did anyone else feel it—the beauty of the moment? It didn't matter. She did and she held on to it, eyes shut tight until the last peal faded away, knowing full well when her eyes opened the moment would be gone. She would be Viola Hawthorne, London's Shocking Beauty, again. But only for one more year.

A little spark of realisation flickered. This was the last year she had to maintain her reputation. After this Season, she'd be a candidate for the shelf—out three Seasons and no husband in sight. She could get on with her dreams. This time next year, everything would change. Her parents would have despaired and been all too happy to send their wayward daughter to

Vienna, where she'd be out of sight, out of mind. And she'd be happy to be there.

She wrapped her arms about herself in a little hug just before she opened her eyes and whispered, 'Happy Christmas to me.'

Around her, groups formed as people drifted towards Brockmore Manor, where, no doubt, hot drinks were waiting on cue to send people off to bed. The fallen snow had become thick enough to make Brockmore's sleigh viable, a sleek red and gold affair with front and back seats for four. Brockmore himself was at the ribbons with two smart blacks jingling in harness. She watched Penrith hand in his beautifully fragile mother and his aunt who was followed by the sad-looking, older man, Lord Truesdale. Penrith took the space in the front seat beside his uncle, but not before he'd tucked warm robes about the passengers and bent attentively to hear something his mother said, squeezing her hand, a fleeting smile on his lips. The moment was surprisingly tender. She almost wished she hadn't seen Penrith like that, so attentive, so caring. It went against the idea he was an empty shell. He *did* feel something, *could* feel something, at least in small increments. What else could he feel if he'd let himself? What could she *make* him feel?

He wished he hadn't seen her like that—Viola Hawthorne outside the chapel tonight, her head tilted slightly towards the sky, eyes closed in approbation, snowflakes dusting her face, dancing on her eyelashes before dissolving. Vale stripped out of his coats, alone in his room. He'd given his valet the night off to enjoy the holiday below stairs. He undid the cuffs of his shirt, put the links in a small dish on the bureau and discarded his shirt. He should have looked away, but she'd appeared *serene*, nothing at all like the vixen who'd sat beside him at dinner.

He was being whimsical now. He had to stop before he started comparing her to an angel, which she most assuredly wasn't. He'd seen her true nature today, twice in fact: atop a ladder, ankles exposed and more, and then again at dinner, the display of her cutting wit. She had not minced any words when it came to how she'd felt about him; an unmarriageable prig. Ouch.

His gaze lingered on the bureau mirror and the bare-chested man in the reflection. He studied his face, searching for signs of his supposed priggishness. Was that what he'd become? He was quieter, he supposed. There hadn't been that much to celebrate, these past years. But quietude wasn't priggishness. It was…restraint, respect, discipline. Only, he hadn't been all that restrained at dinner. He'd given back equal measure. He braced his hands on the bureau and hung his head, recalling his angry words. He'd accused her of being a cheap trick, not exactly the most gentlemanly of remarks. Well, perhaps he'd given her some proof there about the unmarriageable part. Great. Now, he was a prig and sharp-tongued to boot.

He turned away from the mirror and finished getting ready for bed in earnest. He was disgusted with himself. Not entirely for how he'd behaved—Lady Viola *had* been in need of a scolding—he was more disgusted with his reaction, which struck him as rather petty. Why did he put so much stock in the opinions of a girl who had no sense of decorum? If ever there were opinions that *didn't* matter, they were hers.

# *Chapter Four*

⌘

*Saturday, 26th December 1818, Boxing Day*

He'd escaped them! His uncle's guests were insatiable when it came to holiday festivity. He was not. He'd had his fill of looking cheery. Vale breathed a relieved sigh and sank into a wing-backed chair of softest leather in front of the fire in the Brockmore library, but his eyes still darted nervously about the room, landing on dark corners and the heavy folds of curtains at the windows where someone might hide, just in case he wasn't the only one to take refuge here. Not that anyone else would want to. *They* were all having a marvellous time.

After two days of Christmas, that was how he viewed the guests: *them* and *him*. Two distinct groups. Oh, he liked his uncle's guests well enough. Kenelm and Eaton and the other young men were good fun. They'd had some good billiards games after the ladies had retired for the night. But, by Jove, Vale needed a break. After a late Christmas Eve service, there had followed a Christmas Day full of games and feasting, as well as another church service and gift-giving to the children of the estate. This was followed by yet more good cheer as they assembled baskets for his uncle's tenants this morning and tramped through the snow to deliver them this afternoon. He was socially exhausted. He hadn't been around this many people for this long in years. All the politeness and pretence that he was enjoying himself positively wore him out.

It didn't help that *she* was everywhere, she being Viola Hawthorne. When he was in a room, he heard her laughter, noticed her gowns for reasons he couldn't quite name, caught the sound of her voice, the movement of her body always in motion, always at the centre of the party. He had the sensation it was her energy that fuelled the high spirits as much as it was his aunt's exquisite planning. If rooms weren't brighter when she was in them, they were certainly louder.

The clock on the mantel, a beautifully carved wooden affair from the Black Forest a German diplomat had given his uncle years ago, showed three o'clock. Boxing Day was nearly over. Just four hours until dinner and then some of the holiday cheer would ease. He hoped. The clock ticked, the sound loud in the glorious quiet. His papers and notes lay on the long reading table that ran the centre of the room, waiting for him. He'd not touched them since he'd arrived. There'd been no time. His aunt and uncle had kept him and every guest busy, moving them skilfully from activity to activity.

Vale closed his eyes. In just a moment he'd get up and see to them. There was the new translation of a Lapland history that had just arrived before he left. He was eager to read it in the hopes it would help his latest research and he had the report to get to if he wanted sponsors for the expedition by next year. But not yet. It was nice to sit here by the fire, in the stillness and just be with himself, just for a moment…

He must have dozed. It was suddenly five o'clock and someone was at the table looking through his papers. A female someone. Vale sat up. Not just any female someone, but the one guest he wanted to avoid most. 'Don't touch those. I have them in particular order.' Not entirely true, but he didn't want them messed up and who knew what *she* might do with them.

'Are these the "weightier matters" you referred to the other night?' She glanced up, but kept reading through them in complete disobedience with his request. 'A history of the Sami? Whoever they are.'

'They live in Lapland. I'm compiling a report and I hope to launch a northbound expedition next year if I can get the backing. The north is the new frontier these days,' he explained in his defense.

She feigned a yawn. 'Boring.' She rose from the table, hips swaying as she strolled the perimeter of the room, her hand running idly over the spines of books. She turned her head and tossed the words over her shoulder. 'Especially when there are more entertaining diversions at hand.'

The tease was implied in the lilt of her voice, the spark of her eyes—eyes that were always sparking. He hadn't seen them without a spark these past two days. 'Are you supposed to be that diversion?' he replied sharply, moving from the comfort of his chair to the table to straighten his papers.

'I might be.' She laughed and stopped her perambulations in front of the sideboard holding his uncle's brandy. She lifted the stopper from the crystal decanter and sniffed. 'Ah, that's good. Would you like a drink?' She poured a glass before he could respond and then arched an eyebrow at him in query, waiting. What was she waiting for? Clearly not his answer since she'd already poured.

'I was going to say no, but I'll take a drink so it doesn't go to waste.'

Lady Viola smiled wickedly. 'It won't go to waste. I never pour precipitously when there's good brandy at stake.'

It took him a moment to grasp her meaning. She held up the glass, gently sloshing the contents. 'This one's mine. *Votre Sante*.' She took a long swallow, head tilted back, eyes closed, the long column of her neck exposed as she savoured the brandy, not unlike he'd seen her outside the church on Christmas Eve. 'Sweet heaven, that tastes even better than it smells.' She fixed him with a smile. 'Are you sure you won't have some?'

He ignored the request, still processing what she'd done; she'd drank his uncle's brandy! 'What are you doing in here? The party is…' He didn't know exactly where the party was at present. He waved a hand in the general direction of the door. 'Elsewhere.'

'Actually, I came looking for you.' She took a smug sip of her brandy, holding her glass in one hand with the easy negligence of an expert. She held out a slip of folded paper. 'In the spirit of holiday giving and self-lessness, we've all drawn secret admirers, or whatever you want to call them. We're not to tell anyone who's on our slips. We are to get to know our person, without being obvious, select a meaningful gift for them and give it to them on New Year's Day when all is revealed. *I* think it sounds fun.' She threw the last out as a challenge, already assuming that he hated the idea. *He* hated that she was right.

It sounded terribly social. He left the slip of paper on the table. He'd look at it later. 'Thank you.' He infused the words with a sense of finality—her task was complete. She was free to go. He sat down at the table, making all the signs of a man getting down to work. Surely she wasn't obtuse enough to miss the signals. Surely she'd take the hint and depart.

She didn't. She went back to strolling the shelves of books and for some reason he couldn't look away from the sway of her hips in the purple day dress flecked with spots of dark gold. The design of the gown was nothing out of the ordinary—long sleeved with a slight puff at the shoulder, a modest round neckline— yet her movements made the standard gown come alive. Of course they did. This was the woman who'd climbed a ladder and let everyone glimpse her ankles and more. Her body was a tool, an instrument for attraction.

*What else can she do with it*? came the wicked thought before he could push it away. He would not dignify that with a response. No doubt it was what she wanted him to think—perhaps not even him specifically, but what she wanted any man to think.

'I wouldn't want to keep you from the party,' he offered politely.

'You're not.' She smiled to match his politeness. 'Everyone's in their rooms resting and changing for dinner.' Yes, damn it, she was right. Everyone would keep to themselves until seven when they began to make their way downstairs to congregate before dinner. A horrible thought occurred to him. Surely she didn't mean to spend the next two hours in the library *with* him?

'Perhaps there's somewhere else you'd rather be? I don't need you to keep me company.' He gestured to the papers laid out before him. 'I have work, I'd be poor company anyway.'

'Has it occurred to you that I'm precisely where I want to be?'

'No, it hasn't. Frankly, Lady Viola, you don't strike me as a library kind of girl.'

'Tsk, tsk. I thought you were a smarter man than that. Of course I like libraries.' She arched her eyebrow and bit her lip playfully. 'You should have known better, Penrith, there are ladders, after all.' With that, she leapt on one of the great, long ladders that bracketed the floor-to-ceiling shelves and pushed off with one foot, sailing the length of the wall. She laughed then, a sound that was full bodied and loud, the sound of a woman enjoying herself.

'Lady Viola, please!' Vale cautioned sharply, taken aback by the forthright loudness of her outburst. 'Someone might hear.' It occurred to him rather belatedly how this might look, the two of them together, a woman's laughter, all during the quiet time when everyone was supposed to be changing. To be caught would be absolutely compromising.

Lady Viola jumped off the ladder, mocking laughter in each word. 'That would be scandalous! Two people in a library with nothing for chaperons except books. Shocking indeed!' She walked behind him, trailing her fingers across his shoulders. Her touch sent an unlooked-for frisson of awareness through him. 'I wonder, Penrith, are you afraid of being caught, or...' she bent to his ear, the scent of her, all plum and bergamot, sending another spear of awareness through him '…is it the being alone with me you fear?'

It was the audacity that aroused him against his preferences. He'd never been touched so boldly by a woman before outside the bedchamber. Certainly, there'd been lovers but they'd kept their forwardness confined to the proper place and time, which was not the middle of the afternoon in a library where they might be discovered at any moment by almost anyone.

'After all, there is always the question of what might I do?' She was on his lap now, her arms about his neck, a knowing smile on her red lips as she sat him side-saddle, her bottom wiggling as she made herself comfortable, her comfort coming into contact with his discomfort in the process. 'I see you've already thought of what I might do. Perhaps you *are* more man than monolith.' She put her forehead to his, her voice soft, invitingly intimate. 'What is it that you think I might do to you? What do you *want* me to do to you? I know what a man likes.'

Lucifer's tight, aching balls, London's Shocking Beauty was a temptress nonpareil. How did a duke's daughter 'know what a man liked'? Never mind. That was not especially salient at the moment. He could not partake of this particular temptation no matter how his body roused. She was not for him and she was *definitely* not for the future of Brockmore. But she could be whether he liked it or not if he didn't get her off his lap soon, before someone walked in. There was a serious sense of urgency in that regard. The threat of discovery was real. 'If you do not remove yourself from my lap, Lady Viola, by the time I count to five, I will stand up and you will be dumped on the floor.' He offered the warning bluntly.

She trailed a finger down the curve of his jaw. 'You can stand up any time you'd like. All you have to do is pay the forfeit.'

'What might that be?' He had no idea why he was bothering to humour her. She would only see it as a way to prolong this dangerous game.

'A Christmas kiss, of course,' she whispered her *dare*. He should do it; kiss her hard and fast in this chair, call her bluff and maybe scare some sense into her about the sort of man she toyed with. He was no green village boy or a prig as she accused. Just because he was discreet in his dealings as a gentleman should be didn't mean he was unfamiliar with the arts of passion.

'One,' he began. Kissing her was too risky here, his more logical side asserted. There was no mistletoe ball to excuse the behaviour. 'Two.' She was not budging. Instead, she shifted closer, her hip now firmly against his groin. 'Three,' he ground out evenly. He would not give her the satisfaction of counting faster. If he did that, she'd know he was trying to escape, trying to run. It would only suggest he was indeed 'afraid' of her. 'Four.' She gave him a witching smile, her only warning before her mouth covered his, taking his lips in an open-mouthed kiss. A little sigh of pleasure purled softly from her throat as she worked his mouth with her tongue, her body pressed up against his, as she gave herself over to the kiss.

He was aware of all of her in those long moments: the plum bergamot smell of her, the softness of her breasts pressed to his chest, the feel of her in his mouth, her hands in his hair, pulling it loose from its ribbon.

He was aware of himself, too; of the tightness ebbing from his body, of his escalating arousal that went far beyond a simple, physical erection, his want overriding his good sense, his mind forgetting the risks. How long had it been since he'd let himself get carried away just for the sake of being carried away? He was cognisant of his mouth answering hers, his hands cupping her face, framing it, in order to drink every ounce of pleasure from her lips before it was too late. Even so, it was done too soon.

She slid off his lap and straightened her skirts, looking suddenly prim and very proper as if *she* hadn't tried to seduce *him*. 'If you'll excuse me? I have to go change for dinner.' She gave him another witching smile. 'I knew you had it in you. You're a man, after all, Penrith.' But she was wrong, he was all rock; hard rock.

He didn't even remember the slip of paper until well after she'd gone and his body had restored itself to order. Vale reached for it with a sigh. He was not interested in getting to know someone else and, if he knew his aunt and uncle, he'd bet money the name on his slip was the name of some respectable lady whom they wanted to put forward as a marriage candidate.

Vale unfolded the paper and stared. The words, 'Lady Viola Hawthorne' were neatly written in his aunt's elegant cursive. The holiday spirit, if there was such a thing, was certainly a contrary one. Here was the one person he'd least likely wanted to draw and evidence that his aunt hadn't engineered it. His aunt and uncle would not find the likes of Viola Hawthorne a suitable future duchess. Well, if there was some good in all of this, it was that he wouldn't have to think too hard about her gift. He'd get her a bottle of his uncle's brandy and call it square. It could have been worse, he supposed. She could have drawn his name and who knew where that would have led? Well, actually, he knew. All the better it had worked out this way instead.

# *Chapter Five*

❧

*Sunday, 27th December 1818*
*—skating party on the lake*

He was still thinking about those kisses the next day, proof that his foray through the snow to the frozen lake with the other guests for skating was a failed attempt to cool thoughts of hot kisses with the crisp winter air. Vale had held out hope that a turn or two around the lake would succeed where cold air had failed, but he'd found no success in exercise either.

Who could concentrate on ice skating when there were stolen kisses in a library to think about? Kisses so disturbing he'd lain awake most of the night analysing them in a variety of detail; his mind contemplating every aspect from his shockingly lusty and immediate response to the feel of her on his lap, in his arms, pressed against him. It was the immediacy of his response that bothered him most. He'd *enjoyed* kisses from a woman whose behaviour he found appalling in the extreme. Was that truly the target of his aversion? Perhaps it was not *her* passion, but *his* reaction that he found appalling.

What had he been thinking to respond like that? Perhaps he hadn't been thinking at all. For a few moments his carefully constructed armour of polite aloofness had been down and he'd forgotten to be the man he'd become in the wake of R.J.'s death. For a moment, the self he'd tamped down all those years ago—the self that knew the thrill of a fast horse and the excitement of the hunt, and revelled in them, had managed to break free. Probably not the best idea. He'd tamped that self down for a reason—two of them. The heir to Brockmore couldn't go kissing forward girls any time he felt like it and the man he'd once been was tired of hurting, tired of feeling, because to feel good, one had to know how to feel badly. He was tired of sorrow.

Boots crunched on the snow and he turned towards the sound as his uncle came to stand with him. 'You should be out there skating.' His uncle nodded towards the frozen lake, filled with house guests enjoying themselves. 'You still have your skates on. It's good you've been out already, but hopefully not for the last time today. I remember when you were younger, nine or ten, maybe. You and R.J. use to love to skate. Your father and I took you out every day when you'd visit in the winter. The two of you would race from end to end trying to outdo each other. Those were good times when the house was full of children.' His uncle looked at him and smiled. 'The house will be full of children again one day. I look forward to that.' This line of conversation was not subtle at all. Vale smiled politely in response. The Silver Fox was losing his touch.

'I know many men prefer women in the spring, with all the pretty fashions and light fabrics, but I'm a winter man.' His uncle's eyes crinkled at the corners as his gaze returned to the ice. 'I think women are lovely in furs and coats, their cheeks pinched with a touch of colour from wind and cold.' Anne Lowell skated by, arm and arm with her cousin, her colour high, the epitome of his uncle's description. 'What do you think of her, Blackton's daughter?' Oh, his uncle was not subtle at all.

'Anne Lowell?' Vale struggled to get his thoughts on track. He'd been searching the ice for a whirlwind in a maroon coat. 'I haven't thought much of her at all. We've only had conversation at dinner.' Opening with the truth seemed to be a good strategy as long as he didn't have to go into the reasons why he'd not devoted any thought to the pretty Lady Anne. Whatever thoughts he'd given time to had been directed towards a dark-haired minx with violet eyes.

'Perhaps you should,' his uncle said amiably, but Vale knew better than to be fooled. His uncle had the soul of a matchmaker and—how did one put it?—a certain arrogance when it came to believing he knew best what suited others. It was a well-earned arrogance and not without support. He and his aunt had brokered many successful marriages in their three decades of entertaining and he was in no way finished pushing his latest match. 'Lady Anne is attractive, from a good family, well dowered, although you don't need it, her father is politically connected and she's personally accomplished. You'll get to hear her sing at one of our musical evenings. Intelligent, too. She'd be interested in your cultural work. There'd be no running out of things to say at the breakfast table.' He chuckled the way a long-married man does when imparting knowledge to a bachelor yet to take the plunge.

Vale nodded. 'I am sure Lady Anne is a paragon.'

'She is and true paragons are not thick on the ground.' He nodded towards a figure Vale recognised too well. Viola was out on the ice, spinning in circles with Eaton's little sister who had come over for the day. 'Consider the Duke of Calton's daughter.' His uncle shook his head in general disapproval, watching Viola spin with the younger girl. 'She should have been taken in hand long before this. With her fortune and her family connections, there's no good reason she's not married by now, except poor parenting.' It was hard to know if his uncle disapproved of Viola specifically or if his larger objection was with her circumstances. 'They've let her grow wild and wild she has stayed.' His uncle gave him a meaningful but inscrutable look. 'It will take an extraordinary match to an extraordinary man to save her now.'

'A little spirit is an admirable quality,' Vale began, startled by the surge of defensiveness he felt on Viola's behalf. Since when did he feel the need to champion her?

'Most definitely,' his uncle agreed readily. 'But she's taken it beyond "a little spirit". I am not oblivious to what that "little spirit" has got up to since her arrival. I know about her escapade in the hall. I've noticed how she garners all the attention in a room when there's a game to play. There's the right kind of attention a lady should attract and then there's the sort *she* attracts. A gentleman knows the difference. Calton will have trouble getting her off his hands if he waits much longer, duke or not.' His uncle continued knowingly, 'Men will flirt with girls like her, but they won't risk the family line by marrying them. A smart man takes a wife like Anne Lowell, every time.'

Dear lord, his uncle was tenacious! Vale had forgotten, or maybe he'd simply not known, never having had that tenacity turned his direction. Vale knew very well who the 'smart man' was in that allusion. 'I don't think it's an issue of Anne Lowell's qualities.' How did he tell his uncle he didn't need a match made for him? He'd make his own. *When* the time came.

His uncle blew out a frosty breath in the silence and his voice dropped. 'Then what is it a matter of? Don't tell me you're not ready. You're thirty and you've had time to adjust to your circumstances.' In other words, to accept his duty as Brockmore's heir to beget an heir or two of his own. 'Do you do find Lady Anne to be flawed in some way?'

'Of course not. She's all you claim, but my preference is to find my own bride at my own time.'

That did not sit well with his uncle. He raised a grey brow. 'You're the heir, my boy. Whether you like it or not, your time is not your own. Don't wait too long. Your aunt and I aren't getting any younger. If the events of the past four years have shown me anything it's that we're all mortal. We can be called home to our maker at any second. R.J., your father, the Princess Charlotte, notwithstanding. Coronets and kingdoms didn't protect them and they won't protect us either.' He clapped Vale on the shoulder. 'I'm a selfish man in the final analysis. I'd like to see Brockmore full of youth once more before I go, full of laughter and hope. I want to meet my reward knowing my legacy will continue, that my life's work has not been spent in vain.' He gave Vale a long stare. 'You, dear nephew, *are* my life's work.'

Vale swallowed against the rising emotion in his throat. His uncle's appeal was a potent one, logically and sentimentally. He owed a good marriage to the family as much as he owed it to himself, even if the idea of 'good' varied depending on who was asked. Clearly, his uncle equated the idea of a sound marriage with bloodlines and accomplishments. Vale held other ideas about what might be involved—affection, mutual respect among them. But how to respond without provoking an argument or setting himself against his beloved uncle when he hadn't quite sorted through how to let those emotions out for himself? How did he have an emotionally satisfying marriage if he didn't allow himself to give his own emotions free rein?

A flurry of maroon and fur flew past, skates close to the edge of the shore, a gloved hand grabbing for his at the last moment, pulling him on to the ice. 'Come on, there's something I want to show you!' Vale let momentum take him, let it drag him away from his uncle's well-intended matchmaking. Far better to be skating than to be arguing. The rescue could not have been better timed. Had she been watching him?

Viola had him firmly by the hand, leading him across the ice at a fiend's pace. They wove in and out among the other more sedate skaters, her laughter floating back to him. 'You can do better than this! I saw you out on the ice earlier.'

He answered her scold with a burst of speed, dropping her hand as something primal surged in him to prove his superiority in this small way. He could go much faster. He pushed with one foot, flying forward, finding the rhythm of his youth. He sailed past Viola, the blades of his skates whispering their dare on the ice. He knew she was with him. He could hear her own blades take up the reckless pace. The party fell behind them, fading with the shore, the island in the centre of the lake looming closer.

It was his chance to lead and he took her around the leeward curve of the island to the far side, where the island was naturally protected from the wind before coming to a full stop, breathless and exhilarated. He bent down, hands on knees, gathering his breath between gulps of laughter.

Viola skated up beside him a few seconds later, letting out a whoop of delight that was swallowed up in the winter silence. 'That was magnificent! You're a champion racer, Penrith.' The accolade warmed him unexpectedly, like he'd won a silver cup.

She flopped down in the snow at the edge of the lake, falling backwards like a snow angel. There he went again, thinking of her as an angel. Why did his brain insist on doing that when his body knew she was the very devil? She sat up in the little snow drift, the hood of her coat falling back to reveal her dark hair, glistening with errant drops of melted snow. 'Care to join me?'

'I already have. I'm here, aren't I?' His sense of self-preservation warned him to stay upright. If he gave in to the urge to plop in the snow beside her, who knew what might happen? What did he *hope* would happen? Another kiss? Did he want her to kiss him again or did *he* want to do the kissing this time? Wait. *He* wanted to kiss Viola Hawthorne? The discoveries were unending. Earlier he'd been moved to defend her, now he wanted to kiss her? He needed to stop surprising himself like this. If there was to be any more kissing, it would be easier if she kissed him. Then, he could play the victim. He could tell himself he had no control over *her* actions.

Just the thought of taking that route smacked of cowardice. He was not the sort of man who waited for a woman to make the first move. In all of his relationships, he was the one in charge. But if he kissed her, that would change everything about their association. He'd have to stop being appalled by her behaviour and concentrate on his. He'd have to decide what came next. What *did* come next with a woman like her? A woman who was so secure in her emotions, her sexuality? A certain thrill bubbled up inside him before he could tamp it down—the age-old thrill of the hunt.

She leaned back on her gloved hands, looking entirely comfortable in the snow drift, and cocked her head to gaze up at him, 'Suit yourself.'

'Did it suit you to pull me on to the lake?' He doubted there'd been anything to actually come and see.

She shrugged. 'It appeared to suit *you*. You seemed in need of rescuing. There was something about the look on your face, *and* the look on your uncle's, both of you were being so politely determined with each other.' She shrugged. 'Call it intuition, if you want.'

'I suppose a rescue *was* in order,' Vale offered, attempting neutrality and failing. He was finding it impossible to look at her without his gaze falling to her lips, without his thoughts going back to yesterday's interlude.

'What were you discussing so intently?' She was audacious even without trying. No decent lady of his acquaintance would probe so indelicately into a gentleman's business. His uncle's words came back to him. *There's no good reason she's not married by now, except poor parenting.*

'That's not any of your business.' Vale began to skate a figure eight, anything to distract him from looking at her, from thinking of her.

'I will make it my business. Shall I guess?' she persisted. She tipped her head skyward, showing off the long column of her neck. Perhaps she knew full well the pretty picture she made with her dark hair and maroon coat against the stark whiteness of the snow. He didn't want to find it picturesque, but he did. His body did. Even in the cold, he was rousing. She would have his secrets out of him in no time at this rate.

# Chapter Six

⧟⧟⧟

She would have his secrets or die trying, Viola vowed.
It would be part of her larger victory, part of her mission to break Vale Penrith's impenetrable shell. Even if
she hadn't decided to take on the challenge, she'd still
be morally obligated to probe a bit. The 'perfect' gift
was on the line, after all, and she needed some ideas.

Viola slipped a hand into her coat pocket, her gloved
fingers closing over the slip of paper from Brockmore's
game yesterday. She'd drawn Penrith—something of
a blessing and a curse. Well, she'd sort of drawn him.
She'd actually traded Anne for him. She'd originally
drawn Kenelm and Anne had drawn Penrith, which
made Viola think the game might have been rigged.

Viola began to think out loud, confident she would
guess the source of the argument. Was Penrith arrogant
enough to think men were such a mystery to women? Besides, she had an advantage thanks to Anne's information.

'Was it about money? Men always discuss money
and it leaves them in poor spirits. But Brockmore has
plenty. So, no, I do not think it was money.' She tapped
a gloved finger against her chin. 'Love, perhaps?' She

tossed him a coy look, only to be disappointed by the shake of his head. She gave him a pout. 'Not love, Penrith? Marriage, then?'

'Are they mutually exclusive?'

His words caught her off guard. She'd not been prepared for the revelation.

Viola's eyes narrowed in contemplation. 'It's really a case of the possible against the probable. Love *is* possible in marriage, merely not probable, not the way the *ton* does it anyway.' She fixed him with a violet stare. She was on to something. He hadn't denied her guess. 'So, it *was* marriage that had you and your uncle at odds?'

'It's still *not* your business. Marriage is a private arrangement,' Penrith protested, but he was starting to crack. He *wanted* to tell someone. She could see it in the way his gaze flitted away from her, how he couldn't meet her eyes. He was hiding something.

'Then make it my business. Tell me. You look like you need a friend.' She teased the temptation in him, 'Who's to know? We're on the other side of the island, nothing around us but winter. We might as well be the only two people in the world.' She patted the snow again and took a calculated risk. 'Sit down and tell me why you don't want to marry Anne Lowell.'

His blades skidded to a halt, his body plopping down beside her. 'How did you know?' There was fleeting panic in his eyes. 'My uncle hasn't announced it, has he?'

She laughed. 'No. It's just obvious. Brockmore brought her here for you. I'm the only other one here with a pedigree worthy of you and he certainly doesn't want you to marry me.'

Penrith shrugged his broad shoulders in assent. 'I suppose you're right on that account.'

That stung. *She* could point out how unmarriageable she was, but that didn't mean he could. The hurt in her wanted some revenge. 'Anne doesn't want to marry you either. She told me so Christmas Eve.' Viola leaned in conspiratorially. 'She has her sights set on Kenelm and he on her, only his father resists.'

'Well, good. Then she and I are in agreement.' Penrith remained disappointingly unruffled by the news. 'If she and Kenelm have affection for one another, I hope they will be able to marry.'

'Don't tell me, *you* believe in love?' What had he said earlier? That love and marriage needn't be mutually exclusive? Was that what he believed? She wouldn't have guessed.

'And you don't? You think they have to be separate?' He was not afraid to challenge her and she was enjoying it. She didn't *want* to enjoy it, that hadn't been part of her plan. She *didn't* want to like him, didn't want to be looking up into his serious blue eyes and thinking about the straight length of his nose, or the high curve of his cheekbones. She certainly didn't want to be thinking about his mouth on hers, or how his body had felt at her touch, all hard muscle and strength coming alive beneath her fingertips when they kissed, and oh heavens how the man could kiss!

'Look around. How many marriages do you see that incorporate both? Conventional wisdom says I'm right. You'll see. Even your marriage will prove it.' She meant to taunt him with her words, meant to put him on the defensive so she could stop liking him. He'd say something conservative and old-fashioned and she'd remember he was a borderline prig. *Who just happened to kiss like a rake.*

'What about yours? Will yours somehow be different?' It was not said unkindly. He had not taken the bait.

Viola tossed her head, letting her eyes flash with daring to match the audacity of her words. 'I'm not getting married.'

'Why ever not?'

'Why aren't you going to marry Anne Lowell?'

'That doesn't mean I don't want to marry, I just don't want to marry her,' Penrith argued. 'I want to pick my bride. I want there to be something between us besides duty. Don't you want that?'

'I've already established I don't think it exists, not up in the rarefied air you and I breathe, anyway,' Viola shot back. This conversation was not going as she planned. She was supposed to be ferreting out his secrets. But she felt like the one being exposed. She opted for the most shocking revelation in her verbal arsenal. 'I can have that "something else" without marriage. I don't need to marry a man for the pleasure of his bed. After all, men don't marry for it. They seek pleasure outside of marriage and before marriage. Why shouldn't a woman?' Viola grinned. It was clear from the frown on his face that she'd succeeded in irritating him.

Penrith stood abruptly and with an extraordinary amount of grace considering he wore skates. 'To be discussing this with you carries a hint of the absurd. I think it best we end the conversation here.' He dusted the snow off his caped greatcoat with sharp swipes, his agitated gestures a further sign of his unrest.

Viola rose, too fast to be graceful. 'Why? Because I spoke of conjugal relations? Because a woman shouldn't claim as much freedom as a man? No one expects *you* to come to the marriage bed untried. Why should society expect a woman to? I mean, that doesn't work mathematically, does it? It's entirely illogical. Who are the men going to sharpen their prowess on if women can't join them?'

She meant to shock him at his priggish core and maybe she had, but it was his turn to do the shocking. He fixed his solemn blue eyes on her, his voice sternly quiet. 'Why should anyone have to practise at all? Why can't intimacy be discovered together between two people over time? Why should a man's intimacy be reduced to the seeking of cheap pleasures? For that matter, why should the choice to marry be reduced to those same cheap pleasures? Is that all marriage is to you, Lady Viola? An opportunity for intercourse? When I said something more, I meant something more than what you refer to. Quite a bit more, in fact.'

For a moment she was speechless. What sort of man talked like that? Thought like that? No man she knew. A wicked thought occurred to her. 'Are you a virgin, Penrith?' she whispered in part-awe, part-disbelief. He couldn't be. He was thirty years old and he didn't kiss like any virgin she knew. And yet, she had to wonder, with romantic sentiments like that…

'No, but that is yet another item that is none of your business.'

'Don't you think your stance is a little hypocritical?' Viola pressed, ignoring his jab at her invasion of privacy. They were standing close together now on the ice, their argument having decreased the space between them.

'I think society is the hypocrite. Perhaps *it* shouldn't equate manliness with a man's reputation regarding the quality of his bed sport.' His eyes had gone the shade of midnight sapphires, his pupils wide. He was aroused, too, and the recognition was heady knowledge. Perhaps his idea of flirtation was spouting homilies on sexual moral code. It was working.

'Do you have such a reputation, Penrith?' Her voice was breathless. This discussion had moved from the broader scope of sexual politics to personal ones and the shift was intoxicating. It conjured up hot speculation. What would it be like to be in bed with a man who believed as he did? Not just bed, he'd made it clear bed alone was not enough for his finer appetites, but in bed with all that he suggested should be present. She was starting to burn.

'I hear it is, if we're being honest.' His voice was pure gravel now. 'When I bed a woman, it is because she means something to me.' That was the absolute best line she'd ever heard, the best advertisement of the prowess he claimed not to care for. What woman would refuse such an invitation? Not her. Her curiosity was searing her alive. She wanted to know what Vale Penrith could do to a woman, to *her*.

Viola whet her lips. The glimpse of the man beneath the shell was tantalising, to have a marriage that was not the enslavement she railed against. What if she could have a marriage like that with a man like this? A man who wanted more from marriage than a trading of titles and wealth? Would that be enough to change her mind? *What if*? Would her dreams be safe with a such a man?

Oh, no. There were no 'what ifs'. She didn't allow for them. Curiosity was meant to be satisfied. She'd never met a man she couldn't charm into compliance, virtues and ethics notwithstanding. Penrith was still a man no matter what philosophies he ascribed to and that meant he should be just about ready to capitulate. She was not the only inferno here. He was aroused and spouting lines that put Casanova to shame. It was time to move in for the kill.

Her gloved hands gripped the front of his coat as she tilted her face up, lips parted, wet and glistening in invitation. 'I've never met a man like you, Vale.'

His eyes, dark and half-lidded, dropped to her mouth, his hands covered hers, his grip firm. She let a little sigh escape her. His mouth lowered. A kiss was inevitable. She let her eyes close. In three, two…

'No, I don't think I will kiss you.' The firm hands pushed her away, sending her sliding gently backwards on her skates. For a moment she was stunned. He was rejecting her! *He was rejecting her?* For the first time ever, a man didn't want what she was offering. She hardly knew what to do. Failure was not an option she'd considered and yet here it was.

Penrith gave her a curt nod of his head, his shell firmly intact. 'And, I don't recall giving you leave to use my first name. Forgive me, I must return to the party.'

Vale Penrith skated away—before he was missed, before anyone found them together and suspected he actually had claimed the kiss he'd refused, before she could exact immediate revenge for her rejection. That was twice now he'd played her, turning her game on its head. But she'd learned something valuable today. She'd been wrong. Penrith wasn't a prig, after all. He was an idealist. A romantic, even. How novel. Viola kicked the snow with the toe of her skate. Hadn't given her leave to use his first name? Hah. They'd be on more than a first-name basis before New Year's. He'd be screaming her name to high heaven before she was done.

# Chapter Seven

Evening, Monday, 28th December 1818

Raucous yells and boisterous whoops met Vale half-way down the hall leading to the billiards room. It was after midnight. What could possibly be going on? The sound of feminine laughter—laughter he was coming to recognise too well—rose above the rest and Vale found himself hurrying down the corridor out of intrigue, interest and perhaps a little fear—what had she got up to now? Why did he care? They'd parted poorly yesterday on the lake. They owed each other nothing.

Why hadn't she gone to bed like the rest of the guests? There'd been music and wassailing in the music room after dinner, the guests merry but tired after another day filled with non-stop activity. There'd been a special beverage, too—one with rum and other flavours he couldn't identify. He'd imbibed carefully, although others had partaken quite liberally. It was supposed to be good for the vocal cords. Vale thought the drink was likely better for the ears, making the listener more tolerant of whatever 'special' talents were on display.

Surprisingly, those talents hadn't included Viola. She had sat the evening musicale out, letting the other ladies take centre stage, although she'd got plenty of attention just sitting there. She'd worn an enticing red dress and had stationed herself on an ottoman. It did him no credit to have noticed. She had beaux swanning around her on all sides. Martindale and Throckton coming and going on one side, Eaton and Kenelm on the other, even though Kenelm's eyes never left Anne.

Whatever she may have lacked in attention, she was making up for now. The sight of her in that red dress, bent provocatively over a billiard cue, the curve of her derrière displayed, the swell of breasts pressed tight against the low-cut bodice confirmed that rather empirically. All of her 'charms' were on exhibit. Vale felt a bolt of jealousy shoot through him. Her red dress had him seeing green. How dare she flirt with the others the way she'd flirted with him? Did she kiss them, too? Did she dissemble with them the way she had with him at the lake, sharing her unorthodox views? Did her eyes promise them the passion they'd promised him? *Passion you'd rejected*, he had to remind himself. He'd passed on her dubious charms. He had no right to claim them now or to prevent others from claiming them.

Viola sank a ball into the corner pocket and then repositioned herself for another shot, nudging Throckton with her hip to do it. She tossed Throckton a teasing smile and sank another shot, and then another to rowdy applause. She'd nearly cleared the table and the gentlemen were egging her on. He was starting to think 'gentlemen' might be a loosely applied appellation. Martindale was here, Throckton, the aristocrat's bastard, Eaton and Kenelm. With the exception of Kenelm, none of them were of serious rank. Of them all, Kenelm ought to have known better than to let this get out of hand. It was more telling as to who was absent. Lord Truesdale and Captain Milborne would have added some sobriety to the gathering.

'I'm down to two balls, gentlemen.' Viola delivered the allusion in a smoky, whisky-laced voice. The gathering laughed.

Eaton matched her in wit and innuendo. 'I think it's more like six, unless you count Penrith over there in the doorway. Then you've got eight. I'd say that's a handful.'

She straightened and reached for the chalking cube, eyes landing on him. 'Penrith, won't you come in and join us? You're just in time. Martindale has bet me a kiss I can't clear the table. If I sink this last shot, I can kiss anyone in the room. If I lose, I have to kiss him.' Jealousy dug him hard in the ribs at the thought of her kissing Martindale. Across the table, Martindale traded knowing smiles with her and Vale wondered if he already knew what it was like to taste her lips. He wondered, too, if Viola preferred Percival Martindale's kisses to his. It was not well done of him. She could kiss the whole damn party if she wanted to. He just didn't want her to want to.

Viola twisted the chalk, her gaze never leaving his, daring him to stay. She managed to make the gesture provocative before she brought the cue to her cherry-red lips and blew. Good lord, he was going to go hard right here in the billiards room in front of the company. When she flirted, her eyes went straight through a man. That gaze made him feel like the only man in the world even when the room was full of men whose company she obviously preferred to his.

He ought to leave now. Before something happened—something always happened when Viola was around. Being here was *not* in his best interest. Being here was, in fact, the perfect miserable ending to what had not been a good day. This afternoon, his uncle had chastised him, politely, of course, but the scolding had been obvious. He'd skipped all of the day's activities today and most of yesterday after the skating. Uncle Marcus had been 'concerned' about his untimely and lengthy disappearance with Lady Viola at yesterday's skating party, followed by his abrupt departure. He'd absented himself from the skaters' luncheon altogether and only reappeared at dinner that night and this one.

'Makes it look as if you'd had a quarrel of some significance. Have you? Is that the impression you want to create?' had been his uncle's words, which were followed by a lecture on the merits of Anne Lowell and a few not-so-subtle reminders about the character of Lady Viola, not that he'd needed any warnings. He'd seen her 'character' first hand. And yet he couldn't bring himself to cede the room and leave her to the likes of Eaton and Martindale and whatever after-hours entertainment they got up to in his uncle's billiards room. But here he stood, his attentions riveted by a red dress and a pair of flashing eyes.

Viola strolled the perimeter of the table, hips swaying as she surveyed the baize. She bent and stood, moved on, bent and stood again, repeating the movements a few more times. He shouldn't let himself be interested in such tawdry play, but Vale felt his gaze studying the table and assessing her chances—or rather Martindale's chances. The shot was tricky but not impossible if one played a significant amount of billiards and had some experience with banking and splitting. Still, he arrived at the conclusion she was going to lose. Even if he suspended belief for a moment, Vale couldn't imagine Viola had that kind of experience. When would she have acquired it? Surely even Calton's negligent parenting hadn't allowed for such a skill to develop. Maybe she wanted to lose.

She bent and let out a breath, ready to settle. A hush fell over the room, everyone suddenly intent on the shot as if a championship rested on this and not a mere kiss. Throckton's voice broke into the silence. 'Lady Viola, I think you'd have a better shot if you moved just a bit to the left, like this.' His hands were at her waist, his body angling intimately over hers as he guided the cue. Vale felt his blood boil. How dare Throckton take such liberties, how dare she allow it?

'That's cheating,' Martindale growled.

'That's hedging his bets,' Eaton put in good-naturedly. 'If she makes the shot, perhaps she'll want to reward him.' Martindale shot him a hard look. 'What?' Eaton laughed. 'I thought maybe you were saving your kisses for Lady Beatrice Landry, anyway.' That earned him another searing look. He held up his hands in surrender. 'I'll kiss you then, Martindale, if you're so desperate.'

Vale found himself suppressing a chuckle and another stab of envy. This time, not over Viola, but over the easy comradery between the gentlemen. He'd not joked with friends like that for what seemed a lifetime.

'Are you ready, Lady Viola?' Throckton had his mouth at her ear, his body over her like a stallion covering a mare. 'Shall we take the shot together?'

She laughed, shaking off Throckton. 'I'll make my

own shots, thank you.' She drew back the cue and struck true, the cue ball splitting the pair. The first ball had speed and the closer pocket. It dropped with ease. The second ball had further to go. It slowed as it neared the pocket. Vale found himself holding his breath. It paused at the pocket, coming to a near stop, teetering on the pocket and then dropping with the last of its momentum.

'Gentlemen, I win.' Viola laid down her cue stick and held her arms wide. Someone put a brandy glass in her hand. 'To my victory!' She took a long drink while the others cheered. 'Now, to my prize.'

She looked around the room, giving each gentleman the consideration of her eyes. 'I've already had you, Eaton,' she joked, passing over him. 'Under the mistletoe, I recall. I'm not likely to forget it. That leaves Martindale, whom I must eliminate—it is whom, isn't it, Penrith?' She gave a throaty laugh. 'After all, it makes no sense to win a bet and then kiss the same person you would have kissed if you lost,' she teased Martindale with a smile. 'That leaves me with three.' Vale tensed. He did not want her to announce she'd already 'had' him. Eaton's kiss had been public. Everyone knew. But their kisses had been entirely private and he wanted to keep them that way.

She set down her brandy glass, eyes narrowing in a look that sent a *frisson* of anticipation down his spine. It was positively predatory. He knew what she would say before the words were out of her mouth. 'I choose Penrith.'

There was a general manly outcry of disapproval. She silenced it with a smile. 'Gentlemen, he needs it most.'

Fabulous. Now he was a charity case. She swayed

towards him, hips rocking beneath the folds of her red dress, eyes glistening. Somewhere in the house a clock chimed one—it was far past time someone showed a sense of decency. What would happen if one of these gentlemen told his uncle what had transpired and that he'd participated? That they'd all witnessed him kissing Lady Viola, that he'd let her drink brandy and play midnight billiards, one unmarried woman alone with five men. This would all be his fault. He'd be the one to pay. He took Viola by the arm. 'There will be no kissing. Let me escort you to your room.'

'Come on, Penrith, we're just playing,' Throckton argued on Viola's behalf.

'Playtime's over. We should all get to bed.' He'd only meant to be stern, but he recognised his poor choice of words immediately and she didn't hesitate to turn them on him.

'All of us?' Viola purred, tossing a smoky glance over her shoulder at the others. 'That's a mighty big... *bed* you've got then, Penrith.' She lifted a shoulder in a negligent shrug. 'I'm game if you are.' The others laughed. Loudly. The whole house would hear them at this rate. Vale was angry now. He could feel his temper running hot in his blood, feel his frustration rising. Why did she insist on challenging him at every turn? Every word? Why did *he* insist on being her champion when she clearly didn't want one?

He glared at her, she smiled back, undaunted with eyes flashing. The tension ratcheted another notch, the other gentlemen exchanged uncomfortable looks. Kenelm cleared his throat. 'I think I'll head up. Eaton, are you coming?' Matthew Eaton agreed with astonishing alacrity and far too much enthusiasm to be natural. Throckton and Martindale muttered about getting a nightcap in the library. Throckton stopped as they passed Viola. 'Did you want to join us, Vi?' Vale didn't miss the challenging glance Throckton threw his way or the excessive familiarity. It was insulting, really. An aristocrat's illegitimate son equating himself with a duke's daughter. She might allow it, but Vale wouldn't.

He spoke before Viola could even think of accepting one more indecent offer this evening, the grip on her arm tight, in full anticipation of a bolt. '*Lady* Viola is staying with me.'

Throckton hesitated, looking as if he would like to try out that assumption. Vale added, 'I don't think Lady Beatrice would appreciate hearing about your evening escapades.' There was no sense in mincing words. He meant it as a threat and he wanted Throckton to take it as one, without any ambiguity. Throckton moved on.

Vale waited until the group was out of sight. He kept his voice low, his words barely more than a growl as he rounded on her. 'What in heaven's name do you think you're doing?'

# Chapter Eight

'I'm waiting,' Viola replied, eyes wide in feigned innocence. 'I thought you were taking me to bed.'

'Stop it.' The words were a growl. He was angry and it was a ferocious sight. Most angry men she knew blustered. Like her father. Angry men yelled and made horrible but ultimately toothless threats. Occasionally they threw something priceless at the fireplace and regretted it later. Not Penrith. His body went still and hard, his eyes glittering, determined slits as his mind and body worked to keep the boiling anger in check. She heard the effort in the gravel of his voice. She heard the breaking in it, too. She nearly had him, just as she had nearly had him at the lake. That was when he usually slipped away, put himself beyond her reach emotionally and physically. He was proving to be a wily opponent, a man who would not allow himself to be manipulated, a strong man.

Viola twisted her arm, trying to step back, but he wouldn't let her go. 'Stop what?' She was pushing him hard now. She knew how much he hated the feigned innocence, hated being called to bluntness.

'This game, all the games. What do you think happens if word of tonight gets out?'

'I get sent home? Oh, do you think someone might tell your uncle I was playing billiards and drinking his brandy? I do hope so.' She let her sarcasm needle him. She kept pushing. 'Wouldn't that be a shame? I'd get to go home and be with my friends instead of here, being trotted out by parents who are desperate to get me off their hands. They can hardly wait to hand me over to a husband and let me be his problem. I've been a trial to them since the day I was born.' Since the day her mother had nearly died giving birth to the only child her poor body could sustain. She shrugged and slanted her gaze in Penrith's direction. 'It would have been different, of course, if I'd been born with a penis. Then the jeopardy I put my mother in would have been acceptable. Instead, the risk was disappointing, as I have been every day since.'

He let her go, the tension in him coiled tight. 'So that's why you do it? To shame them?'

'Hardly. My rebellion isn't quite that juvenile.' She tossed her head and poured another brandy. 'It's simple. I don't want to be here. I'd rather be at home and the fastest way to get there is to be expelled from the party.'

'I don't believe that. This is not an isolated incident. It's a long-standing behaviour.'

'Next you'll be saying I do it to get attention, to feel better about myself.' She pointed the glass at him, her words starting to slur slightly so that her 'S's came with 'H's. 'You, sir, know nothing about me. If you did, you would know this is a rebellion against the female enslavement also known as marriage, where a woman submits to a man's pleasure in order to preserve her own financial security. But you don't me know at all. So, I'd appreciate it if you kept your assumptions to yourself.'

When he said nothing, she gave a giggle. 'Now I've gone and shocked you.'

Dear sweet heavens, she was a drunk philosopher! She had shocked him, but not in the way she thought. It was the vulnerability behind her rant that him speechless. She would regret that in the morning. She would not like anyone seeing her so exposed, especially not him. 'That's it, you've had enough. Give me that.' He was on her in two strides, wrenching the brandy out of her hand, liquid sloshing on the carpet. He did it more for her than for him. What did he care how much she drank or said? But she made him pay for the intrusion.

'And maybe *you* haven't had *enough*.' She wound her arms about his neck, trapping him against her. 'I'm not so drunk, that I've forgotten you owe me a kiss. I won that billiards game and I get a kiss from whomever I want.' She had her hands in his hair, pulling it loose from its ribbon. 'Why do you grow your hair so long?' She was starting to feel warm and tingly, the world was tilting just a bit and it was fuzzy on the edges, soft. The softness felt good and disconcerting all at once. But Vale Penrith was a solid anchor. As long as she clung to him, everything would be all right. Vale would never let her fall. He was too much of a gentleman, no matter what he thought of her.

'Do you know what I wanted to do to you the first night I saw you? I wanted to mess you up. I wanted to untie your cravat, I wanted to pull your hair out of that black-silk bow. I wanted to spill wine on your shirt.' She had her mouth inches from his. 'I still want to. You're so damn perfect and such a good kisser.' She was beyond warm now, uncomfortably so. She was hot and wet and she wanted him to be hot and wet, too. She kissed him then, hard and fierce, but his mouth would not be enough, not tonight when she was burning. She slipped a hand low between their bodies, finding the intersection between his legs and stroking up, up over the hard length of him, her hand closing over the tip of him where it jutted against his trousers, giving him away entirely. He might be angry, but it hadn't stopped his desire. 'Seems like we might not make it to bed, after all.'

Lady Viola Hawthorne had her hand on his member—his *fully* aroused member. He ought to put a stop to this, but he knew as soon as the thought crossed his heated mind he wasn't going to do a damn thing about it. He'd tried to fight fire the traditional way—with water. He'd tried to douse her enthusiasm with scoldings and warnings. But clearly to no avail.

Now it was time to fight fire with fire and call her bluff. She wanted to play the temptress? So be it. He was in charge here. He'd let her see how a man responded. He took the kiss away from her, his mind and body more than ready to take charge, more than ready to break free of the artificial constraints he'd acquired to hold them in check. He gave his want free rein, his mouth devouring hers in a hard kiss, proof that actions had consequences: *her* actions, *his* consequences.

And yet, it was her hand on him, driving him mad; mad enough to push her up against the billiards table, mad enough to lift her, to settle her bottom on the bumper of the table. He felt her thighs part, her legs gripping him, holding him close as her hand stroked, her other hand working the fastenings of his trousers. She was excited, *he'd* excited her, this minx of a temptress.

It was heady knowledge to know he could arouse *this* woman who liked to hold all the cards.

'Let me bring you off, Vale. Right here.' Ah, those words! It was a rare woman who knew how much dirty talk could turn a man on, even a gentleman, or perhaps *especially* a gentleman. Her voice was all naughty smoke, the slur of brandy gone, pushed aside by the rush of excitement and arousal. He might have let her do it, too, if he hadn't understood her better. He knew what drove her: control. Not attention. She liked to control situations, to control others. But she would not control him. He wouldn't allow it.

'You first,' he growled, pushing her back on to the table, sliding her skirts up to reveal…nothing. Was it possible to get any harder? Vale swallowed. 'You aren't wearing anything.' No petticoats, no pantalettes, *nothing*.

'Undergarments are such a bother.' She gave a coy smile, her tongue running over red lips, giving every impression of a woman not yet ready to relinquish control. He answered with a wicked grin. If he wanted control he'd have to take it. It was to be a siege then, a long, slow assault on the citadel of her womanhood. His thumb feathered the entrance of her core and he felt her shudder, then she whispered the most provocative words he'd ever heard, 'Use your damn mouth, Vale.'

He knelt then, cupping her buttocks with his hands and drawing her forward to the edge of the table with a hard slide. He did not mean to take her easily. It would be a rough siege. She would pay first before he gave her pleasure. He put his mouth to her core, blowing warm breath across her damp curls, listening to the ululation of her sighs as she melted into the caress of his mouth.

But it was a prelude only. He had more in mind than a gentle climax. He would not let her get off that easily.

He began to lick, to suck, teasing her with the nip of his teeth, and she began to rise. Her hands searched for purchase on the flat of the table. Finding none, they anchored in his hair, tugging as her sighs turned to pants, her breath coming in ragged inhalations, her body arching, her mons pressing hard against his mouth asking for more, pushing him to his own limits even as he pushed her.

She was all wetness when she broke, her legs tight around him, holding him to her as she let the pleasure take her. Perhaps she feared he would leave her before she could claim it. But he hadn't the power or the desire to think of leaving her. Watching, feeling, the completeness of her climax was far more intoxicating than any beverage his aunt served. She lay back on the table, gasping, her skirts askew, her hair tumbling about her shoulders, her eyes…her eyes. They brought Vale to a halt. They weren't flashing. They weren't full of fire and mischief. He'd never seen them like this, violet and calm. They were full of peace. He wondered how long that would last.

She sat up, dark hair falling about her, and her eyes began to move, began to flash even before she spoke in her smoky voice. Her hands were at his shoulders, shoving him gently towards a chair. 'Sit. Now, it's your turn and I mean to have my wicked way with you, Vale Penrith.'

He should protest. This had gone far enough. This bordered on a sensual, physical feast far different than his usual sexual venues, but he could not resist. Perhaps he didn't want to resist. Vale was in the chair, his legs wide for her before he could mount a reasonable offence. She tugged at his trousers, sliding them over his hips until she had full access to him.

She took him in hand and he felt himself harden, strain against the cylinder walls of her fingers. Had anything ever felt as good and irrationally so? Why did this minx of a woman rouse him to such heights? These were questions for another time. His brain could only focus on the purposeful glide of her hand, stroking him from tip to base with a rhythm designed to tantalise, driving him to the edge of pleasure and then pulling him back from the brink—something his body both celebrated and resented, his mind torn between wanting to claim the pleasure and prevent its achievement. To claim it meant to end this, to prevent it meant to prolong the exquisite dilemma of her hand.

Her other hand moved to cup him beneath. She squeezed and he groaned. She laughed up at him, her eyes dark. 'Tell me if you like this.' She put her mouth to him, her lips taking the place of her hand. He would explode. Right now. It was the only certainty in his world as her mouth worked him, laving his tip with her treacherous tongue, licking the pearl that beaded there as if she tasted the finest cuisine. Had any woman ever shown him such attention? Or such enjoyment of the act? Treating it as something more than a perfunctory action that had to be performed? That in itself was a heady elixir, so heady, that Vale felt his body tense and gather. She was pushing him to the brink of pleasure again and this time it would be different. He knew instinctively this time he'd go over that edge. He was groaning out of hand now in hard rasping sobs that gave no illusion of control. She'd stripped him of all semblance of order, stripped him down to his most primal, and he relished it. His body arched beneath her mouth, thrusting into her one last time. She moved, taking him in hand, and he spent, in hard, pulsing spurts.

'Dear lord,' he managed in a hoarse voice he barely recognised as his own.

Viola rose and put her fingers to her mouth, sucking each one by one. He could not pull his eyes away from her. He was going to be hard again after only a moment ago feeling as if the very life had been drained out of him. Her eyes slanted like a cat's as she licked the last one. 'You, my lord, taste like victory.' He reached for her, but she moved away, turning her back to him as she sashayed towards the door. 'Hmm. Some say victory is sweet, but I'd say it's salty. Yes, definitely salty.'

# Chapter Nine

❧

She'd gone and turned their exchange of intimate oral pleasures into a game of one-upmanship. A game! Damn it! That was the only reason he didn't run down the hall and drag her back into the billiards room by her hair—his pride wouldn't allow it. And of course, there was the fact that to do so would wake the entire house—something else his pride wouldn't allow. It was bad enough he had to witness his own folly. He didn't need the entire house party to see him chasing after London's Shocking Beauty.

Vale raked his hands through his hair and leaned back in the chair. What a disaster! This was not like him at all. He was always so careful, not just with *affaires* and avoiding the traps of matchmaking mamas, but with himself. He worked hard to keep his emotions in check, his passions restrained, let out only in the proper time and place with the proper sort of woman for those activities; a lovely member of the *demimonde* or perhaps a wealthy merchant's discreet widow. But a woman known for her notorious accumulation of near-scandal?

Viola Hawthorne could not be *less* his type. She

craved attention where he craved obscurity, she was a flagrant flirt where he sought solitude, a daredevil where he clung to the safe and the pragmatic. She was a woman to whom scandal hoped to attach itself, but never quite managed to stick. Scandal didn't dare to even breathe in the direction of Brockmore's heir. He knew her reputation for trouble and her incredible luck in extricating herself from exile. Any one of her antics would have seen any other young woman promptly shuttled out of society's sight, never to return. Yet no one dared to challenge Viola Hawthorne's right to move in society while doing whatever she pleased, with whomever she pleased.

*Whomever she pleased.* He didn't want to think about that. To do so, he'd have to admit she shared tonight's pleasure with others. Why was it so wrong to want to be her only experience with such pleasure? It wasn't his first time with those pleasures, although it might have been the *best* time, especially if she hadn't flounced out afterwards declaring him salty as if it had been a mere lark to put her mouth between his thighs and swallow him whole. Vale groaned. He was getting hard again at the thought. He needed to do up his trousers before someone walked in and thought he'd been pleasuring himself, which was almost worse than someone knowing Viola had pleasured him—the idea that a duke's heir had to make do with his fist.

Vale fumbled with his trousers. He should have left the room and left her to her fate. He should have let her kiss Throckton. Now, he just felt foolish. He'd let himself go, let himself engage in an act that he reserved for a special few and certainly in more private settings than a billiards table, and she'd encouraged him. How ironic, when he'd been seeking the same from her, to teach *her* a lesson about poking sleeping dragons, to show her that outrageous overtures had consequences.

But she'd not been the only one learning that catechism. She'd called his bluff just as he called hers, and she'd raised the stakes: *use your damn mouth, Vale.* She'd been ready for him and now he was reeling. At least he could be assured she wouldn't tell anyone if the vitriol behind her earlier rant could be believed. Marriage was the last thing on Viola Hawthorne's agenda, something she'd reminded him of on two occasions now. The best thing he could do was put the evening behind him and move on.

Truly, he tried to do just that. Vale threw himself in to the party spirit the next day, joining the large group of guests going down to the village for the Brockmore version of a Frost Fair and Gingerbread exhibit. The day was overcast, but without wind, which made walking about the village tolerable if one was properly bundled. The Brockmore guests made a gay addition to the fair; the men in their caped greatcoats and wool mufflers, the ladies with their coats and muffs, although Vale noticed more than one lady had forgone her muff in order to tuck a hand through a gentleman's arm instead.

'The party is shaping up nicely.' His uncle fell into step beside him and followed the direction of his eyes to where Miss Pletcher and Lord Truesdale walked apart from the group. 'I had fancied Truesdale for your mother, but it seems Miss Pletcher and he have found common ground.'

'Mother?' The announcement took Vale by surprise. He'd not expected his uncle's matchmaking efforts to extend to her. 'But Father…' He couldn't quite put the thought into words. Surely his uncle, of all people, wouldn't want his mother to remarry, to replace his own brother.

'Your father has been dead for four years. Not her. Not you. She has a lot of living left, another thirty years, God willing. That's nearly a third of her life. Why should she spend it alone, or as only a spectator to other people's lives? Why shouldn't she start again?' his uncle prompted gently. Put that way, Vale didn't have an adequate response. Yes, indeed, why should she not?

His uncle nodded towards Truesdale. 'He and Miss Pletcher have made that decision.'

'After only five days?' Vale was sceptical. 'Is it even wise to make a life-altering decision in such a short time? They can hardly expect to fall in love in a handful of days.'

'And yet they have. Love does not run by our clocks, Vale. Silas insists on it.' His uncle spoke fondly of his old friend. 'They came to us separately. Miss Pletcher spoke with Alicia yesterday afternoon and Silas spoke to me last night. He was like a young man again, full of a bridegroom's eager worries over pleasing a cherished bride and providing for her.' His uncle smiled wistfully.

'Of course, he is more than capable of providing Miss Pletcher with every comfort. He even talked of children, of wanting to have a second family with her. Silas doesn't think fifty-eight is too old to be a father. Perhaps it isn't when one's bride is twenty-seven and more than able to give him two or three children if they're determined.' His uncle sighed. 'Talking with Silas reminds me that love can find us when we least expect it and with whom we least expect it. To think my old friend has found it with a woman thirty years younger than he is amazing proof of that.' He chuckled, then added slyly, 'We were up quite late in the library talking it over.'

Vale was on full alert now. If his uncle had been in the library, he would have encountered Throckton and company looking for a nightcap. They stopped at a booth to look at intricately frosted gingerbread men, fresh from the oven and still warm. 'I think five days of close quarters is plenty of time to take someone's measure,' his uncle went on as he selected a gingerbread to eat. 'Kenelm and Lady Anne have taken a shine to one another, although I understand some of that polish was already there. At least I can help pave the way with Kenelm's father. Miss Burnham and Matthew Eaton have done well together. I have hopes there. I wasn't sure how that would work out, so far it's been promising. Mmm. This is good gingerbread. Are you sure you won't have any?' Vale shook his head. His stomach had tightened at the mention of the library. He was sure the Silver Fox was working towards something that involved him.

'Love's a funny thing, Vale. Your aunt and I didn't plan the party as a specific venue for matchmaking, not like our summer parties, but we had our intuitions about who might suit if given a chance to discover one another. We had hopes for you, too, although you seem to have gone a different direction, which is fine. I won't force you to marry where I want, as long as you know what you're getting into. Marriage makes up too much of a man's life to be a miserable venture.'

He paused here and Vale waited. It was hard to process that last bit and he sensed the shoe hadn't dropped yet. 'I heard there was a bit of a contretemps in the billiards room last night.'

Lucifer's balls! There it was. Vale felt as though he was back in school again and one of the boys had tattled to the headmaster about private business. 'Throckton should keep his mouth shut, we aren't boys. Besides, he started it with his ridiculous wager long before I arrived at the scene.' Vale winced. That last line hardly supported the former claim. Not schoolboys indeed.

His uncle shrugged and wiped his hands free of gingerbread crumbs. 'Apparently, you finished it.' Had finished and been finished.

'I only meant to come to her aid,' Vale offered in defence. It was true as far as it went.

'An admirable sentiment if it was any other girl. But she's one chit that doesn't need help. She's always *exactly* where she wants to be: swinging chandeliers, climbing ladders, billiards rooms after midnight,' his uncle chided, looking at him askance. 'Lately, with you.' His uncle didn't miss a thing. Damned if Vale knew how his uncle did that. In a house full of people, his uncle knew precisely where everyone was at all times.

'Dinners hardly count.' Vale tried to shrug it off. 'The social gods control that.'

His uncle seemed to ponder the remark for a moment before shaking his head. 'And skating parties? Long disappearances on multiple occasions where neither of you can be accounted for? Wicked wagers in billiards rooms? Do the social gods ordain that as well?' He wondered what his uncle would say if he knew his nephew had drawn her name for the secret-admirer game as well? Social gods or not, it seemed fate had decided to throw the two of them together.

'Step in here with me, Vale. I need to speak with the owner.' His uncle opened the door to a small shop set just off the village green. The bell overhead jingled as his uncle finished his confusing lecture, the second in two days on the subject of Viola Hawthorne. 'If she's the one you've chosen, then we'll talk. I'm not saying she can't be redeemed, I'm only saying it would be a challenge. Certainly, marriage to a duke's heir would go a long way to making her acceptable and we would do our part. Perhaps she's decided it's the only avenue left to her now if she wants to remain in society. On the other hand, I don't want to see you manipulated into a situation not of your choosing. Lady Viola is dangerous, Vale, if you don't know what you're doing.' That was the burning question, wasn't it? What was he doing with Viola Hawthorne? What *did* he want from her? He hadn't had time to think.

'I don't want to marry her,' Vale began automatically. She certainly didn't want to marry *him*. His uncle's voice cut through his thoughts.

'Then stay off my billiards table, my boy.' His uncle clapped him on the shoulder, raising his voice in jovial tones as the shopkeeper approached. 'Mr. Williams, I've come to look at the new stock you promised me. This is my nephew, he'll want a taste, too.'

The 'store' was devoted solely to spirits, Vale discovered as the shopkeeper set out two glasses on the counter. It was an ingenious idea—a shop that carried Madeira from Portugal, ouzo from Greece, French brandies, and other more exotic drinks like the Italian monks' Vin Santo. The shopkeeper even boasted a small supply of absinthe. There wasn't just one variety of each, but several.

The shopkeeper poured glasses of an amber liquid. 'This is what you came for, Your Grace, the Vin Santo.'

'Holy wine?' His uncle held his glass up to the light.

'You'll think so, too, once you taste it.' The shopkeeper produced a plate of gingerbread and plum cake. 'Taste it with these. I call it the Christmas wine, perfect with our holiday treats. Can you imagine how it would taste alongside a mince pie?' He turned to Vale. 'It's a Tuscan dessert wine, been served in Italy since the Middle Ages. I finally got some in. The one you're drinking now is rarer, it's been aged for ten years. Most of what I got in has been aged for five. Still, very good.'

Vale nodded and took a thoughtful sip, letting the liquid roll over his tongue. At the first taste, the dry sweetness of the Vin Santo connected to Viola, his brain registering: 'Viola would love this.' The thought made no sense, other than he'd seen her drink brandy, but his gut knew—she would like this. It was like her: different, unique. He took another sip, instinctively knowing Vin Santo was not to be rushed. A small glass could last a man a long time, much like Viola herself. Too much at once would go to a man's head.

His uncle nodded his approval. 'It is good, everything you said it would be, Williams, and perfect for dinner tonight. The five-year-old will be fine. Have it sent up to the house.'

'And I'll take a bottle of the ten-year-old,' Vale put in spontaneously. 'Make that two bottles. I'm quite taken with it. You can send them with my uncle's order.' He'd just found Viola's New Year's gift and it was perfect.

That feeling of elation over finding a perfect gift lasted all of three minutes until he stepped outside and realised what he'd done: he'd bought alcohol for a woman! He couldn't possibly give the bottles to her in front of everyone. Who gave alcohol to a young woman? Apparently he did and he hadn't even blinked an eye at it until now when it was too late. Even worse, he'd set himself up to have to give it to her *privately* if he gave it to her at all. Added to that, he'd selected a very personal gift that only had meaning between the two of them.

What was becoming of him? This was hardly behaviour he would have engaged in five days ago and it wasn't an isolated incident—there'd been the kissing in the library when he should have dumped her off his lap but didn't; the bit on the backside of the island, a place he never should have taken an unmarried girl; and the exchange of intimate pleasures on the billiards table. *None* of these were things he would have engaged in, left to his own devices. Which meant it could only be her. She was the new variable.

He was changing since he met Viola. The choices he'd made four years ago to keep himself apart from society—something he could not always manage physically, but had succeeded in managing emotionally— no longer seemed enough. His body, his mind, were hungry. They wanted to connect and it was no longer enough to stimulate them through research; reading and writing about other people. They wanted to connect to *someone*. Why had they chosen Viola Hawthorne? She was like choosing fire over the frying pan. Certainly, there were better candidates for socially re-engaging, to ease back into it all with. But there was no halfway with Viola. Was that all he wanted from her, an awakening? Or something more?

His uncle had hinted twice now that he was not against Viola Hawthorne, merely her circumstances.

What had not been clear the first time had become abundantly clear today in retrospect. His uncle was not warning him away from Viola, but warning him to know his own mind before proceeding. That might be easier said than done.

His uncle's questions today had prompted many more on his part. Why had she chosen to flirt with him? Had she indeed decided, as his uncle suggested, a duke's heir was her only way back to respectability—which assumed she wanted respectability—something Vale didn't believe she was seeking, not after last night's revelations—or was it all merely a game to her, one more scandal to add to her collection? He liked to think there was something more between them, but if there was, what would he do about it?

Whoa. That was setting the Christmas sleigh before the horse. Before anything else was accomplished, he needed to determine what Viola was about. 'Uncle, if you'll excuse me? I'd like to catch up with the others.' Vale made his excuses, his gaze already searching the Frost Fair market for his target. He had shopping to do and someone he needed to do it with. What better strategy for picking out a gift for his secret admirer than to see what she liked first hand? Who knew what else he might learn?

# *Chapter Ten*

Viola's hand stilled over the loaf of gingerbread she was selecting, her chatter ceasing, her body freezing in place as she became aware of him. Vale was behind her. Not just merely behind her in a passing crush of people, but *approaching* her.

'There you are, Lady Viola. I've been looking for you.' Vale's voice was at her ear. Not just approaching her, then, but *seeking* her. He smelled good, the sharp scent of winter set against the sweet aromas of the booths. She'd not expected to see him. He'd been angry last night when she'd left him; angry at her and angry at himself.

He wasn't angry now. In fact, he seemed positively friendly and that gave her pause. What could he possibly want? 'If you're looking for a billiards game, I'm busy.' She tried the old strategy of going after him, trying to ruffle him.

'I'm not looking for a game, I'm looking for a shopping partner.' The strategy hadn't worked, although one could argue it never had. Except maybe last night. But even then, those results hadn't exactly protected her. If anything, they'd made her vulnerable. She'd wanted to break him last night and maybe she had momentarily, but the price had been high. He wasn't the only one who'd broken and, this morning, she was still picking up the pieces of that choice. While she was doing that, he was making decisions. 'We'll take that gingerbread,' he directed the waiting vendor. 'Wrap it up for us.'

Then he was leading her off to the next booth, and the next, looking at brightly coloured hair ribbons, carved toys and sweets. Oh, the sweets! There were so many: liquorice drops, peppermints, the gingerbread decorations, artistically frosted biscuits in different shapes, sugared almonds and plums, warm, roasted chestnuts to hold in your hand.

'I think the sweets might be my favourite part of the fair,' Viola said, accepting a paper cone of chestnuts from a vendor. She'd already eaten most of the gingerbread men she'd purchased. Vale tried to pay for the chestnuts, but she was faster. 'I've got my own money,' she scolded Vale, handing over the coins.

But even that didn't faze him today. It merely made him curious, another tactical error on her part, which just went to prove she was still reeling from last night. She'd not expected to enjoy last night quite as much as she had, nor had she been prepared to lose herself as deeply. For all her parting claims of victory, she had not been in control.

'Do you have to be so stubborn about everything?' His hand was at her back, guiding her through the crowd, his voice low at her ear, where she liked it best. Everything he said was just for her. Just for them. Just *between* them, His words were private, as was so much else about him.

'Yes, I do,' she answered almost defiantly.

One of the most difficult realisations about last night was that she'd been wrong about him. He wasn't a shell as she'd originally thought. He was private; his thoughts, his passions, all of them were carefully hidden away from public display and only a privileged few were allowed to see them, to participate in them. Last night, for a brief time, she'd been one of those elite.

'Whatever for?' They stopped in front of a pasty booth for fresh, hot meat pies. This time, when Vale asked for two, she let him pay.

'Because if I'm not, I'll be eaten alive,' she answered honestly, simply. They'd found a place to stand and eat the pies without being jostled by the crowd, but Vale didn't eat. He stared at her, pie forgotten.

'By whom?'

'My parents, society, every gentleman that comes to call. I'd be devoured if I didn't, married off at nineteen and tucked away in someone's country estate. I thought I made that clear last night.' Didn't he see? Everything she did was to protect herself. She'd hoped for better from him. She despised men who couldn't fathom the idea that she might not want to marry them, might not want to give them control over the rest of her life. She didn't want to despise Vale, which was a quiet revelation all its own. Standing here in the snow, it was inexplicably vital he understand her.

Vale lowered his voice. 'I understood the "from" part perfectly the first time. You protect yourself *from* marriage, but *for* what? I think that one word makes all the difference. Prepositions count, my dear.'

'There you go with the grammar again.' She laughed, hoping to dissuade the direction of the conversation.

Vale didn't laugh. He merely waited until she had no choice but to say, 'I'm saving myself *for* me, so that once I'm free of all this…' she waved a gloved hand towards the crowd '…I can get on with what I really want.'

'And what is that?' The question was asked sincerely and it nearly undid her. Did she answer it? She'd never told anyone before, never been *asked* before, not even by her parents. Most conversations didn't get this far, she didn't let them. Usually by now she'd have done or said something outrageous to derail any line of personal questioning. But here she was in the middle of a holiday fair, surrounded by others, being asked to answer the one question that drove her.

She met his gaze. She wasn't London's Shocking Beauty for nothing. If she could climb ladders and hang mistletoe balls from chandeliers, she could answer one simple question. 'I want to travel and to study my music.' She took a defiant bite of her pie. There. She'd said it. Now she waited, waited for him to laugh, or to declare her goal impossible. He did neither. He merely smiled and began to eat.

'Was that so hard?'

She favoured him with a considering glance. It was time to turn the tables. 'You tell me. What you are saving yourself for?'

'Who says I'm saving myself for anything?' He furrowed his brow.

'I do,' she answered smartly. 'If stubbornness is my armour, privacy is yours. You keep yourself hidden away for a reason. It's only fair you tell me what it is.'

He began to move, ushering her out of their space and back into the stream of people shuffling past booths. 'Wouldn't it be more fun if you guessed?'

She gave a short laugh, part-frustration, part because she'd come to know him so well in the last few days. The response was so typically him. He was being evasive, protecting his privacy to the last. They'd stopped in front of a booth selling children's wooden toys and he changed the subject, picking up a boat. 'I used to have one of these.' He smiled and it lit up his entire face, making the serious man look winsome and boyish. To her dismay, Viola felt her stomach flutter. 'My brother and I used to sail them on the shores of my uncle's lake when we visited in the summer.'

'You have a brother?' She was too engaged in learning something about him to think about her response, she only wanted him to keep talking, to keep sharing, to break down some of privacy's wall.

'Had a brother.' He abruptly put down the boat and walked away. She followed, rushing a little to keep up with his long strides. He was suddenly in a hurry.

Had. Yes, right. She'd been foolish not to remember. The great Brockmore tragedy. She knew about it. Everyone did. No one mentioned it. The uncle's brother and brother's son had been killed simultaneously in a sailing incident. She'd forgotten there'd been a brother, too. What had it been? Four years ago? 'I'm sorry, I didn't mean to bring it up,' Viola apologised, but only because she wanted him back, the smiling, laughing version of Vale Penrith who was charming her so effortlessly today at a village fair. She had not meant to chase that man away.

'Are you?' He shot her a sideways glance. 'You've been intent on plumbing my depths since this game has started. Now you have and you want to run from it.' His

voice was ice-hard and he was apart from her: no more
low tones at her ear, no more hand at her back.

'I don't want to run from it. It seems that you're the
one doing the running,' Viola replied sharply. 'Tell me
about your brother. Tell me anything.' She was running
now to keep up with him. He was trying to drive her off
physically, emotionally. The harder he tried, the harder
she pushed. She was close to his secret, close to understanding the core of him. She might not get another
chance. 'What was his favourite colour? What was the
name of his boat? Your boat?' She grabbed for his arm,
stopping him. 'Tell me *something*, Vale!'

He whirled on her then with enough force to send the
hem of his greatcoat swirling against his boots. 'Talking about my brother is not a game, it is not part of this.'

'Game? Who says this is a game?' Viola snapped,
her breath coming in frosty gasps.

'You do.' His eyes were blazing, cobalt coals, his
voice an angry growl. 'Everything is a game to the
Shocking Beauty. Even duke's heirs.' The vehemence
of his reproach scalded her. In that moment she hated
the title she'd worked so hard to create, to truly earn. He
pulled away from her, dusting off his coat sleeve where
she'd gripped him as if he wanted to be rid of her touch.
'Excuse me.' His tone was as cold as the air. He pulled
away and was gone, his broad shoulders disappearing
in the crowd before she could answer.

She wanted to shout it wasn't true at his retreating
back, that he wasn't a game, not any more. Perhaps it
was best she didn't. It made her too vulnerable. The
words were new and they surprised even her. Was that
truly what she thought? What had happened to getting
expelled from the party? What had happened to 'home

by New Year's'? How had this pursuit of Vale Penrith morphed from being a game to support Anne Lowell's covert courtship of Kenelm to something far more serious? It was no longer a chore to sit beside Vale at dinner. It was no longer an effort to seek him out, but a pleasure. Her eyes went to him even in a crowd, as they were doing now. She caught sight of him in the crowd, emerging fifty feet ahead of her, beside Percival Martindale at a booth further down the aisle. Maybe she should go after him and apologise, make him see that she was capable of more than a game. That she was more than what the title reduced her to. But her pride prevented it. Why couldn't he see that all on his own?

'Let him go for now.' A friendly, almost fatherly voice at her shoulder stopped her. A firm hand took her arm and led her in the opposite direction. Brockmore. Damn it all.

They walked in silence, the Duke nodding to acquaintances as they moved to the outer edges of the fair. He stopped at a stand selling hot cider and took two steaming mugs, finding them a place to stand where they could watch the Brockmore chef, Pierre Salois, conduct his gingerbread house demonstration. Under other circumstances, she would have appreciated the feat and the patience it took. At the moment, she was all tense awareness of the powerful man beside her. What did *he* want? More importantly, what did he know and would it ruin her?

'Are you enjoying the party, Lady Viola?' He passed her a mug. Viola wasn't fooled. Cider was a nice way to dress up the pretence of wanting conversation with her. What did he want? To remove her from the scene? To keeping her as far from Vale as possible?

'The party is excellent.' Viola answered coolly. 'But I hardly think that's what you want to talk with me about.' She fixed the Duke with a stare, opting not to be intimidated, hard as it was. Brockmore was an imposing man, but he was just a man, after all. She'd been managing men for years.

The Duke laughed. 'Save your wiles, Lady Viola, for men who will be affected by them. I'm far too old and far too astute to be taken in by such manipulations, no matter how pretty the face who wields them. Like recognises like, my dear.' It was friendly as warnings went, but it was still a warning. She heard the steel beneath the chuckle. 'Lady Viola, it's time you and I had a talk. About my nephew.'

# *Chapter Eleven*

Ominous words indeed, but Viola didn't back down. If Brockmore expected her to drop her eyes and demurely apologise for overstepping herself he'd be disappointed. 'Is this the point where you tell me to stay away from him? If so, let me save you the effort. I do not want him, not in the way you mean.' She tried for neutral nonchalance, the words harder to say than she'd expected. She did not want to denounce Vale, it felt disloyal. She felt like a fraud.

Brockmore chuckled. 'If you want plain speaking, Lady Viola, you shall have it. I've not come to threaten you. I'm not that sort of man. I'm here to guide you, maybe even help you.'

Viola stared, nonplussed. Compliance was always more frightening than conflict. Brockmore laughed. 'I see I have surprised you, which is no mean feat if the rumours about you are true. Surprise is usually *your* business. How do you like the shoe being on the other foot?' Brockmore sipped his cider. 'I know you and my nephew have had some clandestine meetings.' He held up a stalling hand. 'No need to protest. I don't require either good form or explanation. My nephew is a grown man with a mind of his own. He's made it clear he is not interested in Anne Lowell. It must be no secret she was brought here for him to consider.' Brockmore sighed. 'But the young have different opinions about who suits whom.'

Viola tensed. Surely, he wasn't leading up to the idea of a match between them? 'I don't wish to marry, no matter what my parents have told you.'

Brockmore seemed to ponder her response. He nodded. 'Fine. I just don't want to see my nephew hurt in the process, or dragged into scandal. Whatever you do, it must be circumspect. I demand discretion. I demand you be honest with him.' He paused here, his gaze far away, his words halting as he gathered his thoughts. 'My nephew has been dead inside for quite a while. I hoped this party would help him rediscover a passion for living.' He looked at her. 'I think it has. *You* have. But what happens when the party's over? I would not want to lose him again because someone was careless with his heart.'

The sentiment touched her. 'You must love him very much to worry. But as you said, he's a grown man.' She felt an uncomfortable kinship with the regal duke in those moments, standing at the fair with their cider mugs talking about a man for whom they both had feelings. 'I will be as careful as I can with him,' Viola whispered.

The Duke nodded. 'See that you are. Vale is precious to me, even though he can take care of himself.' He cleared his throat. 'There is also the matter of your parents.' Her newly recovered stomach sank again. 'They will be disappointed if there's no match. He's a duke's heir. You're a duke's daughter. It makes sense to them. They will push. I do not want to see either of you compromised into a marriage neither wants. Nor do I want to see my hand forced.' He lowered his voice. 'I am aware you've indulged in certain, ah, shall we say, "behaviour" since your arrival. Others might be willing to attribute this behaviour to the high spirits of the holiday season. However, I do not think your parents are among those tolerant souls. They will use that behaviour to get you both to the altar.'

Viola felt her cheeks heat. 'Shall I stay away from him, then?' Compliance or conflict, the message was the same: stay away from Vale. The Silver Fox was wily.

Brockmore smiled. 'You're being *advised*, nothing more. What you do is up to you. I will help all I can, for my nephew's sake. And for your sake. I know you don't want to be here.' Damn it all, the man really did know everything. 'I am generous to those who support me. I'd like to be generous to you, Lady Viola. For all of your wild antics, you strike me as person very much in need of a friend.' He gave her a bow and stepped apart from her. 'Enjoy your cider, I have other guests to see to.' Other guests to 'advise', he meant. Viola pitied them. Brockmore had a way of getting what he wanted. 'Anne wants Kenelm,' Viola called after him. If he was going to hassle Anne Lowell next, he might as well have the truth.

He turned back and gave her a slight incline of his head. 'Yes, my dear, I know that, too. Just as I know what you did on my billiards table last night.'

*Touché.* Her cheeks burned. Round one to Brockmore. But what had the Silver Fox won? He had not threatened her. She'd expected blackmail along the lines of 'stay away from Vale or I'll expel you from the party'. But there had been none of that. Neither had there been compliance with her parents—'you've dallied with my nephew, now marry him.'

She watched Pierre Salois apply icing to the sides of the gingerbread mansion to created elegant long windows complete with panes resembling the ones at Brockmore. What did the Duke's counsel mean? Did Brockmore find her unsuitable for Vale? If so, why not threaten her? Send her away? If she was acceptable, why not side with her parents and force a match? The third option was that he'd meant it; she and Vale were free to follow their own path, discreetly, of course. He wanted no scandal and no broken hearts. Was he an ally or an enemy? Or was there middle ground? The conversation would have been less curious if she knew. It also raised the question of what was she doing with Vale now?

It seemed her motives had changed. She still wasn't looking for a match, still had no desire to marry. But she no longer wanted to leave the party. Yet, now that caution had been introduced, it would be torturous to be near Vale and not be able to act on that. Public sightings were out of the question. That meant no more feel of his hand at her back. No more rumble of his voice at her ear. No more dinner conversation. She was sure the Duchess would find a reason to rearrange the table after this, as part of the Duke's plan to 'help' her, whatever that truly entailed as enemy or ally. She still wasn't sure. Cheers to the Duke. He'd managed to present her with quite the Sisyphean dilemma. She took another sip of her cider. She was already thirsty.

She stayed 'thirsty' through the dinner, an excellent affair of French-style Cornish game hen for the sixth day of Christmas despite the meal's finale, a dry, sweet, dessert wine Brockmore proudly introduced as Vin Santo, a holy wine from Tuscany. Lord, that was good stuff. Just a sip or two was enough to satisfy, or at least it would have been if Vale had sat beside her. Her instincts had been right. The Duchess had reset the table seating.

Ostensibly, it was because the house party was half-way through. But Viola thought she knew better. If it was any consolation, Vale had been as surprised as she. He'd taken Lady Beatrice into dinner instead. Viola had gone in with her father, a nod to keeping her on a leash, she was sure. She couldn't get up to any trouble with her father on one side and Lord Truesdale on her other side. Thank goodness. She was secretly grateful for the arrangement. Her mother had been waiting for her after the fair, glowing, in fact. Brockmore's instincts had been right, too. 'Vale's attentions,' as her mother put it, 'had been duly noted.' On a related note, her mother had gushed the news St. George's was available the sec-ond weekend in April if they moved quickly enough, followed by did she think Brockmore would be open to a shorter engagement? Viola had not been tactful in her response and much of her joy had gone out of the evening, her thoughts preoccupied. She not only had to explain things to Vale, now she had to warn him.

Around her everyone was in good spirits after a day spent out of doors at the fair. There was plenty of con-versation through dinner and afterwards, but Viola had no desire to linger for cards and music after dinner, espe-cially when Vale didn't emerge with the other gentlemen after port. She waited a decent interval before pleading a slight headache and making her escape with the help of Anne Lowell. With Anne on her arm, acting as an es-cort, no one could doubt her intentions of going straight to bed, least of all Brockmore or her parents. They were the only parties she was truly interested in convincing.

Anne had barely left for her own room—which Viola didn't think for a moment she'd stay in—and Viola was off, conducting a swift, methodical search for Vale. She had to explain. She couldn't leave things as they were from the fair. He'd glanced her way once this evening at dinner and she'd been forced to look away, but not before she'd seen his eyes go to stone. She knew he believed her to be nothing but a game-player and she would not tolerate being thought a liar.

But Vale was proving to be elusive. He wasn't in any of his usual hiding places; the library was empty, it was too early for late-night billiards. She even went daringly to his bedroom. He wasn't there either. Thankfully, neither was his valet. That would have been hard to explain and Brockmore would have been sure to find out about it. She frowned to herself. If he was in the Duke's office or in one of the sitting rooms, she would be out of luck with no chance of getting him alone. The rooms were far too public, too accessible to the Duke.

She wandered through the darker recesses of the house where the party didn't reach: quiet sitting rooms, perhaps used privately by the Duchess, reading rooms, a room devoted solely, it appeared, to playing chess. A long hall loomed, lined on one side by windows, portraits on the opposing wall. She strolled down the corridor, her feet picking up speed when she caught sight of a figure at the opposite end. Her breath caught in her throat. She'd found him.

She'd found him. Vale knew it even before she announced her presence. He heard the determined rustle of skirts invading his sanctuary, the quick speed of feet once she'd spotted him. No one else would come looking. But she would. Viola was unpredictable that way. She'd fought with him at the fair. She'd avoided his gaze at dinner and now she was searching for him.

'What do you want?' He drew a weary breath. He was tired of her games. At least that's what he told himself. But something flickered in him at the prospect that she'd come, even as his common sense warned him this was just another layer of her games to get under his skin and nothing more.

'I want to explain myself.' Her voice was a furtive whisper and he thought she might be nervous for once. She looked down at her hands, laced together and squeezed tightly at her waist. She *was* nervous. That was unexpected. It seemed nothing ruffled her. She had his full attention now. 'And to warn you. There is danger afoot.'

'Danger? Sounds intriguing.' He patted the space beside him on the square, padded bench set in front of the portraits. 'Come, sit, tell me.'

She shook her head. 'I don't dare stay that long. My parents.' Her conversation was a collection of half-started, unfinished sentences. 'I fear they want to push for an alliance between us. Our association has been noted by them, and by your uncle, but for different reasons, I think.'

He chuckled. 'You're being obtuse. But I know what you mean about my uncle. He spoke with me today, too. I'm not sure he's pushing a match or warning me away from it, or just wants discretion.'

'Discretion. It is up to us to figure out what we want,' Viola affirmed. 'It's why I couldn't look at you at dinner,

it's why the seating chart was rearranged. Your uncle be-
lieves he's "helping" by keeping us apart in public. But
you looked so hurt, so angry tonight. I couldn't allow
that. I didn't want you thinking I had toyed with you.'

He let her words rush out. He fixed his attention on
the smallest among them. *We*. A small word with big
connotations. 'Is there a "we", Viola? I confess to being
unsure,' Vale enquired. 'If there is a "we" that is for us
alone to decide. I don't like the idea of my uncle inter-
fering, even if it is meant with good intentions. I am
no man's puppet.' How like his uncle. He had meddled
anyway, despite Vale's own assurances.

'I'm more worried about my parents than your uncle.
My mother came to me tonight. She even has a date
picked out and she can be tenacious.'

Vale gave a wry chuckle. 'So, that's where you get
it. Like mother, like daughter.'

'It's not funny, Vale,' she protested in genuine horror.
'You have to take them seriously. My father is a duke.'

'I know about dukes.' Vale reached for her hand with
a laugh. She was too close not to touch. He pulled her
down on the seat beside him. He'd missed her beside
him at dinner, fight at the fair or not. He'd come to
terms with it hours ago. It wasn't her fault he didn't
want to talk about the accident. That was his own problem. 'We haven't been caught yet. Besides, what would
anyone catch us doing? Looking at portraits? Hardly an
altar-level offence.' It was interesting how truly worried she was.

'Don't you see? It's because you'd be doing it with
*me*. You can look at portraits with Rose Burnham, or
Anne Lowell, and no one will mind. But my reputation precedes me.'

'And you regret that?' he asked quietly, not wanting to push away the moment. This conversation was far different than any they'd had. Their previous conversations had been peppered with challenges, pitting them against each other. This one they were in together. She was vulnerable tonight, worried not only about herself, but about him. He saw it in her eyes and heard it in her words.

'The means justify the ends. Next year, it will all be worth it. My parents will be so tired of me, so embarrassed by me, they'll be all too happy to send me to Vienna. Out of sight. Out of mind. They can forget all about their errant daughter.'

'Unless they marry you to a duke's heir first,' Vale supplied.

'Yes.' Her response was vehement. 'That's why I'm worried.'

A thought occurred to him. 'You really want to study music? I seem to recall you didn't play at the musical.'

'My music isn't for drawing rooms and debutantes.' Of course not. He knew instinctively that for her, it would be part of her soul, that part of herself that shouldn't be paraded out needlessly. He understood that. His grief, his family's tragedy, wasn't for drawing rooms either and yet it had ended up there. It was still there, four years later, every time he walked into a room. He carried the tale with him as assuredly as he carried the title 'the heir'. For society and for himself, the two could not be separated.

'We're not that different, then.' Vale ran his thumb over the back of her hand. 'We both have titles we don't want. I never wanted to be the heir.' When he'd first met Viola, he thought that was the difference between them and their labels. She aspired to hers, he'd thought, and he wanted to be rid of his. He'd give anything not to be the heir.

'I guessed as much today.' Her voice was softer, its edge gone. She did not, thankfully, press for more. Instead she sat beside him and stared with him at the portraits, apparently willing to forgo the risk of being caught unchaperoned in his presence. Which begged the question, would it be so bad if they were caught? He could feel the warmth of her body, smell the subtle fragrance of her. There was peace in his world, until she went and ruined it.

'So, that's your father? Robert Penrith?' she said quietly. 'He looks like you, the same hair, the same eyes, the same chin.' Damn her. She wasn't going to let him off easy. 'Did your brother look like him, too?' There was no picture of R.J., of course. He wasn't the heir while his father was alive and they'd died together.

'Yes. The Brockmore genes run strong.' He swallowed. Maybe that compensated for the fact that the Brockmore ability to sire children seemed compromised either through biology or tragedy.

'It was four years ago?' She pressed, her fingers lacing through his. 'Will you tell me about it?'

It made no sense to tell her, this woman he barely knew and up until now hadn't possibly even liked. It gave credence to his uncle's words that love had its own clock, that maybe a handful of days was long enough to know someone's true measure. Maybe it was the darkness, maybe it was the warm press of her hand in the cold corridor, or maybe his need couldn't be bottled up any longer. He'd never told anyone. But he told her, one of the most notorious women in London, a woman who didn't want scandal, but courted it anyway all for the sake of her own freedom. Maybe *his* freedom needed to tell her.

'They'd gone out on a yacht. The day was clear, the water calm. There was no reason not to. It was early spring. But the yacht's steam engine exploded without warning. They never stood a chance.' His voice broke. 'They never had a chance to fight, to save themselves.' To say goodbye, to make peace with their fate. He felt the tears come. One of them rolled down his cheek. But it was dark, so he let it.

'How awful.' Viola's voice was quiet and stunned. Her grip on his hand tightened and he knew: She *understood* what no one else had grasped: The root of his grief lay in the nature of the death, not in death itself.

His voice was a series of croaks punctuated with breaks as the words struggled to get free. 'They didn't get to meet death on their own terms. They woke up that morning and had breakfast. They read the newspapers and told jokes. My mother had left for her charity work before my father could tell her goodbye. She wasn't in the house when he left and then he never came back.' That was the piece that ate at his mother's heart to this day. She'd been in a hurry to leave that morning with promises to catch up with them that night. She'd never dreamed she wouldn't get to keep that promise. 'I had breakfast with them. They'd asked me to come with them. But I had plans to go to Tattersall's with a friend to look at horses I didn't need.' What if he had gone? Would he have seen the boiler malfunction? Could he have stopped it before it was too late? He shook his head. There were too many tears to worry about wiping them away. 'It was an ordinary day. We were all supposed to have dinner together. Nothing extraordinary was supposed to happen.' He was gripping her hand too tightly now, struggling to keep himself together.

He waited for the platitudes to come: *you were lucky, if you'd gone, you'd be dead too. At least they didn't feel a thing. They'd died not knowing pain.* He'd heard all that at the funeral and from countless people in the weeks following who'd come to offer their condolences. But Viola said nothing. It was what she did next that pushed him over the edge.

Slowly, she took his head in her hands, her own head pressed to his, foreheads meeting. 'Thank you.' There was profound sincerity in her gaze and it moved him. Had he ever received such genuine compassion before? He could not pretend any more. He was falling for her. He closed his eyes and let it happen. He *wanted* to fall. He didn't want to fight the emotions being with another raised in him. Instead, he gave them full rein. He wanted to drink her in, the scent of her in his nostrils, the touch of her fingers at his face. At her touch, a wall inside him began to crumble, slowly, becoming an avalanche of jubilant emotion and thought: he was alive! And whole. For the first time, he wanted to celebrate that instead of apologise for it and he wanted to celebrate it with her, right here, right now.

'I want you, Viola.'

She whispered her smoky offering, 'Then take me. Tonight, I'm yours.'

# *Chapter Twelve*

Viola drew a shaky breath. This was no brandy-fuelled game of Truth or Consequences on the billiards table. This was Vale Penrith unleashed and it was devastating to behold. She had never had a lover with his confidence. She did not have to lead tonight. She couldn't wrest the lead from him if she tried, even if she'd wanted to. But she didn't want to. Sisyphus be damned. She would not go to bed thirsty tonight. The slow burn that had licked at her all night began to build. She *wanted* him to be in charge.

He moved into her, taking her mouth in a lingering kiss as if he could drink his fill from her. Vale gave a low groan, hungry and primal. Yet for all of its growing roughness, this was not one of their usual kisses; there was no competition to hide the passion behind and pretend it was something else. The passion was naked tonight. They'd be out in the open in more ways than the literal.

His hands cupped the rounds of her bottom, drawing her on to his lap, pressing her full against him, taking her core where he wanted it, flush against the hard root of him, core pressed to core. His hands slid up the silk of her bodice, taking her breasts in their palms, thumbs stroking the fabric over her nipples until they were taut and straining, further proof that this seduction was all his. His hands were back at her bottom, this time sliding beneath her skirts and taking a firm grip. She moved against him, pressing hard against his stiffness. Then he flipped her.

In a lightning move, she was beneath him, looking up at blue eyes and loose hair. Gone was the restrained aristocrat, replaced by primal man and raw desire. One hand worked the fastenings of his trousers with exquisite dexterity and thankful speed.

What had started with a slow kiss, had quickly sped up in tempo to match their need. They were frantic now, having teased themselves to the edge of madness with kisses and cupping. Viola gripped his shirt, pulling him down to her, wanting the weight of his body on her, wanting to feel the press of muscle, the contour of manly planes. 'You will be the death of me, Viola.' He was already panting.

'I will be the life of you,' she answered, meeting his eyes, feeling his phallus take up position at her entrance. But who would be the saving of her? If last night had cost her something, how much more would tonight take from her? And yet, in the moment, the price of her desire was not too much. It never occurred to her to turn back from this, from him.

Viola rose up, letting the tip of his phallus brush against her, teasing him as he teased her with a hint of the wetness and heat that waited within. Then he was in. She gasped, feeling the slide of him, long and full, *filling* her, and she was complete just for a moment before he retreated. She groaned her displeasure, her thighs gripping him in a plea to return. He slid deep again and she clutched him to her. There was a brief bout of competition, each of them struggling to gain the upper hand and then deciding they were better together than against. She picked up the rhythm of his thrusts with her hips, her back arching. All she wanted was him, all her body was focused on him, focused on *them* driving towards pleasure together. This was new frontier, never had she been *partnered* so exquisitely, matched so well.

Vale's body was all hard heat above her, the muscles of his arms straining with effort as they bracketed her head, his hair falling forward, framing the primal emotions of his face as he thrust into her, and yet for all the pleasure this act brought him, *her* pleasure was his concern. He *wanted* them to come together, all his effort was concentrated on that aim and now hers was, too.

Her breaths came ragged and irregular. 'Almost,' she gasped, only to inhale sharply as his next thrust came into her hard and fast, the quickening of his pace indicating they were nearly there. Once more, twice, and then completion. He had her in his arms, holding her tight against him, their bodies locked together as it took them in all its shattering brilliance.

He held her for a long time afterwards, wrapping her in the cocoon of his arms, his body still joined with hers, neither of them moving. She didn't want to recover, not if it meant him leaving her. Perhaps this was why people were so adamant about making love in beds as opposed to portrait galleries; so they didn't have to move afterwards. How was she supposed to get up and *walk* back to her room after this? She barely had the strength to sit up, and where she'd find the strength to have him disengage was a mystery to her.

Perhaps they could just stay here until she'd fully processed what had happened. She'd just made love with Vale Penrith. Not 'had sex with'. To describe what had just transpired as merely a physical act was nowhere near adequate. This had not been like any of the other times—all two of them. One had been a dare, the other had been a wager. While not entirely unsatisfying in their own ways, neither had held the promise of this.

Vale shifted his weight. He would leave her soon. She begged him with her eyes to stay a little longer. He smiled down at her, content to do her bidding. 'I've never seen you looking so content.' Viola returned the smile with a sleepy one of her own. She was feeling drowsy and lazy. If he offered to carry her to her room, she wouldn't say no.

'I've never seen you look so beautiful before,' Vale murmured.

'My hair is a mess, my clothes are wrinkled. You call that beautiful?' She was shamelessly fishing for a compliment.

'Yes, I would.' Vale dropped his eyes, gathering his thoughts. She braced herself, willing him not to speak, for fear that words would ruin these moments. Time would do that all by itself shortly. They couldn't stay this way.

She reached her arms up and twined them about his neck, stopping his words with soft kisses, her words interspersed. 'I've never done anything like this before.' The words seemed inadequate. Would he know she didn't mean the physicality of making love out in open?

Vale grinned. '*We've* never done anything like this.'

'*We.*' It was where their conversation had started. The sound of that single word thrilled her as much as it frightened her. What did 'we' mean? More of this soul-searching lovemaking? For how long? She gave him a smile and a gentle push. It was time to go. Before one of them said too much.

How she made it to her room would always remain somewhat foggy. One moment she'd been lying on the gallery bench, the next she'd found the fortitude to wander the halls back to her room, somehow avoiding guests. But fog was preferable to the clarity that came once she was abed, alone. *What had she done?*

She'd never pushed herself so close to the edge of her doom. Taking a lover was always scandalous. Taking Vale Penrith, the heir to Brockmore, as a lover was downright dangerous. He was not some randy squire's son who was looking for a hayloft affair to pass the winter. Neither was he a baron's second son having a fling before he took up his commission on the Continent. Those men posed no real danger to her. That wasn't true of Vale. The danger he had posed to her tonight hadn't been the mere danger of discovery by others, although that risk was certainly present. There was no denying Vale represented the establishment she'd fought so hard against—loveless marriage, enforced motherhood to as many children as a husband wanted, all in exchange for financial security. Surely a woman was entitled to more than that? Surely she was entitled to as much freedom as a man to choose the life she wanted? The Shocking Beauty had been her protection against the establishment and her protest.

But perhaps the other danger was greater. In one night, she had risked throwing all her hard work—every scandal, every flirtation, every wager—away.

What if Vale went to his uncle and told him what had happened? What if Vale insisted they marry out of honour? It was almost enough to make her cringe beneath her bedsheets. To be a duchess was a horrible fate; a woman buried alive under daily menus, seating charts and social calls. But to be *his*? That did not bring the requisite shudder it had brought last week when Anne had proposed her ploy. Some traitorous part of her wondered if the trade-off would be worth it to be the woman who went to bed with him every night. If the days were torture, at least the nights would be exquisite consolation.

*And your dreams*? her conscience challenged. What happened to them? The wife of Brockmore's heir couldn't hare off to the Continent and study music or travel about at her leisure with no destination in mind. She would need to be feathering her nest, taking her place in society, birthing an heir. Vale would want a child as soon as possible. More than one. An idea, that tonight, she didn't find terribly unpleasant—a frightening realisation all its own. Since when did she think about children?

She was letting her thoughts run away with her. There was always the chance Vale would say nothing. A very good chance, too. Why would he want to put himself in a position to *have* to marry *her* when there were more suitable, more biddable girls to become the future Duchess of Brockmore? There was no logic in it and Vale was, if anything, logical. What he wasn't was empty. She'd been wrong Christmas Eve, to assume he was nothing more than a pretty shell. He was merely private. Tonight, he'd let her into that private world for a small, intoxicating glimpse and she wanted more, against all odds. Viola had taken challenges before, but the stakes had never been this high. How ironic that the greatest threats to oneself often came from within.

'You're not out risking life and limb?' Kenelm slapped Vale on the back jovially as he surveyed the racecourse with the other spectators. Guests were taking advantage of the powdery snow that had fallen last night resulting in the perfect sledding conditions. The more intrepid guests had made a 'horse' race of sorts out of it, with the gentlemen acting as horses pulling ladies on sleds in a race around the improvised course.

'No, this sort of thing isn't for me.' Vale smiled congenially. 'Nor you either, I take it?'

'No, I'm letting Eaton pull Anne.' Kenelm's gaze drifted to the starting line where Anne's dark hair and cardinal-red coat showed bright against the snow. The easy-going Kenelm sobered. 'To throw the Silver Fox off the scent, so to speak. Don't want to be too obvious.'

'Why not?' Vale couldn't resist asking. 'You mean to marry her. Perhaps being obvious is the best way to declare your intentions, perhaps even to make it impossible for anyone to object.'

Kenelm elbowed him good naturedly. 'A chip off the old block, aren't you? Already stepping into your uncle's matchmaking shoes.'

'My apologies,' Vale began. 'I didn't mean to presume.'

Kenelm shrugged. 'Presume away. Perhaps you're right. Perhaps Anne and I should stop slinking around. A man who is willing to hide the woman he claims to love sends the message he's not willing to commit to her. Why should anyone take him seriously if he doesn't take *himself* seriously?' He pondered that for a moment, eyes riveted on Anne. 'I think you may have something there, Penrith. Thank you.'

Great. He'd solved Kenelm's dilemma, but was no-where nearer to solving his own: What to do about Viola Hawthorne? He'd slept like a log last night, much to his surprise. He hadn't lain awake wallowing in regret or in retrospection, two activities that usually ate up quite a bit of his nights. Instead, he'd fallen asleep promptly and deeply. He'd slept the entire night. If he'd dreamed of her, he didn't remember.

Could she possibly understand what a watershed last night had been? Last night, he'd shown a lover more of himself than he ever had before, shared with her more. And now he didn't know what to do or what that meant. Did he simply go about his day as if it hadn't happened? Did he watch the races and go up to the library and work on his report? Come down to dinner and take Lady Beatrice in without a glance Viola's direction? That seemed to make a mockery of last night. It had been a watershed for her, too. They'd both transcended game playing. Now they were in new territory. Now, there was 'we', a stunning realisation for a man who'd spent four years alone for all intents and purposes, and he was willing to embrace it.

Vale watched the racers with half an eye to the enter-tainment, already composing in his head a very impor-tant note and thinking through his options. It was too bad he couldn't take his own advice to Kenelm. But he could take the opposite. He needed a covert strategy to give he and Viola time to sort through what 'we' meant without outside pressure. That would require playing a double-layered game where he ignored Viola in public to appease his uncle, but lavished all his attention on her in private. The idea held merit. Anticipation could be a seductive tool. He was already looking forward to the rest of the party. He dared not think beyond that.

# *Chapter Thirteen*

⁂

*Thursday, 31st December 1818, New Year's Eve*
*—Hogmanay*

Anticipation was indeed a potent aphrodisiac, especially when it was turned his direction, a *most* unexpected development. Vale thought of the note tucked in the pocket of his evening coat, hiding a secret smile.

He'd planned to send a provocative note of his own, but Viola had beaten him to it. She'd sent the note during the 'last meal of the year'—a Scottish-themed feast complete with neeps and tatties and a bit of haggis, which had tasted decently enough if one didn't think about the ingredients. It was easy enough to ignore the idea of eating intestines when he had Viola's evening to occupy his thoughts and Viola herself. He'd never had a woman take the lead in his passionate encounters before and the novelty was a heady one.

Vale stole a furtive glance at his pocket watch. An hour until midnight. Time was starting to drag. He'd played the anticipation game before, but not as the recipient. Usually it was him doing the teasing, a role he enjoyed. He'd thought teasing to be the most delectable part of the game, but he'd been wrong. *Being* tantalised was, especially when the role of tease belonged to the incredibly inventive Viola Hawthorne. *Come to me at midnight. I will be waiting.*

Fifty-five minutes. Vale glanced around the ballroom, looking for her. Where was she? She'd been striking this evening in a gold gown, her dark hair piled high, her eyes sparkling, her laughter everywhere as they played favourite holiday games. She'd been inexhaustible, the life of the party. But now, everyone's attention riveted on the excellent bagpiper his uncle had brought in for the evening as part of his effort to celebrate Hogmanay in honour of his Scottish guest. This would be the calm before the party picked up again at midnight with the First Foot, and dancing, Scottish reels, no doubt, although he wouldn't be around to see them. Everyone would be too busy to notice one quiet man wasn't present. But they might miss her. He did wonder how Viola would sneak away unnoticed.

A flash of burnished gold at the door moved on his periphery. Viola! He turned slowly, careful not to alert anyone. She paused at the ballroom door, catching his eye with a wide, wicked smile full of promise. She pressed a finger to her lips in playful warning before mouthing the unmistakable words, 'my room'. Then she was gone, making her escape into the empty hallway. *To get ready for him.* Just the thought sent a bolt of white-hot desire through him. She was preparing herself for him, taking down her hair, loosening her gown. Vale crossed and re-crossed his legs, shifting his position on the little folding chair, trying to dislodge his growing arousal. It would be difficult to explain why 'Amazing Grace' gave him an erection.

Three classic tunes later, the concert concluded. It was time to make his move. He'd sat in the back precisely for this reason. The audience's enthusiastic standing ovation was the perfect cover for slipping away. He was in the hall in no time, checking his watch. Five minutes before midnight, five minutes to reach Viola's room. The further he got from the ballroom, the faster he walked until he was nearly running. He'd not touched her at all yesterday and he was starting to burn.

Her room was unlocked and he stepped inside, out of breath and aroused, a condition that seemed inevitable. If he hadn't arrived in such a state, he would have been rendered into it at the sight of what waited for him: Viola garbed in a dressing gown of red silk, limbs arranged in a provocative curve in the centre of the big, canopied bed, the lines of her body limned in the seductive light of candles, her dark hair down over one shoulder, long and luxurious, a veritable Circe waiting for her Odysseus. 'Happy New Year, Vale.' Her smoky voice reached him from the turned-down bed.

She rose, eyes on him as her bare feet padded across the floor in slow, purposeful strides, stopping several feet from him, her hand working the satin belt of her robe loose. 'Tonight, I want you to see me naked. And I want to see you.' She slipped the gown from her shoulders and his mouth went dry. Somewhere in the house a clock began to strike midnight. He couldn't think of a better way to ring in the New Year.

She licked her lips and let him look before she stepped close and took his hand, putting it on her breast.

He squeezed, caressed. She closed her eyes and exhaled a soft moan. He loved this about her, how she not only embraced her own passion, she *engaged* it. 'I want you, Viola.' His voice was already hoarse. 'I've thought of nothing else all day.'

She kissed him. 'Not yet. Tonight is not to be rushed.' She pushed his coat of his shoulders and worked his cravat loose, his waistcoat, his shirt. 'Everyone is busy celebrating,' she promised. She ran her hands over his chest.'You're beautiful, Vale, so exquisitely made.' Her appreciation was as heady as her touch. She skimmed his flat nipples with her nails and he threw back his head, exhaling deeply at the eroticism of her touch. Then she was gone, stepping back from him and sitting down in a chair near the bed, her legs spread wide in provocative invitation, her eyes glittering. 'Take off your trousers, Vale. One of us is overdressed and it's not me.'

He held her gaze, no mean feat, and worked the fastenings in a tease of his own. He took his time sliding the trousers over his hips, letting the candlelight reveal him part by part until his trousers were off. A coy smile lit her face. 'You are magnificent, so vertically…male. So…mine.' She slipped a hand between her legs, stroking the wetness there. 'Do you see what you do to me?'

Vale swallowed hard. 'Careful, Viola, or you'll have me spending before I can give you pleasure.' He desperately wanted to replace her hand with his mouth.

'Are you going to stand there and watch or do something about it?' she issued the invitation.

He knelt before her, his hands gripping her thighs, his voice a growl. 'Damn right I'm going to do something about it.'

* * *

Viola slid down in the chair, unable to help herself. It was happening again. She was losing control and it was all his fault. She'd half-hoped the other two times had been merely circumstantial; the first time driven by the heat of anger, the second time in the portrait gallery inspired by emotion. Perhaps this time, she'd discover he was only a man, fallible in passion as a man is fallible in much else. But she'd been wrong. Her hands tangled in his hair as she begged his mouth for mercy, as she moaned his name and climaxed halfway out of her chair. He helped her the rest of the way, pulling her into his arms and laying her on the floor beside the fire, his long body stretched out beside her. The bed was going to go to waste.

Vale Penrith was one hell of a lover. Not all of her was disappointed by this revelation. But it did complicate matters. She'd chosen him over returning home. She no longer thought of wanting to get expelled from the party. She only thought instead of how to stay, how to avoid getting caught and still have what she wanted—and that was this gorgeous secret of a man lying beside her, the firelight his only cover.

'My parents would be thrilled if they knew. They'd force your hand and, if that failed, they'd force your uncle's,' she murmured, running a hand along the muscled curve of his hip.

Vale chuckled. 'You make that sound like a bad thing.' He smiled and reached out to wind a dark curl about his finger.

She rose up on one arm and faced him squarely, alarmed by the nonchalance of his response. 'It *is* a bad thing, Vale. A *horrible* thing. You don't want to marry me and I don't want to marry you. It would ruin everything. You have your Lapland expedition, I have my travels in Europe, my music.' Men forgot all nature of things when they were gripped by passion.

A slow fire started to burn in his eyes. 'And this thing between us? Is that a *bad* thing, too?' The conversation was starting to get dangerously near to topics she didn't want to discuss, topics she didn't have an answer for.

Pleasure was the best distractor she knew. She reached for him, taking him in her hand. 'This between us is not a bad thing, Vale, it's the getting caught that's bad.' She slanted him a hot look. 'I have a confession to make.'

He raised a dark eyebrow. 'What might that be?'

'It's New Year's Day now, technically.' She shifted closer to him, letting her breasts brush his chest. 'I can reveal my secret admirer. It's you. Anne Lowell traded me your name for Kenelm's.' She ran her tongue over her lips, watching the angry flames in his eyes give way to more passionate fires. She kissed his lips, the base of his throat, the centre of his chest, making the journey to his navel. She blew against it. 'I have a present for you and I have to give it to you right now.' She kissed the length of his phallus, moving to the tender tip of him, and felt him shudder. She released a sigh of relief: danger averted. She was safe for now.

She was, in fact, safe for three hours. But she was fast learning Vale Penrith was tenacious, even without trying. The fire had died and he moved them to the bed, drawing the covers up over them and cradling her against him. She could feel him starting to rouse where her buttocks met his groin in spoon fashion. 'There's an old New Year's tradition that says whomever you kiss at midnight, you'll end the year with,' Vale murmured against her hair, springing the trap just when she thought she might fall asleep unless he had ideas of taking her from behind.

'Don't, Vale,' she warned with drowsy caution. The allusion to the tradition was just another angle on the earlier question and she had no answer. To discuss the future, would be to fight and she didn't want that tonight. Perhaps it was selfish, but she just wanted to be in his arms, to be in his private world as long as she could. 'If you want to worry about something useful, worry about tomorrow. Tonight was mine. Tomorrow it's your job to find a way for us to be together.'

'Hmm.' Vale sighed. 'Is that a challenge? Shall we make this a competition?' He chuckled in the dark, a warm sound at her ear. 'I'm just thinking how ironic it is that the first half of the party I hadn't wanted to be here and now for the last half, I am dreading it being over.'

'Then don't think on it.' She turned in his arms and kissed him. Conversation was getting dangerous again. 'The future will take care of itself.' But who would take care of him? Of her? When had she started to care about the answer to that?

# Chapter Fourteen

Vale did better than take care of the next day. He took care of the next four. Viola found her days settling into a decadent pattern. Each morning began with a gift, delivered discreetly through her maid, whom Viola assured him was trustworthy. New Year's Day, it had been a small bottle of the Vin Santo she'd enjoyed—and something only Vale would have access to. It made her smile to think of Vale presenting her with wine. The Vale he'd been would never have dared it. But the Vale he was becoming had a wicked side.

The Vin Santo had been the beginning of their double life. In the drawing room that morning when the secret admirers had been revealed in much merriment, Vale had presented her with a 'decent gift' of gingerbread, a pretty box of all her favourites from the frost market. But she knew what paired well with gingerbread—the Vin Santo that remained beside her bed upstairs. It was a tantalising prospect that kept her on the edge of anticipation all day, waiting for night. He was good at tantalising. How had she ever thought he was an empty shell?

He flirted with her when no one was looking, bringing a blush to her cheeks when his eyes met hers, his gaze a hot reminder of what they'd done with their 'holy wine' the night before. Turned out, navels made good sipping cups. Interestingly, it also turned out that Vale knew the Brockmore house better than anyone. On Saturday afternoon, while the others were engaged in the Brockmore Winter Games down at the lake, he lured her to a small unused practice room at the back of the third floor. 'All of my boyhood explorations are paying off.' He laughed as she kissed him to show her appreciation.

'It's perfect, but are you sure no one will miss you?'

Vale had merely grinned, his hands at her waist in a proprietary gesture she was coming to love. She was his when he touched her like that, so easily, so naturally. 'I told my uncle I needed to work, that I'm behind on my report.'

She gave him a sly stare, eliciting a laugh. 'Don't look at me like that, Vi. I *am* behind on it and I *do* need to work on it. I'm just not working on it now. It's not a lie. It's…subterfuge.'

'You'd rather be with me than working on your report? I will consider that progress, all things considered. So, what shall we do first?' It was said teasingly, but there was sombreness that followed, their gazes falling together on the old piano and she suspected he might have chosen this room on purpose.

'Will you play for me?'

The request touched her. She knew him well enough by now to know that he understood the intimacy of his request rivalled the intimacies they'd already shared. Playing for him was another way of being naked before him, of being exposed. Viola nodded slowly and walked to the piano bench. She sat, closed her eyes, her hands resting just over the keys as she contemplated the piece. She'd play the Bach for him, the 'well-tempered clavichord', with its nuances; surging *crescendos* and quiet *pianissimos*, a piece that spoke to intensity and mood.

She risked a glimpse at Vale as she neared the end only to find that he'd never looked away. His eyes were riveted on her, as if he could see into her very soul or because her soul was so nakedly on display. And he *liked* what he saw. There was awe in that gaze. She finished and gave him a tremulous smile. Now that he'd seen her, *truly* seen her, what would he think?

He didn't offer accolades as he strode towards the bench and offered his hand to help her rise, and she was glad for it. People had tried to classify her playing before with words—stunning in some cases, overwhelming in others. Some had even called it 'different' simply because a young woman didn't play such pieces or play them with such passion. A young woman should limit herself to polite pastorales. But Vale offered her the words she'd offered him. 'Thank you. I think I understand now, as much as someone can understand another, anyway.'

'Now, it's your turn. Tell me about Lapland.' She wrapped her arms about his neck. 'Do the Sami have interesting sexual rituals?'

He laughed down at her and she was relieved to see some of the awe fade, his eyes starting to sparkle. 'I don't know about that, but they do have female goddesses like Maderakka. She gives humans their bodies and she has dominion over all the women of the tribe.' He paused in thought, remembering. 'And dominion over boys until they become men, if I remember correctly.'

'Ha! Everyone starts life as a woman then.' Viola grinned smugly. 'I think I like the Sami. Very liberated in their thinking.'

'I supposed you could look at it that way.' Vale led her to the fire and she sat down on the floor, tucking her skirts around her and taking in the pleasant warmth. 'They also believe the deceased and the living are merely two halves of the same family.'

'The dead are always with us? I like that, too,' Viola said softly. She feathered his cheek with her touch. 'I can see why that appeals to you. There's no need to say goodbye. What else appeals? I want to know everything.' She wanted to draw him out, wanted to see his soul.

He showed it to her, there before the fire that afternoon, pouring out tale after tale of a people who lived simply with nature, in a world unbothered by cities and so much of the needless complexity that governed life as they both knew it. 'To be sure,' Vale said, wrapping up his exposition, 'they have their own rules, their own organisation, but it seems much purer to me, more straight forward than London and dukedoms.' He gave a thoughtful sideways glance and she pushed aside the warning in her head that this was becoming a courtship in truth.

This was becoming too real. In her honest moments, she had to acknowledge she wanted Vale in ways that superseded the physical. It was true of Vale, too. He wanted her in ways no one else had. Surely, Vale understood that what had begun in earnest at the stroke of midnight on New Year's would end on the stroke of midnight on the Twelfth Night? But what if he didn't? What if Vale thought this was more than affair? Why didn't that thought frighten her? Why did she no longer see the risk in that?

A girl could only change a man like Vale Penrith so much. But her mind started to play the 'what if' game. What would she do if he started to think of this as more than a casual holiday affair? What if *she* did? Perhaps she already was. The idea was already hovering on the fringes of thought and it stayed there as the days passed along with the growing realisation of exactly how careful they had to be.

In public, they allowed themselves no words, no errant touches, no glances. Viola no longer thought of wanting to go home; the absence of interaction became a foreplay of its own, an adult version of the 'opposite game' played by children, where what one said meant the reverse. When Vale told Miss Philippa Canningvale how lovely she looked in her green velvet before the Victor's Supper after the games, Viola knew who the compliment was really for.

Vale's secret room became their sanctuary, the one place they felt safe in being together and they stole away as often as they could; sometimes for stolen kisses, other times just to be in one another's company. She'd sit at the piano while Vale worked on his report. He'd moved all of his work here, out of the library. She had her music books here as well and those little touches seemed to make the room theirs in truth, and the domestic fantasy spun by a 'place of their own' was potent indeed. Was there a way to have this? To have her music and Vale?

Their efforts made Viola wonder if they weren't the

only ones playing various games under the cover of politeness. What other courtships were going on beneath her nose? There was no arguing that the party was changing. In the days after New Year's the atmosphere shifted, underscored by a new tension. Men were disappearing for intervals to meet with Brockmore in his office. Women were in close tête-à-têtes with the Duchess, hands tightly folded in their laps as important discussions took place. Even if Brockmore insisted this party had not been a matchmaking event, it seemed many of the guests had taken up that thread anyway and matches were resulting.

There were also those who became less careful. Miss Pletcher and Lord Truesdale treated everyone to an announcement of their engagement at the Victor's dinner after the Winter Games. Kenelm and Anne were quite obviously together now, sitting beside one another at every event. At the box supper on Sunday before the village theatrical on Monday, Anne bid an insane amount of money on Kenelm's dinner. Viola had felt a twinge of jealousy, wishing she could have bid on Vale's dinner. She consoled herself with the practicality of it—she wouldn't have had time to eat anyway. She was one of the leads in the play and there would be 'dessert' later.

They were running out of 'laters', though. It was the first thought Viola woke up to on Tuesday. Monday night had been heavenly, right here in this room, all rosy candlelight and pleasure. Dessert indeed. There'd been more gingerbread, and more Vin Santo, some of which they'd drunk, some of which they'd lapped from each other's bodies. He'd even brought her roses as if she were a fine Drury Lane actress worthy of acclaim.

They'd found things to do with the rose petals, too. Very soft, rose petals were. She smiled and stretched, trying to hold on to the night and its memories, trying to shake the feeling that something was amiss. But her intuition wouldn't let her.

Her maid entered with a tray of chocolate and a roll. 'Here you are, Lady Viola.' She set the tray down and began bustling around the room, picking up discarded clothing and costume pieces from last night. Viola sat up. Her maid was never quite this brusque. There were usually questions about the previous night: how was dinner? How was your fellow? Sally was the only one who knew about Vale. She didn't know everything, of course, but she'd been ferrying the morning notes.

'How is everyone, Sally? I can't help but feel something is not right this morning. Has something happened?'

Sally stopped fussing with the clothes. She dropped the items in her hands and turned, her face crumpling. 'My lady, your parents have requested an interview with His Grace this morning.'

Viola felt her stomach grow cold. 'Why?' How could they know? She and Vale had been careful. The Twelfth Night ball was this evening. They'd been so close.

'I thought you'd want to know.' Sally was trembling. Viola stood up and began to pace. She could not give in to panic. She had to think. The Shocking Beauty never let others dictate her actions. She wasn't going to start now. For now, she had to assume the worst: that her parents knew about the *affaire* and were attempting to force Vale's hand.

Oh, God. *Vale.* She clutched the window sill, her knuckles white with realisation. This was worse than any scandal she'd ever sought to create. Those scandals had actually been helpful tools. Not like this where a scandal would bring down another person.

She knew how the morning would play out. Brockmore would call Vale to the study and tell him. What would Vale's reaction be? She feared it would be anger. He would feel betrayed if it happened this way. He'd think she'd used him all along, that she'd been covertly in on her parents' ploy to snag a duke for their daughter, that all of her protests to the contrary were for show. How could a marriage even survive if it was started under a cloud of such doubt and mistrust? There'd be no hope for the beauty they'd shared over the past week and that tore at her heart. She couldn't bear to lose those moments, to have them ruined by matchmaking contretemps.

Who could she go to in order to stop this? Viola considered her options; she could go to the Duke and plead her case, but she was unsure of his response. Their conversation at the Frost Fair had indicated he had empathy for her, but it had also indicated that he was not opposed to her spending time with his nephew. Did that mean he'd sanction a match if he thought it suited his nephew even if it didn't suit her? No, the Duke was too big of a risk. There was Vale. She could go to him right now and explain everything, but he might opt for the honourable route. Hadn't he indicated as much? He wanted to talk about a future, refusing to see the drawbacks to that future. A duke-to-be like him could not be saddled with a girl like her. But she'd put him off. She was regretting that. How could they talk of the future now without those plans being tainted by outside interference? No, she could not go to Vale. She had to solve this on her own.

Viola looked out over the white and black expanse of the winter landscape, the Brockmore lawns deep with snow, but the lanes were black, wet and clear. *Roads* were passable. A coach could travel. An idea began to form. It was not an easy one. But what choice did she have if she meant to protect Vale? And herself? And their dreams? Vale couldn't marry her by force or by want if she wasn't here. It was time to go home and get on with her plans.

The old Viola would have seen the benefit to this turn of events. The scandal of walking out on the Duke of Brockmore and his nephew would be too great. Her parents would be too glad to let her go. They'd pack her off to Vienna willingly now, just as she'd wanted all along. The old Viola would say this was coming along as planned. But the new Viola, the woman she'd become with Vale, wanted none of it. Viola pushed her maid aside. 'Sally, quickly, get my cranberry travelling ensemble out. We must pack as fast as we can. Send for the coach as quietly as possible and then bring me some paper.' She would leave, but not without saying goodbye. Perhaps the letter could be her absolution.

It wasn't until she started to write did she realise how deeply she'd fallen. At last, she'd found love. She'd never thought to find it and she'd certainly never thought it would hurt this much to give up the man she'd found it with. Perhaps in time Vale would understand, or perhaps he'd simply be relieved. She would never know. She'd be a continent away in Vienna, playing her heart out, or what was left of it.

## Chapter Fifteen

❧❧❧

'Where is she?' Vale burst into his uncle's office without permission, not caring that he'd trampled over the butler to get here. He cared only that Viola was gone. Her trunks were missing, her room was starkly clean, the bed made, the clothes picked up, so different from the tumbled sheets and rumpled garments that had littered the floor last night. Something sick and cold had taken up residence in his stomach at the realisation. This was *not* how it was supposed to end. He didn't know how it was supposed to end, but this was not it.

His uncle looked up, something alert passing behind his sharp eyes. 'I have guests.' He nodded to indicate Matthew Eaton and his newly arrived parents who had driven over for the Twelfth Night ball and quite possibly to meet Rose Burnham, their future daughter-in-law.

'If you would all excuse us. I need to speak with my uncle. There seems to have been a misunderstanding.' Vale sent an apologetic glance at Eaton. He liked Eaton. He didn't want to ruin any betrothal talks, but this was important. If Viola was gone, he wanted to know why.

His uncle waited until the room was empty to scold

him. 'You've cleared *my* office, Vale. Now, what is all this about Lady Viola?'

'This!' Vale shoved the note at him, impatient. Time was of the essence, especially if he meant to go after her and bring her back. 'I want to know what happened. Why did you do this after all the subtle encouragement? You never condemned her,' Vale challenged.

His uncle glanced at the clock, ignoring the accusation. 'It's been a busy morning, Vale. Her parents were here two hours ago, as soon as it was decently possible. We had breakfast together.' His distaste over the interview was evident in his tone. His uncle did not care for Calton and his wife. 'They want a marriage between you and Viola on the suspicion you've been spending clandestine time together. They say you've compromised their daughter.' He winked. 'If it's any consolation, I don't think they know about your secret room on the third floor or the billiards table, or New Year's. I think they're bluffing with their "suspicions".' Some time later when he was not panicked, he'd want to know how his uncle knew. But not today. Today, he was only concerned about finding Viola.

'You had nothing to do with it?' Vale pressed.

His uncle shook his head, suddenly serious. 'I've been in here all morning, meeting with guests. I was unaware Lady Viola departed earlier this morning. If she did indeed leave, she did so of her own volition. I had no hand in it, nor is it something I would have wanted. I told her parents I would not force your hand, that in light of no witnesses to any indiscretion and only their hearsay to go on, this was a matter for the two of you to decide.' He paused. 'I hope that was appropriate? I wanted to respect your wishes to do your own bride choosing, Vale.'

His uncle's sincere support calmed his anger to a manageable simmer. 'I am sorry I accused you.' Vale slumped into a chair. 'She left to protect me, to protect us. She didn't want any great sacrifices made.' That was the more difficult piece to decipher. Had she done it altruistically or had she decided to take advantage of the drama and make her escape out of self-preservation and the lure of Vienna? Was all of this really just about her in the end?

'What does your heart tell you, my boy?' his uncle put in quietly when he'd finished airing his thoughts.

'I've never known anyone like her,' Vale answered truthfully, words forming from ideas he'd only dared try out in the privacy of his mind.

'She's beautiful and outrageous, quite a departure from London's usual offering,' his uncle said. 'I can see the appeal, especially when you've been living like a monk.'

'I have *not* been living like a monk,' Vale protested. 'She's more than her reputation, Uncle. She's funny and insightful. She listens when I talk. I'm more than an heir to her, more than a man who carries a tragedy with him.' The attributes were tripping over themselves as they poured out. How had he ever thought her appalling? 'She's talented. Have you ever heard her play? She's inspired and passionate. She's *alive*. For the first time since R.J. and my father died, I want to be alive, too. I want to be alive *with* her.' But did she want to be alive with him? Could he bear it if he went after her and she refused?

'Does she know any of this?' his uncle prompted,

his eyes mysteriously glassy. 'Have you given her a reason to stay?'

'No. I tried. She didn't want to talk about a future. She says marriage is a trap,' Vale began. That's what had him reeling now. Did she still feel that way? Was marriage to *him* a trap to her? He wanted to go after her, because it was what he wanted. But he also wanted to give her what *she* wanted and if that was freedom, he wanted her to have that, too, even if it hurt him.

His uncle leaned forward over the desk. 'Then try again, Vale. You know, your aunt refused me the first time I proposed. And the second. She said I was too arrogant.' His uncle smiled. 'She was likely right. But her refusal humbled me. It made me see that it wasn't about *her* getting to marry *me*. The real bargain was that *I* was getting to marry *her*. Once I figured that out, nothing was going to stop me from winning her.' He was silent for a moment. 'You're good for each other, Vale. She's calmer when she's with you. And you've come alive these last days. You're more like yourself than you've been in years. If she's the one who can bring you back to happiness, you have to risk claiming her.'

Even if she chooses Vienna, was the unspoken risk. Vale was out of his seat. He'd had his conclusion before talking with his uncle, but now he was centred. The conversation had given the shattered pieces of his plan direction. 'I'll need my horse. It's going to be a cold ride.' He folded the note and put it in his pocket.

Twenty minutes later, Vale swung up on his horse, a strong Cleveland Bay with winter shoes for icy roads. He gave his uncle a nod, not wanting him to see how much his words had resonated with the doubt in him.

'I'll bring her home.' He'd found a woman to love, the woman he wanted to spend his life with. She was not going to get away from him, especially when he had a plan that would give her, give *them*, everything they wanted. There was no turning back from the future now, whatever it held.

She should go back. It wasn't the first time Viola had entertained the thought since the coach had set out. But there was no logic for it. She couldn't plead the weather. The coach was luxurious, the interior warm and supplied with all possible comforts, from blankets to warm bricks and a basket of food. Neither could she plead that she'd made a mistake. Vienna was within her grasp. This was the opportunity of a lifetime. One she'd worked towards for years. Why would she go back? And for a man? Hadn't she spent her adult life avoiding entanglements like this? No woman should ever be held back by a man. It was the height of irony that she of all people would be considering that now. So, Viola kept going. Mile after mile.

There was no reason to turn back except a tall, handsome man, with blue eyes and a secret smile, who had made her no promises. *That was your fault.* Her conscience was relentless. *What would you have done if he had?* How many times had she tortured herself, mentally replaying that moment New Year's Eve when he'd talked of tradition and ending the year with the one you started it with? What if she'd allowed him to spin out his fantasy instead of silencing him with a kiss?

Logic came to her rescue. Maybe it wouldn't have mattered. He had his work, his Lapland expedition. Additionally, Vale Penrith was going to inherit Brockmore.

He needed a suitable mate by his side. Only the accident of her birth recommended her as that mate. She'd ruined herself long ago. She'd never regretted becoming the Shocking Beauty until she'd met Vale.

There was a rap on the ceiling from outside. The coachman wanted her attention. Viola opened the window. It was starting to snow again. 'There's a rider coming up behind us, my lady. He's signalling for us to stop. Shall I?' The roads had been deserted all day. Her driver was likely worried about highwaymen. Who else would be out in the weather? Viola looked behind her at the approaching rider. On second thought, why would a *highwayman* be out in this weather if there was no guaranteed quarry? Only a man on a mission would choose to be out. She squinted, her pulse starting to race. Or a man in love. 'Stop. He means us no harm,' Viola gave the order, trying to collect herself. Vale Penrith had come for her.

# *Chapter Sixteen*

She stepped out of the carriage to meet him, using the cold air to steady herself. 'Out for an afternoon ride?' She didn't want to appear too desperate, or too glad to see him until she was sure why he'd come.

But Vale had no such compunction. He swung off his horse, his emotions an obvious storm of turmoil on his face. 'You left.' He was mad, this man who had hidden every emotion until she'd broken through. Now, he wore this one all too plainly.

Viola swallowed. 'I left a note explaining why. It's for the best, Vale. I will cost you too much.' She'd not thought she'd see him again. It was almost too much right now to see him, so tall, so confident and commanding. 'I didn't want you to think I'd had any part in my parents' plots.'

'I know you better than that. I thought you knew me better than that, too, that I would be unlikely to believe such a thing of you after all we've shared.' He advanced towards her, boots crunching on the snow. 'When I went to your room and saw that note, it undid me. I didn't know where you'd gone or why. Or what I had done to drive you away.'

She tried to break in. She couldn't have him taking all the blame. She was the one who had run. But he shook his head, a cue for her not to interrupt. 'I know what happened. I spoke with my uncle about your parents. But I won't let them ruin our decisions. I should have settled this with you before now. I gave you nothing to believe in, Vi, no promises, nothing to weigh against your dream.'

No, not nothing. How could he think that? 'Vale, I…' She tried to override his words, tried to tell him leaving had been a mistake. She should have come to him no matter what the price. She pressed a cold hand to his lips. 'You gave me nothing? Is that what you think? You gave me too much. You saw beyond the scandal, beyond the façade. You didn't care how ruined I was and you understood why I had done it.'

He had her bare hand in his gloved one, kissing each freezing finger, warming it with his breath. 'I never thought of you as ruined, Viola. Just the opposite. You are so much more than me, more alive, more courageous. Nothing daunts you.' His confession came in fast words. 'I should have told you. I should have shown you that you don't have to choose between me and your dreams. We can have it all. I will see to it.'

'You tried to. I put you off. I didn't want to hear it. I'm not as courageous as you think, Vale. I was too afraid.'

He squeezed her hand. 'I'm afraid, too, Viola. I'm afraid of going back to Brockmore Manor without you, afraid of going on without you. You make me feel alive, Viola. Not just in bed.' He tapped a finger to his head. 'In my mind.' He tapped his heart. 'In my soul.' He paused, letting out a frost-laden breath. 'And I'm afraid right now of what you'll say, when I ask you this. I want to marry you. Do you want to marry me? I promise it won't be a trap.'

She'd never thought a proposal would happen this way, here in the snow beside a coach on the edge of a road, just the two of them. She'd always imagined it as a very dry occasion, with paperwork and her future husband walking out of the study with her father and a smug smile on his face as he contemplated the enormous dowry he'd just signed for. She wasn't a commodity to Vale. The realisation caught her off guard. He wasn't a commodity to her either which was why she had questions, too. 'What about Lapland and the Sami? That work is important to you. I can't ask you to give it up.'

'I don't recall you asking.' Vale's eyes were serious. 'I won't ask you to give up Vienna.'

'But how?' The words were nice, but she didn't understand how that was possible.

Vale smiled. 'Have you ever heard of a honeymoon? Vienna is beautiful in the spring.'

'And the Sami?' She would not have only her happiness upheld.

'The next spring. It will take at least a year to organise the expedition and I can do that from Vienna.'

'You have it all worked out.' The tension was starting to leave her.

'I had plenty of time to think it all through on the ride.' Vale's smile widened and it gave her confidence. 'Now, all I need is for you to say yes.'

'Two years. That will be a very long honeymoon,' she teased, contemplating the question.

'I'll take that as a yes.' He drew her to him and kissed

her, a long, lingering kiss that had her wishing they were closer to home. 'Be warned, Viola, I intend for that honeymoon to last longer than two years, more like the rest of my life.'

'What next, then, Vale?' It was one thing to dream of the future, it was another to live it, step by step.

'We go back to Brockmore and we dance, and on the way, we just might try out the coach's hospitality.' He held open the door and helped her up.

'I think life with you will be an adventure. I hear you have a penchant for all sorts of unusual locations.' Viola laughed, already reaching for him as the door shut behind him.

'You're the adventure, Viola. *My* adventure,' he assured her as she pulled him down the leather seats.

She giggled. 'Together, we'll be unstoppable.'

'I plan on it.'

She laughed against his shoulder. Of course he did. Vale Penrith was that sort of man. It was a good thing she always had plenty of surprises up her sleeve, because once one got past his outer layer, he was a vast wilderness she'd get to map and she wouldn't have it any other way.

## *Epilogue*

The Twelfth Night ball might have been the most lavish entertainment the Duchess had ever thrown. The ballroom was swathed in velvets of deep, rich blues and violets, shot with silver. White winter roses in vases populated the niches of the room, letting off a light fragrant floral smell among the forest scents of pine. Not all of the green had been taken down and the ballroom held the last remnants of the holiday season.

The Duke and Duchess had led out the first dance, a surprising waltz, or not so surprising if one considered how many matches had been made over the past twelve days. What better than a waltz, a dance of love, to start the last festivity of the party? Everyone wore masks, but no one was under the impression they were dancing with a stranger.

'You've outdone yourself, Alicia.' Marcus pressed a kiss to his wife's hand. She looked stunning tonight in a dark violet gown, diamonds in her hair, at her ears and about her neck, his very own star in a dark sky.

Alicia laughed. 'It's you who've outdone yourself. We weren't even trying to make matches!'

'Silas and Marianne,' the Duke said as the couples sailed by. 'Rose and Matthew, and Throckton and Lady Beatrice—a most excellent match, it will be the making of that young man. He has talent, all he needs is a bit of confidence.'

'Those are triumphs indeed,' the Duchess agreed smilingly, 'though not as astonishing, I have to say, as Miss Canningvale's, if it comes off.'

'You are in the right of it there, my dear,' the Duke replied, eyeing his dear niece Verity's rather outrageous friend Philippa Canningvale circling by in the arms of Captain Milborne. 'You had a word with the chit, regarding the nature of the Captain's condition? Those headaches of his, the uncontrollable tempers…'

'The Captain himself has left Philippa under no illusions,' Alicia replied. 'She says she admires him more for his honesty.'

'A rare enough quality.' Marcus sighed heavily. 'And as for that pair,' he said, eyeing Drummond MacIntosh sailing by with Joanna Forsythe in his arms, 'thanks to them, I shall have to be brutally honest myself with Wellington when we meet in a few days, and I can't say I'm looking forward to it. Twice now, he's begged the favour of having one of his men here at Brockmore and twice the outcome has been very far from what he intended. Are you really set upon becoming a patroness of this school those two are talking about?'

'Yes, I am. I think it a marvellous idea. It will be in the Highlands, too, such a romantic place, a perfect setting for a couple so clearly in love,' Alicia said, eyeing the pair indulgently. 'They could be quite alone in the room, for all they are aware of the rest of us. Do you remember that feeling, Marcus?'

'My love, I only have to look into your eyes to feel the very same way. If only it were the same for everyone here,' Marcus said with a sigh, nodding towards the corner where Margot Penrith sat alone. Not for long, though. Viola's mother was on her way over to chat. They had a wedding to plan between them. That would give Margot purpose for the immediate future and, with luck, grandchildren shortly afterwards. Marcus hoped perhaps her soul was on the mend. In time, maybe she'd find someone. He'd keep looking. It was what Robert would have wanted.

Alicia patted his arm. 'We did well, especially where Vale was concerned.' She leaned in close. 'Tell me, Marcus, did you have that planned all along?'

Marcus chuckled and feigned innocence. 'How could I have? I had Lady Anne Lowell here for him.'

'For him or for Kenelm? I think it might have been a ruse. I know you too well, my dear.'

'I should think so, after all these years. Love is a remarkable thing, is it not, Alicia? Do you recall our last Midsummer Ball, how meticulously we planned the matches?'

Alicia chuckled. 'And though many matches were made, I don't think any of them were the ones we had in mind,' she said, smiling reminiscently. 'Now this party, where we had not a single match in mind, yet love has blossomed between the most seemingly disparate couples. A most remarkable and unpredictable thing indeed, my dear.'

'It is fifty years this spring we have been married. Can you believe it?'

Alicia sighed, shaking her head. 'It feels like fifty days, my darling. Where has the time gone?'

Marcus smiled. Life had been mostly…extraordinarily…good. Vale danced by with Viola. There would be youth at Brockmore again, soon. It would be a blessing to see it. Life was good. He'd been luckier than most and he wanted to share that luck with others especially when it came to love.

'Does it matter, Alicia? As long as there's tomorrow and you're there to share it, that's all that matters to me.'

\* \* \* \* \*

*If you enjoyed this story
you won't want to miss these other great reads
by Bronwyn Scott,
in her* WALLFLOWERS TO WIVES *quartet*

*UNBUTTONING THE INNOCENT MISS
AWAKENING THE SHY MISS
CLAIMING HIS DEFIANT MISS
MARRYING THE REBELLIOUS MISS*

## Author Note

Happy Christmas from Brockmore! The Duke and Duchess are at it again with romantic hopes for their friends and family. What better time of year to give the gift of love than Christmas, a season of love and hope? And a Christmas house party is the ideal venue for creating two classic, regency holiday tales that should appeal to lovers of traditional holiday regencies. We loved returning to Brockmore. Fans of our first anthology, *Scandal at the Midsummer Ball*, will enjoy revisiting the marine drawing room, the elegance of the Brockmore dining room and catching up with the Duke and Duchess who are more in love than ever before.

We had a great time planning an agenda of holiday fun that highlights the best of English regency Christmas traditions from a holiday fair in the village to Twelfth Night revels. These activities give the stories a cozy feel to them and conjure up the best of Christmas Past. Against this warm atmosphere, we let the Duke of Brockmore weave his holiday magic with a guest list of those less fortunate in love. In each of our stories, Brockmore extends a second chance to those who have given up hope of finding the security that comes with being loved, proving that love conquers all, even in the depths of winter. We set the anthology shortly after the death of Princess Charlotte, when the whole country mourned for 6 weeks. Mourning would have ended just in time for Christmas, so the themes of winter and darkness and loss of hope are sharply juxtaposed against the cozy festivities and warm atmosphere of Brockmore at Christmas, allowing Brockmore to become a place of re-birth.

There's something for every reader at Brockmore this year: a little sophistication as we respect the historical context of the times and play with some literary themes, a little holiday cheer in the warm festivities of the party, a little hope for those who might also feel alone this time of year, and in the characters of our house party, readers will definitely find something a little naughty and a little nice—because what is Christmas without a little spice! We hope you enjoy our Christmas gift to you.

Sincerely,
*Marguerite Kaye* and *Bronwyn Scott*

## HOMETOWN HEARTS ♥

**YES!** Please send me **The Hometown Hearts Collection** in Larger Print. This collection begins with 3 FREE books and 2 FREE gifts in the first shipment. Along with my 3 free books, I'll also get the next 4 books from the Hometown Hearts Collection, in LARGER PRINT, which I may either return and owe nothing, or keep for the low price of $4.99 U.S./ $5.89 CDN each plus $2.99 for shipping and handling per shipment*. If I decide to continue, about once a month for 8 months I will get 6 or 7 more books, but will only need to pay for 4. That means 2 or 3 books in every shipment will be FREE! If I decide to keep the entire collection, I'll have paid for only 32 books because 19 books are FREE! I understand that accepting the 3 free books and gifts places me under no obligation to buy anything. I can always return a shipment and cancel at any time. My free books and gifts are mine to keep no matter what I decide.

262 HCN 3432 462 HCN 3432

| | | |
|---|---|---|
| Name | (PLEASE PRINT) | |
| Address | | Apt. # |
| City | State/Prov. | Zip/Postal Code |

Signature (if under 18, a parent or guardian must sign)

### Mail to the **Reader Service**:

**IN U.S.A.:** P.O. Box 1867, Buffalo, NY. 14240-1867
**IN CANADA:** P.O. Box 609, Fort Erie, Ontario L2A 5X3

* Terms and prices subject to change without notice. Prices do not include applicable taxes. Sales tax applicable in NY. Canadian residents will be charged applicable taxes. This offer is limited to one order per household. All orders subject to approval. Credit or debit balances in a customer's account(s) may be offset by any other outstanding balance owed by or to the customer. Please allow 4 to 6 weeks for delivery. Offer available while quantities last. Offer not available to Quebec residents.

**Your Privacy**—The Reader Service is committed to protecting your privacy. Our Privacy Policy is available online at www.ReaderService.com or upon request from the Reader Service.

We make a portion of our mailing list available to reputable third parties that offer products we believe may interest you. If you prefer that we not exchange your name with third parties, or if you wish to clarify or modify your communication preferences, please visit us at www.ReaderService.com/consumerschoice or write to us at Reader Service Preference Service, P.O. Box 9062, Buffalo, NY. 14240-9062. Include your complete name and address.

HHBPA17

# Get 2 Free Books,
## Plus 2 Free Gifts—
### just for trying the Reader Service!

**HARLEQUIN®** Western Romance

# Get 2 Free Books,

## Plus 2 Free Gifts—

### Just for trying the Reader Service!